Nuclear Crossfire

We Choose to Stay and Fight!

Stephen L. Thompson

Nuclear Crossfire

Books by Stephen L. Thompson

The Crossfire Series

Colorado Crossfire
Believer's Crossfire
International Crossfire
Israeli Crossfire
Spirit Crossfire
Faith Crossfire
Chinese Crossfire
Texas Crossfire
Dark Crossfire
Island Crossfire
Jagged Crossfire
Violent Crossfire
Russian Crossfire
Nuclear Crossfire
End Times Crossfire
Revelation Crossfire
Gates of Hell Crossfire
Assassin's Crossfire
Albatross Crossfire
Global Crossfire
Far East Crossfire

The SFO Series

Station Force One -Onset

Nuclear Crossfire

The Crossfire team tracks a resurgence Arab Strike Force now armed with stolen Russian MIRV nuclear missiles. A major Biblical Event changes the entire world. Demons in Jerusalem and the Peruvian Jungles threaten life across the globe.

-    Stephen L. Thompson

Nuclear Crossfire

Published by
Stephen L. Thompson
Facebook.com/CrossfireNovelSeries

ISBN- 978-1-943879-15-1

Published in the United States of America

Foreword

To my Christian readers –

The Crossfire series of action/adventure stories include depictions of violence which are unusual in Christian literature. It would be nice if there were no conflict or violence in our world. But we live in a time when evil is increasing instead of diminishing, when some men seem to be controlled by selfishness, madness, or evil forces. When the enemies of decent mankind are bent on subjugation of other men and women, righteous men and women must stand against evil. Please remember that the yoke of oppression is not lifted by prayer alone. God is our shepherd and we are his sheep. As long as there are wolves about, God will use some of us as sheep dogs to defend the rest of us. These stories are about people like that and the forces they fight against. The stories describe violence because it occurs in the real world and it is active in the lives of all people whether they recognize it or not.

To my non-Christian readers –

The Crossfire series include depictions of spiritual warfare and spiritual activity with which the non-Christian may not be familiar. These stories describe the realms and activities of both God and Satan because they are real and active in the lives of all people whether they recognize it or not.

Steve Thompson

CHAPTER ONE

Benjamin Gorman was elated. He truly felt vindicated after the weeks of effort without any reportable results. He replayed the climatic event in his mind. The well-dressed Arab man and his partner that Benjamin had been following had, at last, coughed up a lead that would of great value to his country.

Benjamin walked slowly after his assignment in the late October sweltering heat of Tymeria, the capital city of Zyngola. Ben knew he was still a "newbie" spy in his first year of field work but he carefully practiced the art of spycraft he had learned from the experts in the Mossad. He continued to watch the man in the reflections in a window or casually glancing past the man as if he was interested in someone, or something else nearby.

The directional microphone brought the man's voice clearly to the earpiece in his right ear. Against the background of the grabble of street sounds and traffic noises he listened to a running discourse on the virtues of the Zyngolan state religion, the perfidy of the non-Zultarians, especially the Zionist pigs. Ben's Jewish background gave him a strong sense of superiority when the man recited a list of Zultar's magnificent qualities. Ben disdained the concept of the Moon God that was the idol of worship in this middle-eastern country. A few minutes ago the litany of prattle had been interrupted by a cell phone call.

Even though Ben could only hear one side of the conversation he was rewarded with the comment that the avenging swords of Zultar had arrived at the cave in the hills. That was very important because Ben knew which cave the Arab terrorist was talking about. He had followed other suspects to that particular cave in the hills north east of Tymeria. That comment he overheard had to mean that the stolen Russian ICBMs that everyone was looking for were in that cave. Ben felt pride swell inside of him that he was the one that cracked the case.

1

Ben's happiness melted as his target was stopped by two swarthy, bearded men who looked like they were probably some kind of security. Ben stopped to examine a wedding dress in a window. He saw one of the new men point at him. In his earpiece he heard the man say, in Arabic, "Guiding spirits say that man is a Zionist spy!"

Fear drove a knife through Ben's guts. "That tore it" he thought, taking off away from them as fast as he could run. He had to plan as he sprinted under the burning heat of the African sun through the poor district of Tymeria; His hopes to lose the pursuit were being contravened by the population of this definitely anti-Jewish city. His anger mounted as many of the people he passed pointed out his path to the men pursuing him.

Running through a deserted section on the western edge of the town he realized that he had gotten far ahead enough that he was out of sight of the pursuit. He slowed down and walked casually. He tried to slow the rapid beating of his heart as the sweat flowed freely down his face. He acted as normal as possible so as to not draw attention.

Glancing around, he didn't see any of the men pursuing him and he hoped that none of the locals were watching him. Grabbing the roughhewn and sun-dried top rail of a fence he hopped over the fence into a large field of grain which was higher than his head. Slipping in between the rows he quickly moved toward the other side of the field. When he saw men running to the fence on the far end of the field he stopped in place. Frustrated, he crouched and ran to his left towards one side of the field only to be disappointed again as men appeared there also. Fear sent a chill over his whole body when he realized that he was surrounded.

A stray thought caught his attention. He wondered what "guiding spirits" had given him away to the security forces, thinking back to that morning after he got dressed and checked out his appearance in the mirror in his hotel room. He saw good-looking young man, physically fit and dressed casually in tan slacks and a light brown pullover. The man in the mirror was in his early twenties with a prominent nose and wavy black hair combed back over a receding forehead. Ben knew he easily passed as an Arab and thereby could avoid suspicion.

In the wheat field, Ben straightened up to his full five foot nine inches in height and peered though the plants. Another stray thought struck him that he had been losing weight in the heat of Tymeria and the long hours of stakeouts. He dug out his cell phone

It was at that time Ben knew he was probably going to die and it was more important that the vital information would not die with him. As far as he knew he was probably the only one who had a definite lead to the stolen ICBMs and that information was crucial to Israel. He punched in the correct access number and was rewarded with an immediate pick up. Glancing around he knew he only had a few seconds to get everything to his contact. In Hebrew he rapidly summed up the information about what he thought was a definite lead on the ICBMs and the comment about the "guiding spirits" that had blown his cover.

His contact asked his situation. Ben didn't hesitate. "I'm surrounded by at least twenty men that mean to kill me. This will be my last transmission." The contact's voice was soft as he told Ben "May God be with you."

He destroyed the phone and wanted to angrily tell God that it wasn't fair. But, Ben knew that God was fair and this was only a step in his life. He knew that God wasn't surprised by this turn of events. He prayed softly that God would take his soul.

He watched six swarthy men spread out and then they slowly walked through the field with only a few yards between them. Each man held a nasty-looking Shafra, the eight-inch curved knife favored by the Zyngolans. Ben could tell that they knew their quarry was trapped in this field and they laughed because they knew he couldn't get out. Ben's blood ran cold as he heard them casually made bets as to who would the first to find him and kill him.

Ben realized he was so scared he couldn't swallow even if he had had any spit in his dry mouth. He had gotten the vital information to his people that he had needed to get to them. Now. How could he get away? His mind spun in frantic circles with no conclusions.

Sighing deeply, he sadly came to the conclusion that he would not get away. He prayed to God to take care of his parents and realized he was glad he hadn't taken a wife or had any kids to leave behind. He prepared himself for what he was sure to come. He moved slowly toward the group coming from behind him in the hope he could get slip past them without being seen. He was sure they were too close together and they would surely see him. He made himself as small as possible until they were upon him.

He rose up and struck the closest pursuer in the left temple with a knuckle punch which killed the man instantly. He grabbed the man's knife and stood up to face the other Arabs. Three of the attackers trampled the wheat stalks as they rushed him. All three of them started striking at him with their knives. Ben fought back as well as he could as they surrounded him but he was overwhelmed by the number and the sheer violence of their attack. He got in one good slash before a knife struck him in the back and slammed through his heart. In his mind Ben heard the curses and insults fade away as the pain and shock made him pass out. He felt the presence of God in the brilliant light that flared in his mind. The knife that ruptured his heart quickly robbed his brain of blood and Benjamin Gorman died in that split second.

He never knew it when another knife beheaded him or when his killers danced a celebration dance around his body as they spat on his head.

CHAPTER TWO

In a small warehouse in the city of Tymeria in Zyngola, Africa, twenty men assembled in anticipation of their pay. They had pulled off one of the most impossible jobs of the century. It was very risky but it paid very well. They were here to meet with their sponsor. Each of the men thought of himself as an expert in the acquisition of rare and expensive items. This was the supreme caper of their careers and they could all retire now and drop out of sight.

Their paymaster agreed that their dropping out of sight was a good concept as he pushed the little red button on his remote control unit. The blast destroyed the warehouse and made sure that the twenty men disappeared permanently. The paymaster looked at the forty, one-million dollar US bearer bonds that the men were to be paid with and chuckled as he thought to himself, "No use in blowing up so much hard currency." A tall, thin man of indiscriminate age he had a hooked nose and deeply recessed eyes. He liked the term "hooded" when describing his eyes. He had an olive complexion with a sparse patch of dark brown hair which he kept cut short. His thin lips rarely reflected his feelings although right now they were spread in an unfamiliar shape for him, a grin.

Picking up the package of bearer bonds he furtively glanced around the motel as he was leaving and then he seemed to simply slide out of sight. That was one reason he was nicknamed the "Serpent". The twenty dead men now knew the other reason he was nicknamed for a snake.

Two hundred miles away, the late afternoon sun over Zyngola lit up the desert in waves of heat. But the filtered light was dim in the massive limestone cave. The atmosphere was uncomfortably hot and damp since the only entrance was completely covered in a huge tarpaulin to keep the cave a secret. That cover also kept any cooling breezes from entering the space.

Kazim Nabech and Hamid Ridha stood in glorious rapture as they contemplated the four missiles on their launchers. Through the services of the "Serpent", their god

Zultar had provided them with the means to finally rid the world of the hated Jews. It would be a glorious victory for Zultarism and the righteous Zultarian people of the world.

The mysterious man they called the "Serpent" had charged a gigantic fee to supply the remnants of the Arab Strike Force with not one, but four, nuclear multiple independently targeted reentry vehicle (MIRV) ICBMs. It was now within their means to destroy the Zionists four times over. The man had earned his fee and would always be remembered in their history for his supreme efforts for the Zultarians. Kazim had heard the reports that the man had killed all the people that had worked with him on this mission. That would keep their secret from leaking out. The man was morally reprehensible but very efficient at the same time. One had to tie up loose ends, or in this case, any possible loose lips.

Kazim was six-foot-tall and had a non-athletic body that tended to store fat regardless how he dieted. The lack of exercise kept him in a state of constant hunger to keep his weight down. The Arab skin tone was complicated by the blue eyes. Somewhere in his background there was a non-Arab. He still managed to organize the group he controlled better than anyone else had done in years. He smiled cruelly and drew in a deep breath as he turned to his fellow zealot. "Hamid! Do you really understand that we have the means to remove the Jewish state completely from the map?"

Hamid was sweating in the dampness of the cave. He turned feverous brown eyes to his mentor and great friend. "Yes! I do understand that Kazim. I also understand that every western power and military unit is hunting for these missiles at this minute. We have seen their accursed efficiency as they destroyed most of our friends and comrades. They always have managed to interfere with our earlier operations against Israel. We must make the most of this opportunity before they find their way here! We should launch all four of these missiles immediately!"

Kazim understood his good friend's urgency but knew they had to wait a little while longer before they could extract vengeance on the Jews.

Kazim studied his partner for a second. The man was short, maybe five foot seven inches tall; perpetually overweight and he dressed poorly. But, he was faithful and willing to do anything for the cause. His swarthy skin looked more African than Arab.

"Hamid, I agree with you in principle, but, we don't have the expertise to program these missiles to strike the Zionist cities yet. As we have planned, the programmer will be here in three days. Our job is to keep these weapons safe and secret until then."

Hamid sighed a large sigh. "Yes, I know that. I just have a horrible feeling that we will be robbed of our victory again if we wait too long."

There was the loud report of a shot outside the cave. Hamid's eyes grew wide and he moaned. "See! I told you that they would find us!"

Kazim frowned but held his hand up to quiet his friend. "Let us go see what is happening before we assume the worst."

Slipping out of a small vent in the tarp into the hot African sun but also into cooling breezes, the two men cautiously made their way down the path to where their guard was standing. He had his rifle at the ready and was looking out over the northern desert of Zyngola.

Kazim asked him why he had fired his rifle. The guard replied he thought he had seen movement and the shape of a man, "There! By that big rock.". The three men looked at the spot where the guard had fired and saw nothing.

Kazim was upset that his enjoyment had been disrupted, he chided the guard. "Don't get so spooked by the wind in the sand. Just keep a watch out for any real people." Kazim and Hamid went back into the cave leaving the guard to watch.

Four hundred feet away from the guard, shielded by that particular big rock, a thin man in khaki pants a tan shirt, and hat; crouched on the sand of the desert. His brown eyes darted back and forth in pain and anger. Joseph Metzler used his right hand and his teeth to bind a handkerchief over the wound to his left arm. He wrapped it tightly around the muscle in his arm so that it covered both the entry and exit wounds. He thought that he was very fortunate that it was a "through-and-through" wound and hadn't hit the bone or a major artery. Still, it was bleeding and that wasn't good.

He carefully covered any traces of blood from the sand and rocks around his observation place. Then, he awkwardly and slowly crawled a hundred yards away from the covered cave area and into a shallow wadi that ran at a diagonal from the cave. Each time he had to lean on his injured arm it hurt terribly and he had to stifle any moans his body wanted to make.

He could walk now without being seen and that took the pressure off the injured arm. He knew that he needed to get his wound treated and soon or he would pass out and there would be no end to the sleep he'd get then.

When he was over a mile away from the cave and behind a jumble of boulders he climbed out of the wadi and walked on a trail for almost another mile until he came to a small pull off on a dirt trail where he had left his car. He checked all the tell-tales and they weren't disturbed. He opened the trunk and got out the first aid kit. He sat in the shade of the vehicle and used the Sulfa powder on both sides of the wound to prevent infection. He then bandaged both sides and wrapped it in gauze. It hurt like fire and he was pretty clumsy with only one hand but he got the job done.

He opened the driver's door and grabbed the small cell phone from a compartment in the door. He went back and sat down in the shade and leaned back on the car while he made a call. He explained that he had not gotten to see what was being guarded at the covered cave but that there was only one guard and a couple of other men so it may not be that important.

He completed the call and felt faint. After looking for scorpions or centipedes, he layed down on the ground in the cool shade of the car. After he was laying there for a few minutes he started to feel better. But, realizing he needed to husband his strength the best that he could, he still continued to lie in the shade and rest.

Watching for the feet of any intruders he looked under his car and what he saw turned his blood to ice water. Attached to the framework was a large bundle with a wire attached to the starter motor. It was probably Semitex plastic explosive. If he had started the car, he would be very dead right now.

Joe Metzler thought carefully about taking the wires off of the bomb but he didn't know if they had put a tamper circuit on the bomb which would set it off if he messed with it. He slowly got up and put on his coat which covered his wound nicely. He picked up his backpack and stuffed the first-aid kit into it. He grabbed a bottle of water and then the newspaper from the back seat.

He carefully closed the driver's door and the trunk and walked away from the car. When he was behind some major rocks he used the remote starter button on his key fob and was rewarded with a very loud explosion that shook the rocks around him. He looked over the rocks and saw that his car was all over the place and the main part was thoroughly engulfed in flames.

He continued to wait concealed in the rocks overlooking his car. He made himself comfortable and prepared himself to wait. It actually only took twenty minutes before a four-wheel drive truck tore by him and slowed down near the burning wreck. Three men got out of the truck and stood looking and pointing at the burning wreck. They were all of Arab descent with the dark features found in Africa.

Joe used his cell phone and explained to the party on the other end about the events so far. They asked him to describe the truck and he did. Then he hung up.

Joe knew that the people that came in the truck were there to make sure he was dead so he quietly opened his backpack and took out the 9MM automatic and two extra clips. He doubted that they would see him, but, just in case.

The men outside the truck were frustrated because they couldn't check the car until it stopped burning. Their wait would probably be long enough. Joe checked his watch for the third time and then heard the noise he had been waiting for. The sound of helicopter rotor blades.

The desert camouflage colored helicopter came in fast and low from the desert and approached the burning car. The three men outside the truck near the still burning vehicle could be good Samaritans seeing if they could help the hapless driver except for the automatic weapons they held. They were now facing the helicopter and waving it off.

An amplified voice came from the helicopter in Arabic. "Throw down your weapons and place your hands on your heads."

The three men conferred and suddenly broke into a run, each man in a different direction. As they ran they fired their weapons back at the helicopter.

There was the slamming sound of a heavy machine gun and one of the men was thrown off his feet in a bloody spray that left him sprawled on the sand. The helicopter rotated to its right and the machine gun fired again. The second man was smashed into the ground and stopped moving. The third man had reached the cover of the rocks and was climbing over them to escape the fire from the helicopter when Joe stood up in front of him and told him to give up. The attacker's eyes got big but he tried to haul his MP5 submachine gun around toward Joe so he could fire on his new threat.

Joe fired one shot and the man fell backwards off the rocks with a new hole in his forehead and no expression on his face anymore.

Joe waved to the men in the helicopter and it landed. Two men with automatic weapons ran to the truck and threw a package into the driver's window and waved at Joe. He ran with them back to the helicopter and it lifted off immediately. It was about a quarter of a mile away when the truck blew up.

Joe clapped one of the men on the arm with his right hand and said, "Thanks, I was in a bad way there."

Gerald Glisten of the Israeli Defense Force smiled back. "Just part of the job, I think you need some more help." He pointed to the fresh blood leaking through Joe's jacket sleeve.

Back at Mossad headquarters Joe's action got some definite attention. Even though Joe had not been impressed by the cave, the attempt to kill him and the ensuing battle raised interest in the cave by others in the defense of Israel. After a consultation, a combat team was assigned to check out the cave. That evening a report was forwarded from the IDF to the Mossad that their team had been destroyed. Note was made that the team was detected and partially destroyed by an "unknown" and "indestructible" force. At that point a Mossad manager made a transatlantic phone call which was received deep in a mountain outside Denver, Colorado, U.S.A.

CHAPTER THREE

In the multilevel structure built into the center of a granite mountain to the west of Denver, Colorado the call was answered by a strikingly pretty blonde woman with a statuesque body that was six foot tall and athletically muscled. Her green eyes showed wisdom and a great deal of experience for one so young. She was wearing a pale blue pullover top over a set of ripstop nylon pants both of which gave her freedom of movement while being very serviceable. The .40 caliber Smith and Wesson autoloader on her right hip was a definite hint as to her abilities.

Laura Malone reached up and pushed the "talk" button on the bone-conduction Jawbone blue-tooth microphone/speaker resting on her right ear and cheek. "Crossfire Team, Laura Malone, how may we help you?"

"Ms. Malone? Hiram Meir from the Mossad. Nice to speak to you again." Laura had met Hiram several times in the Mossad headquarters in Tel Aviv on two previous missions. "I've got a situation that your team's talents might really help us with in Africa. Is your team available presently?"

Laura guessed that Hiram was talking about the present sore spot in Africa, Zyngola.

She told the Assistant Director of Mossad Operations to "Hold one". She keyed in her husband's number and pushed "contact". On the firing range in the lower level of the "Fortress" as they called their headquarters and home, Jack Malone saw the blinking light on his phone. Standing six foot, four inches tall and strongly muscled, the blonde-haired man dominated his area as a physical force. His gray-green eyes had become penetrating in the last three years of combat with terrorists and demons. He put down the autoloader he had been firing and grabbed his phone. Walking out through the double set of doors separated by a short hall he exited into the weapons room of the Fortress. Taking off his ear protectors he keyed the phone. "Yes Laura?"

She explained the reason for the interruption in his pistol training. Jack told her to conference him into the call. He said hello to Hiram and asked him to explain his request.

Hiram knew he was in contact with the most successful combat team that was able to handle dual dimensional problems in the war on terror. The Crossfire Team had earned high marks with the Mossad on numerous occasions by their efforts on behalf of the Jewish nation. He knew they didn't seek fame or even money for their efforts but were anointed by God to combat the forces of hell when they interfaced directly with the human world. No one else in the local area had shown a similar capability. This made the Crossfire Team in great demand and usually on an immediate basis. Very much like this situation. He started with a little background. "We were notified by your State Department that there was a breech in the protection of some of the old Soviet-era nuclear MIRV ICBMs from one of their breakaway republics."

Hiram paused to look at his documentation. "Oh, I see that you were the source of the information. That, along with a request from Russia to help locate four missiles along with their launchers. Your information indicated that these missiles were probably headed to Zyngola with our name on their targeting programs. To say the least this has consumed our efforts for the last two weeks."

Hiram's British education surfaced again. "Our agents in Tymeria have had a rough go of things recently. One agent was tasked to shadow a middle-eastern financier who has ties to terrorism, possibly remnants of the ASF. Benjamin Gorman had located his subject, one Kazim Nabech who figures prominently in a transfer of fifty million U.S. dollars in petro assets of Libya and Iran to an unknown source possibly an arms merchant. Benjamin was one of our brightest and most capable young agents. He was discovered and killed today. But, not before he was able to give us the information that Nabech had also identified a possible location of the missiles."

Jack could hear in the tone of his voice that it obviously bothered the career Israeli security defense man that they had lost a good agent.

Hiram continued, "Not only that but he said that his cover was blown by something Nabech's security forces called a "guiding spirit". We also had another agent, Joseph Metzler, who was investigating a reported sighting of a truck convoy at the same location that Ben Gorman reported. It is a remote location in the desert several hundred miles away from the capital. Metzler is also a very good agent at surveillance but after following the trucks to a remote cave, he was wounded by a guard. "

"Metzler thought that he was able to maintain his cover even though he got shot. He hid himself again and the guards didn't search him out as they would if they had truly seen him. He managed to get away only to find his car wired with explosives. One of the IDF teams working in the area extracted him after a gunfight with three armed assailants. Metzler didn't feel that his initial discovery was natural. He felt that he had been pushed out from behind a rock and briefly exposed to an armed guard that shot at him."

Jack asked, "Why did agent Metzler feel he had been exposed?"

Hiram checked his notes. "He was well concealed behind several large boulders when he says he was pushed into the open view of the guard. He swears that there was no one there to do the pushing."

Hiram continued with the narrative. "Due to the information from Gorman and the unexpectedly heavy response to agent Metzler, the IDF tasked a five-man team to investigate the desert location which is apparently a large cave with the opening covered by a tarp. To be perfectly honest, we have no proof that this is anything other than another terrorist training facility. The reason we're calling you is because the response team was killed by an "unstoppable" force that reeked of "evil" according to the last transmission from the team."

Jack prayed that Yahveh would direct him as to the need to get involved in the situation. He definitely felt a leading to pursue it. "All right Hiram, we will coordinate with our government and I will contact you when we are approaching the desert location. Can you keep eyes on the desert location to see if all the activity makes them relocate or scale up their defenses? And, send us all the data on the location. We'll be in touch soon."

Hiram thanked them and rang off. Jack told Laura, "See if you can get Mark, Sarah, and David and bring them up to speed. I'll get Su Li to warm up the Shrew and prepare for a half-hour depart."

Laura concurred and broke the connection with Jack.

In the SOG assembly area, Mark Connelly and his wife Sarah were conducting a training session for the twenty five members of the sensitive operations group. This group of God-selected believers was some of the most talented combat troops that had come from all the branches of the U.S. Military in response to an unadvertised recruitment two years earlier. They had been seconded to the Chairman of the Joint Chiefs of Staff, General Miles. During a Satan-inspired political revolt against the operations of the Crossfire Team they had been ordered not to support the team any further and the military was to also avoid interfacing with the team. All twenty-five members of the military SOG resigned their commissions or took early termination of their military careers and joined the Crossfire Team as civilians.

Each man or woman that had been part of the original SOG was a rock-solid Christian and tops in their particular branch of the service. Some could have run their own groups but were humble enough to serve as a member of the Crossfire SOG. Intelligence ran to the high end of the scale and they were totally dedicated to their job. The team used all the members of the SOG in investigation efforts, interdiction efforts against the enemy, and in combat when required.

Under close questioning as to why they had volunteered for this particular assignment, each one had a vision, a dream, or a leading of the Spirit that led them to call. There were ten women and twenty-five men between the ages of 24 and 31 in the original SOG. Experience ran to the extreme in SpecOps and elite groups. There were now nine Navy SEALs, none with less than four years' service; two team leaders and two squad leaders. Five top Army Rangers of which three were women from the clandestine division. The Rangers are an all-male force as far as the world was concerned until recently. At that time a special operation of the Rangers recruited women and trained them covertly along with the men. There were also six Force Recon Marines all with extensive combat service. The last five members were U.S. Air Force Special Ops personnel, three of them were women from the Psychological Operations or PysOps group.

Mark was saddened that four of the original SOG had been killed in action, two in the battle with the leaders of the Omicron Cartel in the Egyptian desert, one in a battle near the Fortress, and one in an assault against team members in Denver. But there were over two hundred requests to join the SOG and replacement of the missing members was facilitated quickly.

As the combat leader for the Crossfire Team, Mark's experience in field combat and tactics were extensive and he took every opportunity to pass them on to the rest of the team, including the SOG. His goal in life was to defend the innocent and to wage war on the people that tried to steal that innocence. Mark could bench press over four hundred pounds and run for miles carrying a full pack and a load of weapons and ammo. He worked out every day to maintain his physical condition. He had developed his condition as a team leader in the U.S. Navy SEALs. His brown eyes took in every detail around him and had to because he had recently added three most important goals to his life. To love the truth, hate unrighteousness, and be ready to die for Yahshua.

His wife, Sarah, had experience as an IDF soldier and more years as an assassin/spy and field agent for the Israeli Mossad. This experience gave her the lead in spy stuff. She was very bright as well as beautiful. After her marriage to Mark he felt that they had become an extremely effective team.

Mark's cell phone chimed with the IDIOT tone. IDIOT stood for "Important! Don't Ignore Our Transmission" It was only used for critical communications.

Stepping away from the group he keyed the cell phone, "Yes, Laura?"

Laura explained the situation to Mark and asked if he knew where Sarah and David were.

"Yes Ma'am. Sarah is right here with me and David is in transit to Israel at the moment by commercial air to see an old friend who may have some information on the missing nukes. I think Alexis is with him also."

Mark grinned; the increasing affection between David Zahavy and Alexis Taggert was an open secret that he concurred with because in this battlefield they needed each other for support.

Laura answered, "Okay, I'll get in touch with them. Can you and Sarah get the weapons, ammo, and desert uniforms for the six of us to the Shrew in the next twenty minutes?"

Mark agreed and hung up. He explained that class would be continued in the near future but that they had to run. As they jogged to the armory he explained the mission to Sarah.

CHAPTER FOUR

The "Shrew" was the codename for the team's new transportation aircraft. The aircraft combined the luxury of a normal CitationX corporate jet with the performance and weapons of a modern fighter aircraft. It was actually the CIA's newest covert fighter aircraft. While the corporate business jet look made it look innocuous, the combination of stealth, supercruise, maneuverability, and integrated avionics, coupled with hidden weaponry and improved maintenance support, represented a new dimension in hidden warfare capability. The only reason the Crossfire Team had, not one but two, of the advanced aircraft was because Congress had reduced the "hidden funds" for black ops for the CIA. The CIA had taken receipt of the other three aircraft each of which the cost of over two hundred and twenty million dollars but they couldn't pay for all five.

The Shrew shared a great deal of its critical components with the most modern air dominance fighters. The development time and cost of the Shrew had been cut by seventy-five percent due to the parallel development of the F-22 Raptor and a few technologies from the F-35 Lightning II. The Shrew used the Raptor's combination of sensor capability, integrated avionics, situational awareness, and some of its weapons to provide a first-kill opportunity against threats. The CF-88 Shrew also uses a variation on the Raptor's sophisticated sensor suite allowing the pilot to track, identify, shoot and kill air-to-air threats before being detected. Significant advances in cockpit design and sensor fusion improved the pilot's situational awareness especially in the use of helmet mounted display from the F-35 rather than a heads-up-display as in the F-22.

The CF-88 engines produced more thrust than many current fighter engines. The combination of sleek aerodynamic design and increased thrust allowed the CF-88 to cruise at supersonic airspeeds of greater than 1.5 Mach or, as it was called "Supercruise". Supercruise greatly expanded the CF-88's operating envelope in both speed and range over most known current fighters, which must use fuel-consuming afterburners to operate at supersonic speeds. The sophisticated CF-88 aero design, advanced flight controls, thrust vectoring, and high thrust-to-weight ratio provided the capability to outmaneuver almost anything currently flying except for fighters of the F-22 Raptor's level.

The Shrew's wingspan was only ten feet wider than the standard Citation X at 74 feet, 6 inches due to the increased body width. The length was stretched to 75 feet and 1 inch, and the height is still 16 feet, 8 inches. The Shrew looks lower because the cabin is larger to accommodate the bigger internal engines and weapons bays.

The four warriors met at the helicopter bay at the top of the mountain. Mark and Sarah had already loaded the weapons, ammo, and other necessities onto a Blackhawk helicopter which was prepared and with its rotors turning it was ready to fly. They climbed into the body of the helicopter as the hydraulic lift raised the chopper to the launch deck located on the actual top of the mountain the fortress was located in.

Mark went forward to the front of the chopper and sat down in the co-pilot's seat next to the pilot. Mark could fly the chopper and land it if necessary but he much preferred to let the team's pilot fly. He looked across at Su Li and nodded that they were ready to go.

Mark admired the beautiful Oriental woman that looked too young to handle the controls but she had actually logged hundreds of hours in this and other helicopters, not to mention several modern fighters such as the F-22. Her Chinese heritage showed in her face which had delicate features and did not give a clue as to her ability in combat or martial arts. She nodded back to Mark and smoothly lifted the chopper off the launching platform. She transitioned into forward flight as she talked to the Air Traffic Controller at Denver International Airport. She had already filed two flight plans with the FAA by computer. One for the helicopter trip to DIA and the other for a supposedly civilian flight out of DIA. A similar flight plan was sent to the Military ATC and the U.S. Air Defense system at NORAD Mountain in Colorado Springs for their use of the military flight corridors.

Mark was amazed at how much Su Li had refined her handling of the helicopter over the last several months. It was now at the point that it was a work of art, stable, even relaxing on a flight that only took twenty minutes.

Mark got clearance from the Air Force Security team at their hanger located at the Far East end of DIA, Su Li flared out and set the helicopter down on its landing pad near the hanger and well within the newly reinforced barrier walls and fencing surrounding their present hanger and the second hanger being built next to it.

Mark was expecting Mike White, formerly of the U.S. Air Force in the next ten days with the second Shrew and while they would both fit in one hanger, prudence directed separate housings to prevent the loss of both aircraft if security was breached and a hanger invaded.

Mike's inclusion into the Crossfire Team would expand their capabilities to be in more than one place at the same time. A situation that was starting to be required as the end of days approached and the enemy was taking more and more liberties that needed to be confronted. After disembarkation and unloading one of the security team took off in the Blackhawk to return it to the Fortress.

The five team members entered through the newly rebuilt hanger office and walked into the hanger to a real surprise. There were two Shrews in the hanger.

CHAPTER FIVE

The second Shrew looked identical to the first one with the exception of one number on the tail. Mike White poked his head out of the second aircraft's doorway and waved to the team members.

Mike was a physically fit specimen for his advanced age of thirty-eight. He had a receding hairline of sandy colored hair neatly trimmed. He had blue eyes that missed nothing and a nice smile on an unlined face. Highly educated and intelligent, his exploits with the team had included battles and airborne incursions into foreign countries and hot landing zones. He trotted down the stairs and jogged over to the crew. He shook hands all around and said to Jack, "Hello boss."

Jack smiled and asked if Mike had informed them that he was arriving today. Mike frowned and said, "Yeah, I called the Fortress and talked to Charlie. He told me you guys were headed this way and you'd be glad to see me. Something about a long trip and Su Li having to drive by herself."

Jack nodded and looked at Mark, "Charlie. Well, that fits. It's probably his idea of a joke to spring Mike on us like this."

Mark put his hand up to his Jawbone microphone. Tapping the talk button he said, "Call Charlie". In a few seconds the ex-Chinese agent was on the phone. "Yes Mark."

Mark said, "Charlie, what's going on with the second Shrew? I understood that Mike called you and said he'd be in today and now no one can find him or the aircraft."

Charlie laughed, "Good try Mark. But, I watched him land and taxi up to the hanger. He put it in the hanger twenty six minutes and two seconds ago."

Mark smiled, "Okay, you win this one. But, don't do that again. We are on a combat mission and something like that could cause problems. Understand me?"

Charlie realized he had overstepped protocol for his joke. "I understand you Mark, and I apologize. No more jokes."

Mark realized that Charlie was contrite about the problem. Enough said. "Charlie, I need you to get in touch with Hiram Meir at the Mossad and get the location of the cave he referred to in his call to us. Then see if you can keep a watch on that area. The Israelis are probably doing an "eyes on" program but I want you to watch for any signs of demonic activity. If you see any, track it as much as possible and see where it goes."

Charlie said he'd get right on it.

Mark broke the connection and officially welcomed the Texas-born aviator to the team and suggested he get his belongings and assist Su Li in loading and preparing the first Shrew for the international flight. The first Shrew had already been tested in battle and the new one needed to be serviced before a new flight.

While Mike was far more experienced in the world of combat flying he was brand new to the team and would work as Su Li's student for this mission to learn the ropes.

The whole team moved the equipment into Shrew number one. Su Li and Mike White preflighted the aircraft while the others set up in the office space of the plane. Mark paged David Zahavy.

David was on a United Airlines commercial flight from New York to Israel. His satellite cell phone chirped. He picked up the in-flight phone and entered Mark's number. Mark greeted his second most recent inductee to the team. "Hi David, how's your flight going?"

David had been Sarah's direct supervisor and control agent when they both worked for the Mossad. Hearing David's voice reminded Mark of his first impression of the man. David was a trim man in his early thirties who was always dressed in style and he was calm and collected even under fire. A nondescript man who could blend into a crowd and be forgotten immediately, he had pale blue eyes that took in everything. He had dark hair stylishly combed back and delicate hands. He was an experienced field agent in his own right. He had taken life and saved life as needed. As a task manager at the Mossad he had a wealth of knowledge about middle-east politics, terrorism, and the culture of the area. His counsel as an associate from the Mossad had always been helpful to the team. That was until a previous enemy got David cashiered by the Mossad. A week later he was in Colorado as a member of the Crossfire Team.

David told Mark, "Fine, Mark, fine. What can I do for you?"

Knowing the vulnerability of cell phone communications Mark kept it generic. "We've got a situation that will require your talents and those of your friend."

David smiled at Alexis Taggert who was sleeping in the seat next to him. "Okay, should we head back?"

"No, we'll meet you at Ben Grunion and explain everything."

David's eyebrow went up. "All right then, we'll see you soon."

Mark hung up and watched the staircase and hatch rise into position and seal the aircraft. The engines started and in five minutes the aircraft rolled out of the hanger and down the tarmac through the armored gates that had been moved out of the way by the Air Force Security detail. Eight more minutes and they started their takeoff roll and lifted into the blue Colorado skies.

Su Li took it slowly until they could move up towards the military air corridor headed east. She then slid the plane up until they were flying just below the speed of sound while they crossed the continental U.S.

Once they cleared the eastern seaboard she opened up the throttles until they were flying at twice the speed of sound. She and Mike alternated the piloting duties as they raced towards the Med. Two in-flight refuelings provided by the USAF gave them the ability to maintain their rapid transit.

Jack made a call to the Mossad and arranged for a secure hanger and permission to land at the Jewish field. It was dark when they landed and rolled out. Su Li taxied the aircraft towards the private hangers until they had a truck pull out to lead them. Jack got a call confirming that it really was the Mossad's truck. They had been suckered on the team's first arrival at the Jewish airport. This time they were able to pull directly into the hanger. The door was shut behind them even before the engines wound down.

Jack exited the plane and had one of the Israeli agents take him to the gate where David and Alexis' flight was just pulling up.

CHAPTER SIX

David studied the young woman he was working with at the present moment. Alexis Taggert was both beautiful and very talented for a woman working in a man's arena. David was intrigued by the blonde who had a body that was a cross between a swimsuit model and a triathlon runner. He knew she could turn heads to the point men tended to walk into things staring at her. But, she didn't let that distract her. She was mission focused and David knew that was because it had been pounded into her during her training and now it was her life.

David knew he was falling in love with her. He recalled reading in her file that Alexis had gone to college for a degree in law enforcement and graduated fourth highest in her class at Yale University. She had earned a second degree in History. She was capable of speaking and writing in English, Arabic, Russian, and Hebrew. She excelled in physical sports in college and in her last few months of her senior year she had been contacted by a representative of the U.S. Army. He explained to her that her physical strengths and talents could be very helpful to the Army and very important to her country.

After careful consideration she agreed to join a clandestine division of the army where she trained in a secret facility which matched the criteria of the U. S. Army Ranger's basic and advanced schools. As a member of the Mossad David had been aware that even though the U.S. Army Rangers only took men, at that time they had a secret cadre to train women. Alexis' training and that of the other women she had enlisted with were kept secret to protect the identities of the women who, many times, would be the first in the line of fire.

She learned hand-to-hand combat as well as weapons and tactics and competed with both women and men as she progressed. Again, she had graduated at the top of her class and went on her first mission the next week. She had been inserted into Iran to keep an eye on a possible shipment of advanced Russian ground-to-air missiles that Russia was denying were sold to the Iranians.

Alexis had discovered the missiles and following orders she destroyed them which is saying a lot because there were seventy of the highly guarded items. She exfiltrated out of Iran and was ready for her second mission three days later. She put four years into a very distinguished Army career in spying even though her contributions were only known to a few in the special forces world. But her capabilities had been noticed and she was watched carefully during those four years. She was then recruited by the Directorate of Operations of the National Clandestine Service.

David's inside knowledge vis-a-vis the Mossad detailed her new service. The Directorate of Operations houses special groups for conducting counterterrorism and counter narcotics, for tracking nuclear proliferation, and other tasks. Administrated by the Directorate, the Special Operations group maintains an elite cadre called the Special Activities Division, that are highly skilled in weaponry; covert transport of personnel and material by air, sea, and land; guerrilla warfare; the use of explosives; and escape and evasion techniques. They are prepared to respond quickly to a myriad of possible needs, from parachute drops and communications support to assistance with counter narcotics operations exfiltration and infiltration. Special Activities maintains a symbiotic relationship with the Special Forces, and is run and manned largely by ex-Special Forces soldiers like Alexis."

After more than three years with NCS, Alexis had been tasked to run clandestine backup support for an operation of the Crossfire Team. She was more than surprised to learn a whole new dimension of combat, the spiritual kind. After clandestinely assisting them on several missions she asked to be reassigned and joined the Crossfire Team.

David had to chuckle to himself because she had never been much of a church-goer or really acknowledged God, but she quickly found out that fighting demons tends to radically polarize one's religious and moral understanding of life. Laura had explained to David that Alexis had weighted her options in this new battleground and decided to give her life to Jesus, her Savior. She now used her considerable talents to help the team on their assignments for God.

David and Alexis rode back to the private hangers with Jack who explained what was going on and why they were needed immediately. Neither he nor Alexis had any checked luggage because their stay in Israel was only to gather information. They were scheduled to return to the U.S. that evening. So, they were free to join the team without delay. They changed into the combat gear and got weapons from the supply that Mark had brought with them in the Shrew before they joined the others in the hanger.

Mark then explained his plan to check out the cave in the desert. With both Laura and Sarah as part of the team they felt capable of handling any of the demonic influences if they ran into them.

They were about to switch to a U.S. Navy Osprey for a trip to an aircraft carrier in the Med when Mark got a call from Charlie Wu at the Fortress. "Mark, don't head out to the desert just yet. I've got six demonic disturbances moving away from there. I can't tell if they have one or more missiles with them or this is just a ruse. They are all traveling on tracks or roads and moving slowly enough to have a missile launcher with them. I will keep you up to date as to their location."

Mark told the troops to stand down and said they'd have to wait to see where the different movements with demons covering the missiles were headed.

As they brainstormed the situation Laura kept praying for direction from Yahveh. Alexis said, "Why don't we take one of the movements and jump it. That would at least cut down the possibilities."

David demurred. "That would also tell them that we are aware of their movements under demonic cover and that could hurt any future efforts of ours. It would also show them who we are and what we can do. If we guess wrong, then it will be exposing our operations and capabilities with no effective results."

Jack added, "We don't even know for sure that these are the missiles. This whole thing could be a giant ruse to get us committed to actions that are only a distraction while the real operation is going on somewhere else."

Jack's cell phone vibrated and he answered it. "Jack Malone."

Carol Moffet said, "Jack, I have a warning for you and the team. I've been drawn to the Heavenlies for the last four hours and one thing is certain on this one. If the team doesn't stop this demonically backed terrorist thrust completely, Israel could be hurt very badly. Be in prayer and trust your instincts."

Jack chuckled, "Carol why is it every time I hear from you I get some kind of performance anxiety? Pray, follow my instincts and I can prevent some amount of destruction for Israel? Do you have anything more concrete to give us?"

Carol sighed, "No, not now at any rate. I just followed the pattern of this attempt which has been in the works for two years. There is a point coming up in the very near future where the future divides. One path from a meeting with the team and the terrorists leads to the elimination of much of the Jewish population." She sounded fatigued. "I had to watch the bombing and the results. It was so horrible I can't even begin to describe it. But, it's only one of two possibilities. The other leads to no such destruction. It is the team's actions that determine which path is followed. I will call you back if anything more substantial is forthcoming."

Jack suddenly realized the agony of her "gift" and he apologized to her and told her they really appreciated her efforts. He passed on the message to the rest of the team. Laura decided to lead them all in prayer because it wouldn't be their actions that determine the outcome but rather, Yahveh's will. She pointed out that God says in His Word that Israel will not be destroyed by anyone.

While they were in prayer Alexis saw a light growing in her mind. It swirled into a mental vision of the angel Rose. Rose looked at Alexis and told her, "Alexis, I have a message just for you this time. Your actions will be pivotal in the confrontation with the enemy. They will attempt to delude you to think that you are not part of Yahveh's will but that you actually know better than anyone how to resolve a major event. Stand rock solid in your faith in the Savior and Yahveh. Your decision will be made in a split second and it will determine the outcome of this battle.

Remember always, you are a sister to the others on the team and you are the beloved of the Lord and He will never, ever, abandon you or forsake you." Rose faded from her mind and Alexis prayed her thanks to the Son and the Father and a beautiful angel named Rose.

Jack told everyone, "I've got a confirmation from Charlie as to the probable course and destination of the demonically-shielded transport which is currently the only one left. The other tracks disappeared after we didn't show up. Let's load up and get to the carrier."

CHAPTER SEVEN

A flight of five U.S. Navy helicopters spread out over a three mile pattern and flew nap-of-the-earth protocol through the night over Zyngola. Their flight through the countries surrounding Zyngola had required landing several times to avoid airborne patrols and satellite detection. They carefully passed around Tymeria and flew out into the desert. The target was a cluster of buildings twenty two miles south of Tymeria, the capital city of Zyngola.

Mark had been talking with Charlie who had been casing the buildings through the use of his computers and various satellites. He had a reasonable floor plan and a solid indication of missile radiation in the southern-most building. Mark called the troops together and used a secure channel to the other two troop choppers to keep the IDF and Mossad members of the assault in step as he outlined his battle plan. Both the Israeli and United States governments had agreed that the site was a terrorist training camp and had given a green light to both the Crossfire Team and the Israeli teams to attack the base.

Jack plugged his headset directly into Mark's and explained something only he had heard from Charlie. "Twice this flight of helicopters would have been detected by satellite but Charlie was able to intercept the detection signals and blank out the data from the satellites. We're running right on the edge of being seen."

Mark assigned Jack and Laura to the main entrance in the south side of the building they were targeting. He and Sarah would come in from the rear of the building where there appeared to be a second set of doors. David and Alexis were to take a covering role on the west side and Su Li and Mike White would take the same role on the east side. This was not merely an assignment by seniority. There were definite signs of dimensional rifts which meant demons.

Earlier in their history God anointed Laura Malone to physically battle demons legally in our dimension by giving her a physical version of the Armor of God. When Laura was in prayer and a demon entered our dimension the armor would appear in a golden hue along with a shield and a sword that streamed with the glory or esteem of God to protect her and give her the power to defeat the demon. When Satan begin to attempt to overwhelm her in battle, God then anointed Sarah with her own armor and sword.

Since Laura and Sarah were anointed to do battle with demons, they therefore they got the lead roles.

The choppers set down at one and a half clicks, or kilometers, away from the dark base. There was a full moon out tonight and the scene was easy to make out without thermal imaging goggles. One of each sub-team wore them anyway so as to pick up any heat signatures or IR emanations.

Running with a full combat load felt very good to Alexis as she had done this for years in training and several times in combat. She breathed in through her nose and out through her mouth of the dry desert air and ran in an easy lope that didn't tire her.

The twenty-four members of the combined teams came to the perimeter wire fence and settled quietly to the ground. The IDF troops opened a wide section of the fencing after determining that there were no sensors or voltages on the wiring. Another short run and the teams divided with the Kido/Mossad/IDF teams branching off to the other two buildings in the complex.

Alexis moved up to where Mark was. "It doesn't make sense that they would put something as important as nuclear missiles in a building with so little defense. They're either not here or these people are dumber than I thought before."

Mark was able to respond in a casual voice as he also hadn't tired as they ran. "Maybe, but then again, maybe not. They just got here and either haven't had time to set up elaborate defenses or they think that it would draw too much attention. I'd guess the first and expect that they would mount a real strong internal defense. We'll see."

The Crossfire Team quickly arranged themselves according to Mark's plan and moved toward the target building.

As they moved to the west side of the building, Alexis began to wonder if they were really doing this right. She had much more experience than Laura or Jack. They really should have let her and David take the front of the building. She slowly shook her head, a motion unseen by David who was still wearing his thermal imaging goggles.

Alexis now realized that the whole assault was poorly conceived and probably illegal. They had no proof that there were any missiles here. Plus, they were basing their authority on God's word. That just didn't make sense. There were much better ways to do this! Alexis realized that she wasn't sure that God was always right. She was breathing deeply and becoming confused by the bombardment of conflicting thoughts.

She came to the conclusion that she had to stop them from assaulting the building. She saw Jack and Laura almost up to the main doors and they would ruin everything. She had to stop them now. She started to raise her rifle to aim at them when a one crystal-clear thought cut though her confusion. Yahveh was reliable and He would never abandon her nor forsake her. In her mental maelstrom she decided to see if that was correct. She turned to the one truth she knew. She prayed in her mind, "Father, please tell me what to do and order my mind so that I know the truth."

It was as if a gale blew into her mind, stilled the questioning voices, and cleared her thoughts. She realized she was on the verge of destroying the mission and possibly killing two of her best friends. That thought scared her and that it made her really mad. "Father, I pray that you protect my mind from the evil one's thoughts and put a hedge of protection around all of the troops who are fighting in your name!"

Clarity came immediately and she concentrated on doing what she had come here to do which was protecting the others.

In the still quietness of the early morning darkness, Alexis watched Jack and Laura slide up to the roof-high doors and carefully fix explosives to the two large hinges on each door and on the central locking mechanism. She knew Mark and Sarah were doing the same at the rear of the building. She watched Jack and Laura back away while they waited for the signal from the Israeli troops that they were ready. Even at her distance Alexis saw the tiny green light lit up on the detonator. She knew that Jack and Mark would push their detonator buttons at the same time.

The small, muffled explosions were sufficient to completely disconnect the doors from the walls and from each other. As the doors fell to the ground with a crash Jack threw a flare package into the dark interior of the building as Laura hurled two flash bang grenades.

The flash bangs went off first with a painfully bright light and a huge slamming noise. The flares lit up the building from end to end since there were no interior walls.

The four team members moved into the building only to encounter rifle fire from a half of dozen places deeper in the building. As Jack lined up his return fire a six-foot high demon ran out of the dark, grabbed him, and threw him onto the ground back out of the building. Laura's armor flared into sight and she advanced on the large black demon. The demon ducked under her sword swing and tackled her around the torso. They fell to the floor of the building and Laura tried to get her sword to strike the reptilian monster. He grabbed her sword arm and prevented her from striking him. She punched him in the throat but it didn't seem to bother him.

Jack jumped back to his feet and ran towards the battling pair. As he got there, a rifle round struck him in the helmet which knocked him to the floor again. This time it caused a real headache. He fought through the pain as Laura and the demon continued to battle. The demon grabbed a black knife from behind itself and stabbed Laura in the stomach with it. The blade hit her golden armor and slid off harmlessly. He pulled it back and raised it to strike her in her unprotected face. The stench of the demon was immense and his drooling was distracting Laura but she saw the knife and raised her golden shield to block it. This demon was really fast and she didn't know if she could deflect the blade in time. Just then a bullet slammed into the right side of the demon's head. Since he wasn't in our dimension legally it blew the other half of his head off and he started dissolving into an ugly black goo-like smoke.

In the meantime, the IDF had reached the blasted door frames and started firing at any muzzle flash or movement they saw. The volume of incoming and outgoing fire was immense.

Laura pushed the disintegrating remains of the demon off of her and rose to her feet. Bullets flew past her and Jack as a man with an AK-47 ran at them, firing as he came out of the back end of the building. Laura deflected his bullets with her sword until he ran out of bullets. As he closed with her he swung the rifle at her. Laura dodged the rifle and used her right foot to knock the man's legs out from below him. He slammed to the ground and lost the rifle. Laura put the point of the glowing sword to his throat and she continued to pray in her mind as she asked him, "Where are the missiles?" The man was still stunned by the contact with the floor and confusedly said, "They are right here."

Laura looked and saw two of the missiles on their launchers. "Where are the other two?"

The man was back to thinking his usual way. "They will be on the way to Israel before you find them. I'm not going to tell you anything. Hail Zultar!" He threw himself upward onto Laura's sword hard enough to run the sword completely through his throat and spine. He gasped and fell off the sword to the floor. His eyes grew large and then glassed over as his body shut down in death.

She stared at the man for a few seconds and then looked around for more attackers from either dimension. Gradually her armor and sword faded from sight. She turned and helped Jack to his feet. He shook his head to clear the pain. Laura thanked him for taking out the demon but he shook his head. "I didn't do it. I was down for the count."

Laura looked around and Alexis walked into the doorway with her M-8 up and searching for more targets. "Did I get it?"

Laura grinned and said, "Yes you did, and I'd say you were just in the nick of time too."

Mark and Sarah with the help of the IDF had killed the other twelve defenders and the two of them came over to the trio. Mark said, "Well, it looks like we were partially successful." He indicated the two Russian missile launchers and their MIRV ICBMs.

Jack shook off the fuzzy feeling in his head and reached into his backpack. Pulling out a radiation counter he checked each of the missile heads. He nodded. "Yeah, these two are the real thing."

At that point one of the Mossad agents came into the building. "We've subdued the rest of the camp." This meant that there were no survivors. "Oy! Look at those hummers." He had just seen the missiles.

Mark called Charlie on his cell phone. "Charlie, we've only got two of the missiles here. Any hope of finding the other two?"

Charlie thought for a few seconds, "Could be. Let me get back to you."

One of the IDF men came into the building. "The two heavy lifters are coming in now. Help me get these things outside."

The rest of the Israeli teams came over and helped the Crossfire Team move the huge missiles and launchers. It went quickly due to the use of a tractor they found to pull the launchers with their missiles out of the building and into the open. Obviously well trained in this operation it was only a matter of ten minutes before the two missiles were detached from their launchers and secured to cables below the helicopters. The heavy lift choppers had been tasked to take two missiles each and had no problem easing upward with their delicate cargo. They quickly disappeared into the night. The Israeli teams quickly packed explosives into the framework of the launchers, the buildings, and anything else of value.

The troop chopper landed next to the building after the Chinooks had left. The troops all boarded the chopper which also lifted off. When they were a half mile away there were six major explosions that completely destroyed the camp and the missile launchers.

Two hours later the troops disembarked onto the deck of the American aircraft carrier in the middle of a battle group. The missiles were to be transshipped to an American nuclear facility to be dismantled and destroyed as they should have been several years before.

Mark breathed in the salt air and was flooded with a host of memories from his days as a Navy SEAL.

CHAPTER EIGHT

The wind blowing in over the bow of the carrier brought the smell of the deep sea along with a hint of the rain falling several miles ahead of the ship. The aircraft fuel mixed with the myriad of warship odors touched off a remembrance of a special mission in Mark's mind.

-----------------------******-----------------------

The sky had been very much like it was now. Scudding clouds mixed with rain, lightning, and spray over the bow as the carrier bore into the storm forming around them. The ready deck launched two F-18s with the usual roar from the fighter's exhaust in full military afterburner mode mixed with the roar from the steam catapult and a clap of thunder. Mark remembered he was moving to an attack helicopter as the carrier cruised just off the coast of Libya thirty miles off of the city of Surt.

Mark was buffeted by a gust of wind and planted his feet firmly on the deck. He grabbed the arm of another SEAL whose poncho acted like a sail and almost lifted the man off the deck. The man nodded his thanks to Mark and grabbed the ladder and pulled himself into the chopper. Mark checked to see that all the men were on board and climbed in himself.

The chopper struggled off the deck and fought the winds. They gained some altitude and then slid off into the gathering gloom towards the coast. Mark was near the open door as they went "feet dry" crossing over the coast at an altitude of only fifty feet to foil the Libyan air defense radar.

Mark had briefed his team as to their target and the rules of engagement. They were after a stolen shipment of deadly anthrax toxin. The CIA had traced it to a remote laboratory seventy miles into the Libyan desert and had men watching at the camp at the moment. Their problem was that they didn't have the men or the firepower to wrest the deadly cargo from the reinforced terrorists at the camp. Hence the call for the SEALs.

Mark worried about faulty information which had happened several times in the last two years of supporting the CIA. He had a special call put into the Admiral in charge of this mission and explained his misgivings. The Admiral felt that they needed to take the chance because of the danger of the terrorists using the toxin. But, he did give Mark the leeway to use his best judgment based on the action.

Mark had made some adjustments on the game plan and hoped his insight would serve both America's interest and that of his men.

The helicopter settled quickly to the sand three clicks away from their target and the men jumped out quickly and formed up in three man squads. Mark had them all hunker down while he found their contact. His second in command, Sergeant Morris shadowed him a dozen yards behind him to prevent any "surprises". Mark saw the small red light blink four times and then two more. That was the prearranged signal and he moved up to the source quickly.

The CIA man was an ex-Army Ranger and was very competent. He outlined the camp and the number of troops. He had a good idea where the toxin was and the major problem facing them. He was about six foot tall and completely covered in desert camo. A powerfully built man he had a full two-day stubble covering his face. He grinned at Mark. "Here's the problem Commander. We tracked the toxin and the ten men that brought it in from the submarine. After they settled in we were going in that night. That would have been two nights ago. But, just as we formed up, a four-truck convoy came in from the direction of Tripoli.

Mark didn't like the way the tale was going. "Regular army?"

The CIA man's estimation of the SEAL leader went up a notch. "Yep. Forty eight new bodies fully armed and carrying heavy weapons including a bunch of RPGs. They immediately set up a perimeter and a roving patrol. It was like they knew we were here and about to attack."

Mark thought back to his briefing, "There are eight of you guys, right?'

The man shook his head, "Seven, and we lost one yesterday to a stupid scorpion. Got into his sleeping gear and stung him when he was asleep. It was a young, little one too."

Mark knew the little ones had much more concentrated poison. "Didn't he yell or thrash around?"

"Nope, the bug jabbed him in the eye and it flooded his nerves right away. Never woke up, at least not in this world." We found him this morning.

Mark thought over his revised plan. "Okay, we can take these bozos. Here's what I need your team to do."

After he explained what he wanted to do the CIA man nodded his head, "Yes Sir! That's flipping brilliant!"

Mark smiled, "We'll see."

Using his communications gear he advised the other five teams of the new wrinkles in the plan.

They waited until two a.m. local time so that the guards would be at a low point. Then they came at the camp in a coordinated strike. Mark was counting on the dissension between the original terrorists and the government troops. He had deliberately set up nine of his men as snipers with silenced rifles and sub-sonic ammo. At his signal all the troops on the perimeter died within seconds of each other. The snipers worked each quadrant one at a time. Nine men died each time the sniper corps fired. Then they moved to the next quadrant. The fact that they had an advantage in a slight elevation made the tactic even more effective although they couldn't tag everyone in the far quadrant.

The enemy force had just been cut almost in half without an alarm being raised. The snipers then fanned out and took out any roving guards and stationary men like the two, two-man teams on the heavy machine guns. Another eight men gone and all was still quiet.

Mark signaled his two three-man teams and then led them over the perimeter and into the camp proper. Thirty paces behind them the second wave moved in quickly.

Mark and the CIA men took the suspected tent with the toxins and the rest of the troops took the other tents. At Mark's signal everyone moved into the tents and eliminated anyone inside.

At this point Mark had made a major modification to the original attack plan. None of his men relaxed or dropped their attack formations. Mark and the CIA troops determined in less than ten minutes that the Anthrax toxin was not in any of the tents. At that point Mark told his men to man the heavy machine guns and to creep back to the perimeter and take guard duty.

He used his MBITR radio to call the information into the system network. Then they waited.

About a half-an-hour later there was an unsilenced round fired from the outside into the camp. That one shot was quickly followed by dozens of rifles firing into the tents and the sand all around the camp. None of the American troops were hit nor did they fire back.

The outside fire tapered off and desert troops started to move out of their hidden positions and close in on the camp. Mark estimated that there were at least a hundred men moving towards the camp in the pre-dawn dark. He pushed the button on his radio and held it down for three seconds.

There was a sudden flash of light that lit up the entire area like daylight. The four airborne flares were like mini suns. The four fast movers came out of the night like midnight terrors. The attacking forces were bombed, shot, and concussed into leaving this earth. The F-18s were configured for ground attack and carried a lot of bombs. Three passes and there weren't many men outside the camp still moving. The nine snipers who had dug into the sand outside the camp and remained hidden as the enemy passed them made sure that none of the remaining troops survived the on-slough.

Mark sent four of his SEALs with night vision goggles out to make sure that none of the enemy that had attacked them was functional.

While they were putting explosives in all the tents Mark got a message from the one of the two Cobra attack helicopters that had followed the F-18s just in case they missed anything.

"SEAL leader, this is Howler One, we have six command types who were attempting to flee. There were ten of them but one of the APCs fired on us. The others are on the ground and eagerly awaiting your tender ministrations. Two clicks from the camp on a heading of two-seven-zero."

Mark keyed his microphone, "Roger that Howler One. Be right there." He pointed at two of his troops and four of the CIA types. "Let's go."

It only took the seasoned troops fifteen minutes to cover the mile of desert sands. They quickly disarmed and bound up the Libyan Army officers. They also searched the APCs.

Mark and the leader of the CIA troops had a quick conference. The Captain in charge of the CIA troops threw the orders he had found on the ground. "This is a total screw-up! There never were any Anthrax toxins according to these papers. The whole thing was a setup to suck us in and capture us. They even knew that we were coming and when! There are going to be heads rolling over this."

Mark could tell from the man's eyes that he wasn't kidding. "Okay, but we're not done here. I smell a rat. This could be a cover up for the original operation. Didn't your people verify that there were Anthrax toxins stolen?"

Captain Young nodded his head, "Yeah, so?"

Mark smiled at the man. "Look, you are the spooks, I'm just a sailor, but it seems that if they went to the trouble to acquire inside information they weren't just trying to set up a CIA team. I still think they have the toxins here somewhere. Let's "talk" to the leader of this little group and see what we find."

Captain Young looked at his watch. "We're running out of time. We're supposed to be gone by now. This could blow up into an international incident if we're discovered."

Mark shrugged, "So? Let's be fast."

The Captain nodded, "Okay, but don't take the leader, he won't know anything. Find the one that is the political officer. He's the one that will know what's going on."

Mark grinned a grin that made the Captain step back. "Fine, go get him and we'll "talk" to him."

CHAPTER NINE

Mark pulled out a small kit from his side pocket and prepared the syringe.

Captain Young and Sergeant Morris brought a short, somewhat timid man into the low light Mark had set up. Mark came over to him and had Morris roll the man's sleeve up.

The man's eyes grew big when he saw the syringe in Mark's hand. In very good English he said, "You can't do this thing. It is against the Geneva Convention!"

Mark smiled as he tied a band around the man's arm and said, "I'm sure you were just as concerned about the Geneva Convention when you were going to spread those toxins among innocent civilians. If you don't like this complain to someone who cares." He located a vein and injected the truth serum into the man's arm.

Five minutes later Mark started the interrogation. Fifteen minutes later they were headed back to the camp on the double. As they ran the Captain used his thumb to indicate the tied up officers behind them. "Are you going to leave them to die in the desert heat?"

Mark shrugged his shoulders, "I doubt that it will be much after sunrise when they are found by the troops that are on the way here right now. Get the chopper into the camp and have everybody on board." What Mark left unstated was the high probability that all of these officers would be killed by their superiors simply because of their failure in this matter.

The orders were given and by the time they reached the camp the last of the troops were boarding the helicopter. They had room for the seven remaining CIA troops and would ex-filtrate them.

The Captain and Mark went to the latrine marker and walked ten steps into the camp and started digging. It only took three tries and a total of five minutes to find the case with the toxins. Mark was going to load it on the chopper when the Captain said, "No, we were tasked to destroy this stuff and we're going to do it."

41

Mark opened the case and took one of the small vials out. "We need to take a sample back to make sure we got the right stuff and don't have to come back to look for it again."

Captain Yound shrugged, "Don't break that vial. We're all dead if you do."

He put two thermite grenades in the case, pulled the pins, and closed the case tightly. He placed the case back into the hole and used his boot to cover it with a bunch of sand.

They ran to the chopper as the pre-dawn light started to light up the desert.

After an uneventful trip back Mark gave the vial to the chemists on the carrier it was determined that they had definitely found the right stuff.

-----------------------*****-----------------------

Mark snapped back into the present and walked after the others toward the carrier's interior.

After a thorough debriefing and some rest the team met to brainstorm any possibilities as far as the remaining two missiles.

Jack called Charlie Wu back at the Fortress and asked if he had any ideas"

Charlie laughed a short laugh, "Yeah, Jack, I've got lots of ideas but few leads. The Israelis raided the original cave and it was empty. There were indications that all four launchers, and by extrapolation, all four missiles were in the cave at one time. So, I believe they split them up and one, or two, of the other leads I was tracking could have been hiding a missile."

Charlie looked at his information and continued, "I checked out all the other tracks and I think I've found the trick they used. There were two movements using the same covering. One had the missiles and the other one was a diversion. They reached a place of physical concealment and the missiles stopped. The covering went on to mislead us. Crayton figured the odds and we think that they stopped at a small village south-south-east of Tymeria. I'll send you the coordinates right now. Remember this is a hunch and it could be way off base."

Jack thanked him and hung up. Turning to the others he related what Charlie had told him as his cell phone chimed to tell him he had received the coordinates. He looked at his phone and read the GPS coordinates to Mark. Mark placed it on the map and they all looked at the possibilities.

Mark shook his head. "Great! That has to be the toughest place in Zyngola for us to operate in. The men, women, and even the children in this sector south and east of Tymeria are Zultarian fanatics, every one of them. We would have to have an army to take the place just to see if the missiles are there."

Sarah and Laura had been praying about their next move and when Mark made his assertions about the city of Wad Farina they both got a word from Yahveh. Sarah said, "Mark, we need to get a look at that area for the missiles and we need to do it without them knowing we're there. This will have to be a spy operation and we have to do it so that they think we're part of the neighborhood."

Mark thought about that for a few minutes and nodded. "David, are there any Mossad operatives in there that we can work through? Or, Laura, are there any western assets in the area that can help us if we go in?"

David shrugged and took out his cell phone. He placed a call to the Mossad while Mark rang up the NSA and Laura called the CIA.

CHAPTER TEN

David's call to the Mossad was routed to Hiram Selamon, a man that was on the level above where David had been. Hiram was guarded with the ex-manager until he heard what the Crossfire Team was involved in at the moment. He had David wait for a few minutes while he got clearance to discuss the matters at hand.

Hiram listened to the details of the team's need to get into the Zultarian enclave to search for the missiles. Then he asked, "How do you expect to approach the search?"

David had been doing what he was good at. After thinking of several possibilities he asked his own question, "Do you still have Ben Adid in prison?"

Hiram laughed, "Until his future home freezes over. Why?"

David referred to a plan he had designed while he was there and had Hiram pull it up and read it. After reading it Hiram said, "Risky, potentially lethal if you make one slip. We do have some assets in the enclave but they can only operate outside of the operations by the ASF. The paperwork and the records are still in place and you can use them if you want to take the risk. What about his two protectors?"

David said, "I can cover that aspect fully."

Hiram thought, let me check this out. But, I believe that the management will go along with it. If they do, I'll set up the escape and let the news leak out that Ben Adid has escaped. I will also send the clothing and the history to you by courier. This is a big thing you're doing for Israel, we won't forget it."

David smiled, "I would expect no less, goodbye" and hung up.

The others had not fared as well. There were no viable assets that any of the other organizations would admit to that could be used.

David recapped his conversation and then elaborated on the Ben Adid operation. "There was the possibility that we would have to go into the Zultarian operation and I devised the plan that we referred to as the Ben Adid operation. After Yahveh demonstrated His power in Zyngola we captured the number two man in the ASF, Ben Adid. He was tried and convicted of multiple operations against the State of Israel and confined for life at facility 1391. My plan was to create a fake escape that the ASF would hear about and impersonate him in contacts with the ASF."

The others nodded and concurred with the idea. David held up his hand to silence the chatter."There is an additional requirement that concerns me and I need to ask your help. Ben Adid had two guardians with him at all times. Very lethal and devoted to Adid. They were Arabian women of great capability. Both of them were killed in the battle when we captured Ben Adid. If he shows up again he will have replaced them. It's a major signature of his that we would have to create."

Sarah shrugged, "So? I'll be one and Alexis the other. We can both speak flawless Arabic." Then she realized what she was saying. She turned to the blonde-haired woman. "Oh! I'm so sorry Alexis. I don't have the right to volunteer you for this assignment."

Alexis smiled, "No problem, I want to be involved anyway. Somebody's got to keep David safe. You know how men are." Both women laughed and David grinned because he was fairly sure he knew better.

Laura spoke up, "I can get Alexis treated so that she looks Arabian in skin coloring and hair color."

Mark had reservations at letting his wife go into harm's way without him but the job description didn't include him. Mark knew she was capable of going on such a mission and coming back alive. He knew Sarah was as capable as him, but his heart cried at the possibility of her loss. He silently prayed for guidance from Yahveh and felt the peace he needed to allow her to accompany David. "Okay, let's get started."

Over the next six hours Alexis turned into a dark-skinned, black-haired Arab beauty. and the clothing they needed was delivered to the carrier. Alexis wore dark brown, almost black, contact lenses to complete her disguise. After David and both women were dressed they presented themselves to the others. The effect was startling. If they hadn't known it was David, Sarah, and

Alexis they would have thought they were local residents in any of the major Arab cities. They maintained their cover and only spoke in Arabic and used the conventions they knew were practiced in Zyngola.

Jack fielded a call from Hiram and passed the information on to the trio. "A captured ASF helicopter will be here in about ten minutes to take you to the enclave. The Mossad agent you will contact is named Rav and he will meet you at the heliport with a limo to take you to the active ASF headquarters building. This building has been built since Ben Adid was captured so you shouldn't be familiar with it. Rav will have the contact information for you when you get there. He will also set up a couple exit strategies for you. Go with Yahveh and our love."

The three warriors walked out to the flight deck escorted by four Marines so that nobody interfered with them. The helicopter with the Arab markings landed on the deck and David entered it, followed by the two women, as it should be done.

The flight was only thirty minutes until they were over land and it was less than twenty more minutes before they were within range of the heliport. There had been six challenges by the Zyngolan Air Defense forces but the pilot was well trained in the required codes and information to penetrate the Zyngolan air space.

They landed neatly on the assigned spot and the pilot hustled out of the aircraft to open the door for Ben Adid and his companions. As he opened the door David muttered in English, "Show Time."

Flowing robes flapped behind him as he strutted to the limo standing near the field like he was an important man not to be toyed with by anyone. The two women behind him were dressed in all black which covered everything except their eyes. Eyes that took in every detail and had seriousness that allowed no exceptions.

The driver bowed to Ben Adid and opened the back door to the limo for the three of them. He closed the door and entered the driver's seat. As he drove carefully but quickly toward town he spoke in Hebrew to David. "You need to talk to Walid Faisal. He is the current leader locally. He was a middleman before the ASF lost most of its upper controllers. He is a toad and tries to bluff anyone he meets with his importance. Watch out for Hakem. Hakem is Faisal's main protector and a truly evil person. He has tortured many Israelis in his time. None of them lived either. Tall Arab with a Van Dyke dyed red. Remember, no one we know of here has ever met Ben Adid but that doesn't mean they don't have pictures of him."

David sighed, "It's never easy, is it? I resemble the real Ben Adid superficially and can explain any differences due to the despicable torture and treatment by the Israelis."

Rav pulled the limo over to the curb and said in Arabic. "Exalted Sir, we are here." He jumped out and went to the curb side and opened the back door to the big car. David climbed out and adjusted his robes as the women exited the vehicle. David said quietly to Alexis and Sarah. "I think we may need to make a statement when we enter to quiet any dissenters. If Hakem threatens us, take him out.

Then he stalked into the building as a commanding force that couldn't be bothered by rules or stopped by anything. He passed the security desk without bothering to speak to the two officers there. One of them ordered him to stop immediately and pulled his handgun out of his holster. Sarah silently knocked the weapon out of the man's hand and cross chopped him on the throat. The man collapsed to the floor with his hands to his throat. The other security man started to stand up only to find Alexis' knife at his throat. He sat back down and raised his hands. Alexis hit him with a palm-heel strike to the forehead that knocked him unconscious. The two actions were so quick that the women flowed after David without much of a pause.

CHAPTER ELEVEN

David knew where to go because he saw a sign that indicated the door to the office of Walid Faisal. In true monarch fashion he never broke stride as he heard the commotion behind him. By the time he reached the door Sarah had moved ahead of him to open the door.

As he walked in David ignored the receptionist and walked into the large, expensively decorated office behind her by knocking open the door with one shove.

They entered the office much to the surprise of the smallish man behind the big desk. Looking up in anger at this intrusion he made a motion of cutting his throat with his right hand and his surprised look turned to a smirk. Hakem came off a chair in a rush drawing a large sword from a sheath. There was murder in his eyes and a smile on his cruel mouth.

Both Sarah and Alexis rotated towards the big man and their right arms snapped out and down. Two throwing knives glittered in the air and slammed into him. One hit him in his throat and the second one sank into his forehead all the way to the hilt. Hakem dropped the sword as his brain fizzled out. He fell to the floor and slid across the tiles leaving a trail of blood.

Ignoring the short battle behind him David walked up to the desk of Walid and stated bluntly, "My name is Ben Adid; I am the supreme leader of the ASF at this time. I need information from you and I will not tolerate any delay. Do you have a problem with this?"

Walid was embarrassed on many levels and the wind was totally gone from his ego. He had just watched as the two tall, black forms behind the man had silently killed his most effective butcher with almost no effort and definitely with no emotion. His mind noticed that they were so sure of their capabilities that they had completely ignored the already dead enforcer as Hakem slid to a halt behind them. They simply continued to walk toward the desk. Walid had heard many tales about the lethality of Adid's companions. Now he had seen it for himself.

He swallowed twice and took a deep breath. "I thought that you were a captive of the Israelis."

David simply said, "I escaped and you are trying my patience."

"No, no. I'm simply surprised to see one as great as you in my office."

David held up one ring encrusted finger and a very sharp knife appeared in Alexis's hand in front of her robes. Walid started to sweat as David held up his second finger. He almost shouted, "What information do you require?"

David said, "Where are missiles we paid for?"

Walid was between a rock and a hard place. He knew to reveal the location of the missiles would be a death sentence by his superiors unless, of course, he didn't live long enough to die at their hands. He knew he had only a few seconds to make this most important decision.

There was a bang and the door to the office flew open and four military guards rushed through with their rifles up.

Alexis and Sarah exploded into action as each rotated outwardly from their standing positions. Alexis threw the knife she was holding and it slammed into the chest of the last guard as he was taking aim at her. She took the rifle away from the front guard by grabbing it by the forestock and raising it quickly upward into the man's face as she kicked him in the crotch. She grabbed the rifle the guard dropped to attend to the intense pain in his privates and sent him to la-la land with a butt-stroke to the man's bent over head. He dropped like a rock to the floor of the office.

Sarah had ducked under the third guard's rifle and slammed the hilt end of her knife into the man's groin. Holding the screaming guard as a shield she side kicked the second man in the side of the head which ended his interest in the intruders and rendered him unconscious at the same time. She then dropped the first guard to the floor as she pulled out a new knife. The guard had passed out from the pain.

All of these actions were accomplished in silence and so quickly that the officer behind the guards was still stepping into the office when he found himself without any troops and with two knives at his throat.

Walid's eyes almost popped out of his head. These women weren't normal, they were supernatural. He made his decision. He stood up and told the officer to leave and not to bother them again. He watched as the women easily picked up the dead and disabled guards and tossed them out of the office and closed the door. They then turned and flowed back into their positions behind David leaving another pool of blood. Walid swallowed hard as he noted that even after eliminating Hakem and the four guards there was still a glinting knife in Alexis' hand as she stared at him and waited for Ben Adid's order.

The officer in charge of the defeated guards stared at the closed door and made a command decision. He could go back into the office and exert his authority over these people or he could use a safer method. Shaking with just the thought of going back in there, he instead hauled out his cell phone and called for major reinforcements.

Inside the office Walid took a deep breath and said, "The remaining two missiles, with their launchers, are at the mountain base six miles east of Majra, Jordan. The launch programmer will be there tomorrow. We will launch both missiles within twenty-four hours after they are programmed."

The small man's eyes widened when he realized that the deadly man in front of him had been a prisoner when the new base was built. "A thousand pardons Ben Adid, let me show you on the map where the base is located."

He pulled out a detailed map of the mountainous area and pointed to the location of the base.

David stared at the man for several seconds before he asked, in an icy, cold voice. "Exactly what do you mean by "the remaining two missiles?"

Walid sighed; it was obvious that this piece of bad news had not reached Ben Adid's ears as yet. "To keep the Zionists from finding all the missiles we separated them into two groups. Unfortunately the group still in Zyngola was discovered and eliminated." Walid tried to look confident that his part in the operation was the good one.

As he watched the anger building on Ben Adid's face, he realized he was running out of options. So, Walid decided to take control of the situation and stood up. David stared at the smaller man and shook his head. "So, now you are going to commit suicide?"

Frightened by the graveyard words Walid reached into an open drawer and pulled out a pistol. Alexis' knife slammed into his neck so hard it severed his spinal column as it came out the back of his throat. Walid dropped the gun and collapsed onto the floor like he had become boneless. His eyes glazed over and he quit breathing with a gurgle.

David hurried around the desk and grabbed the map. Lifting his cell phone he pushed two buttons at the same time. He waved to Alexis and Sarah and they all retreated to the back of Walid's office. The three of them quickly affixed a small bomb at the base of a large window and moved to the side of the room behind a large couch.

The commander of the twenty-man reinforcement team told the personnel carrier to pull up on the sidewalk in front of Walid's building next to the large limo in front of the building. Then he told his troops to alight and enter the building quickly.

The troops started to disembark from the APC as the limo driver jumped out of the car and shouted, "Bomb! There is a bomb in the car! He ran away from the vehicle as quickly as he could. The other civilians on the street did likewise. The troops dismissed the bomb threat as a diversion and simply ignored the people running away from them, which happened frequently when they showed up.

Not following their logic, the car blew up spectacularly and the explosion slammed the troops and the APC into the building across the street from Walid's building. At the same time it blew in all the glass and shattered the front entrance. Timing out the blast, David triggered his bomb and it blew out the window and part of the wall. The sound of the window explosion was lost in the much larger explosion out front.

Kicking some of the cinder blocks out of the way David stepped out of the building into the alley behind it. Sarah and Alexis jumped through the opening and they all ran for the end of the alley away from the back of the building.

Stopping at the end of the alley they waited until a large sedan pulled up and they opened the doors and jumped inside. Rav gunned the engine and they left the area quickly.

Reaching the heliport all four of them left the car and got in the helicopter whose blades were already spinning. The chopper left the ground and headed back towards the sea. This time the pilot kept the chopper almost on the ground until they reached the Mediterranean Sea. He then increased the altitude until he was operating at a normal height for the helicopter. Forty minutes later they reached the carrier and landed. The pilot exited the chopper after he shut it down. Several of the deck crew used a crane to lift the chopper over the side of the carrier where they dropped it into the sea. Within three minutes the helicopter had sank completely out of sight.

David watched the machine as it sank. "Ah, deniability was a wonderful thing." He thought to himself.

CHAPTER TWELVE

After a hot shower and a thorough cleaning up, Alexis found Sarah in the small conference room on the carrier that they were using as a common command center. "Well done, Mata Hari!"

Sarah looked at her friend who was still sporting the darkened skin. She'd removed the black wig and the brown contact lens. The skin tone gave a startling but, strangely beautiful new look to the blue eyed blonde. "Hey, what a team. I'm sorry we had to take those lives but it was literally them or us."

Alexis nodded. "I'm not sorry about Walid or Hakem, they deserved it. But I regret killing that military guard. I know he was only doing his duty but he was too far away and drawing a bead on me.

Sarah knew Alexis had comparable experience to her history and therefore didn't try to counsel her on the necessities of dealing death to another human being in their chosen lifestyles. Instead, she went over and hugged her friend. They were agents but they were still women and it occasionally hurt on the emotional level when they had to do what they had to do.

Alexis patted Sarah on the back for the support. They had just sat down to eat a snack that Sarah had put together when David, Jack, Mark, and Laura walked into the room.

David waved them on to continue eating as the others sat down. Mark said, "I want to thank all three of you for your contributions on that operation. You went straight to the heart of the missile location problem and got the information. We get to stand down for a few hours while Washington and Tel Aviv figure out the proper approach."

Sarah mumbled through a bite of chicken salad. "I know that they are aware of the timeline but do they realize that our raid will probably make them move up the schedule for firing or make them relocate the missiles?"

Mark nodded, "Oh yeah! They are very aware of the situation. They've got six different satellites and at least one predator drone watching the base as we speak. The problem is that the base is in Jordanian territory and the Jordanians are stonewalling everyone, especially the Israelis. If we strike without their permission, then it is an act of war that Jordan will use to drum up to another Israeli-Arab war."

David snorted. "Let me tell you something. Tel Aviv is not going to wait for the Jordanians to keep them from attacking the missile site regardless of their protestations. To do that is tantamount to allowing the total destruction of the Israeli population and that will not be allowed. I can assure you that there are bombers in the air right now."

Mark nodded, "I understand that David, and so does everybody else. The Iranians are on the brink of declaring war against Israel and this would be the trigger they could use to say, "See! The Israelis are attacking our neighbor Jordan." The rest of the Arab world is seeking the destruction of the Jewish nation and all they want is to be seen as defending against an unwarranted attack by Israel. Everyone knows it's a set up and that the rest of the world's Muslim nations are the audience that will decry anything Israel does. They don't care that the terrorists in Jordan are about to launch an all-out missile attack against the Jews, that doesn't fit their understanding that the Muslim radicals have been selling them for years."

David slammed his fist on the table. "SO? I was born in Israel and my children are there. If I could attack and destroy those missiles I would. Right now!"

Sarah nodded her head, "True, as would everyone in this room if we could do it David. We need to seek Yahveh for the right thing we should do at this point in this crisis. I'm afraid that we won't have much of a role in the next forty-eight hours."

David looked desperate but nodded his head. They all bowed their heads and started praying to a God they knew was loving and in charge of everything.

They had been waiting to hear from Yahveh for about twenty minutes when Jack felt a presence and opened his eyes. Hugo sat at the end of the table looking like a quiet, peaceful older man. One that radiated confidence and an assurance that was palatable.

Laura had opened her eyes and smiled, "Hello Hugo. How have you been?"

Hugo smiled faintly and tipped his head to the right. "I have been fine for many years of your time Laura. I understand the frustration you all have with the situation but understand that there is major warfare in the Heavenlies over this exact problem. That is why I was honored to speak to you. Caleb and Rose are in the thick of the battle. The enemy is doing everything it can to allow the destruction of the State of Israel. But, I must advise all of you warriors to stand down and watch what happens."

David furrowed his brow and asked, "Why?"

Hugo smiled. Our heavenly Father selected Israel as his chosen people and history demonstrates the absolute certainty of Yahveh's word and the punishment awaiting all who have mistreated or attempt to mistreat or destroy His people. Nothing can break the Lord's promise to protect His people from complete destruction. Yahveh's ultimate purpose is to establish His eternal kingdom. The people supporting the ASF, including those in Jordan and any nation that mistreats people that love God will be punished, regardless how invincible they appear. You have been obedient and have offered your lives in His service. He will take care of the ASF in a way that will show the world that He is the God of the universe. This will demonstrate to all who have the ability to understand that they shouldn't mistreat or attack Israel. Also, this will cause Yahveh's will to move mankind as He has willed it and as it has been written in His word."

David was in awe of the angel but had to ask, "Hugo, if I may ask how Yahveh will do this thing?"

Hugo stared at the man, or rather, through the man for a few seconds. "David, you can ask but I can't answer. Yahveh doesn't have to seek approval of his plans like the rest of creation. Therefore, I haven't been told what is to be. But, I can tell you that it will be spectacular beyond anything you've seen before. Yahveh has permitted the enemy to use this group of terrorists for as long as his patience will permit. They will disappear from the world after this. Never to be remembered or heard of again. I hope this will encourage you all to have faith and watch

Yahveh's mighty right hand as he smites the attackers." Hugo faded out of sight.

Jack thought about what Hugo had said and pulled out his pocket PC and accessed his Bible software. He read what he'd looked up and laughed. Everyone looked at him. He smiled, "I thought I recognized what Hugo was telling us. This is exactly what happened to Edom after they mistreated the nation of Judah roughly six or eight hundred years after Yahshua was born. Edom had raided the Jewish state and gloated over their miseries. And guess what, Edom thought that they were "invincible" in their mountains. Those are exactly the same mountains where this ASF base is located."

Laura trembled, "Guys, this is going to be very terrible for anyone threatening Israel."

David's cell phone rang. He answered it and listened. He hung up and looked thoughtful. "That was Hiram. The IDF has notified the Mossad that none of their fighter bombers destined for the ASF base will start. Any alternate aircraft they try for this mission also fail to respond. I guess Yahveh isn't going to allow the world to see an Israeli preemptive strike."

Mark's eyes glittered. "I would say that's also probably so that no man can brag about their part in the ASF's demise."

CHAPTER THIRTEEN

Kazim Nabech watched as the Russian-trained programmer worked with the old missiles to program the launch sequence and the target selection of the multiple independent reentry vehicle or MIRV warheads. Each of the two SS-18 ICBMs were equipped to carry 50 warheads-10 MIRV warheads and 40 decoys that behave just like the warheads.

Kazim had carefully instructed the programmer to target four of the warheads in each missile to suspected Israeli nuclear weapons facilities and launch sites. The other twelve warheads were to be targeted at the twelve largest populations in the Jewish state. Starting with Jerusalem and the Haifa/Tel Aviv complex the multiple warheads would eliminate ninety percent of the Zionists in one blow. The Iranian and Syrian ground forces which would follow the missile strike would finish the job of erasing the Jewish nation from the world's maps.

Kazim was particularly pleased by the Iranian demonstrations of the last weekend which were attended by a half million Iranians demanding the elimination of Israel. That would keep America and the other European nations from retaliating against anyone. He was also pleased because Iran was the largest source of the funds they'd used to purchase the missiles.

Hamid Ridha came scurrying into the large barn-like structure with a wad of papers in his hand. He had a frightened look on his face and he was obviously looking for Kazim. Kazim thought, "I have just about had all I can stand of Hamid's paranoia."

The small, weasel-faced man rushed up to Kazim waving the papers in his hand. "Kazim, have you seen this?"

Kazim ignored the papers and asked his partner, "No, I probably haven't seen anything lately Hamid, I have been busy preparing the missiles for launch. What is the problem this time?"

Hamid sputtered several times and then started talking, "Our base outside of Tymeria reports that Ben Adid escaped from the Jews and showed up at the office of Walid Faisal. He was accompanied by two women. There was an explosion, apparently a car bomb in front of the building. Twelve soldiers were killed at the front of the building in the explosion. The first brief says that Walid Faisal, his head of security, Hakem, and more security personnel were killed. Ben Adid disappeared along with his female accomplices! Our plans have been jeopardized and we need to launch these missiles immediately or we will be attacked here! Do you hear me?"

Kazim put his hand on Hamid's shoulder. "Calm down my friend. Our spies in Israel have not alerted us to any Israeli warplanes being launched. The same thing goes for their American allies. There have been no missile launches by anyone other than the Indians and they are not our enemies. If Ben Adid managed to escape from Facility 1391 of the Zionists, a truly prodigious feat in itself, then his visit to Tymeria would follow his latest information as to our organization. The multiple deaths and destruction are his calling card as are the two women. He never raises a hand to anyone. He lets his "protectors" take care of the dirty work. When did he visit the base at Tymeria?"

Hamid stared at his calm mentor. "Ten hours ago."

Kazim thought for a few seconds. "Then I expect Ben Adid got the information about the missiles and this base from Walid before he had him killed. Walid was never more than a puffed up weasel anyway and won't be missed. Adid will have to travel carefully because he knows the Israelis will be intensely searching for him. I don't expect him here before tomorrow afternoon and that will be well after we launch these missiles."

Hamid shook his head, "What if that wasn't Ben Adid. What if it was an Israeli agent?"

Kazim smiled, "No my friend, of all the vile things the Israelis are they aren't given to wanton murder. It is not their way. No, the mess at Tymeria sounds like Ben Adid and if we don't want him to repeat that effect here, we need to get on with what we are doing. Go monitor the situation and bring me news of anything that changes with the Israelis and their war machine which will be a thing of the past very soon."

Hamid stared hard at Kazim and finally nodded his head in agreement. Pacified, Hamid relaxed somewhat and walked away.

Kazim knew what he had told Hamid about Ben Adid coming to their base was very true and he would both launch the missiles and accept Adid's blessings or he would not be here. Hamid would have to look after himself.

The programmer finished the work on the first missile and moved to the second one. Kazim looked at his watch, "Good", he thought, "He is ahead of schedule."

CHAPTER FOURTEEN

Malik Hazim, the supreme ruler in Iran had his staff beating the anti-Jewish drums and attempting to whip the entire population to a frenzy of hatred against Israel. Thousands turned out in Tehran and some of the lesser cities to denounce the Zionist state and demonstrate for the total elimination of the small country. A natural antipathy against anything Jewish learned from birth made it easy for these people to follow the government's urging to denounce them.

In a major surprise to Hazim and his people, over several weeks many of the citizens in Iran pleaded with their neighbors and the government to stop the talk of war and learn to live in peace with their neighbors. Some known prophets also warned of disasters from the Hebrew God and suggested it would be wise to seek atonement and absolution by praying to Yahveh.

At the instigation of the leaders and their activists, the dissenters were jeered, shouted down, beaten and some were even killed. Any indication or hint of dissent was effectively run over and silenced by the radicals with the support and encouragement of the government. Strangely, no prophets had been seen in the last week and the people that wanted peace were silenced and resorted to prayer. True, it was not a good time for protesters that had any agenda other than to destroy Israel and for survival they had retired from the visible scene. The majority of Iranians had to choose between their radical government or try to leave. The angry mass of radicals crowed about their victory over the troublemakers and Jew-lovers.

The major western news outlets had multiple teams in the capital city of Tehran and scores of the lesser cities. They were broadcasting to the west the demonstrations and the hatred for Israel being spoken by all the leaders of Iran and affirmed by the radical populations who knew how to use the Western press to their advantage. Most western intelligence agencies felt it would be less than a week before there was an Arab-coordinated attack against the

Jewish homeland led by Iran. In Israel there were massive preparations for the expected attack.

While his face was on all the Iranian TVs and his pronouncements were constantly on the radio, Malik Hazim, the Supreme Leader of Iran was living in the lap of luxury in one of two completely unknown bases in the remote Iranian desert. His lifelong hatred of the Jews provided the drive to eliminate Israel. This passion was being directed from his base and the means prepared in the other hidden base. As the leader of Iran, Malik Hazim had spent billions of petro-dollars creating his version of Paradise on earth in what he called his grand bunker. Buried in the sands of the desert the opulent "bunker" was actually a small city completely dedicated to Hazim's comfort and control of his country.

The other multi-billion-dollar site was the underground base for the manufacture, storage, and ultimately, the launching of Iran's first nuclear missiles. All the overt activities that the west thought were the nuclear refinement and preparation of nuclear fuel by the Iranians were just shams to divert the NRC and other interests such as the Americans and especially the Zionists. The real material and weapons production had been completely hidden and unknown at this site for over two years.

Hazim had arranged for all the top radicals to attend him at his hidden base while he prepared to strike the Jews in less than four weeks. His nuclear missiles would destroy Israel and render it uninhabitable for centuries. He didn't care about how many of his brother Arabs would die in the West Bank or Gaza. He didn't care about world opinion. And most of all, he didn't care about the Zionist's God. The Arabs that would be killed were to be martyrs for the cause of his ambition.

One of the grand sculptures that adorned his palace in hiding was a secret pride and joy of Hazim. It had been created by a Swedish artist several years ago. It was a sculpture made out of gold rods and formed into a beautiful three-dimensional line drawing of Hazim's face. He had to admit that the infidel had captured his magnificence wonderfully. The ten-foot high golden image was made up of over a hundred twenty-four carat gold rods three inches thick. Hazim had coveted the statue and occasionally prayed to it in private. He had a special room created just for the sculpture. The walls of the room were deep black and non-reflective. In the middle of the huge room was the sculpture highlighted by hidden miniature flood lights so that it looked like it floated above its base. It was a sight to behold and Hazim never failed to display the sculpture to all the people he invited to his lair.

Today, he led the forty-three chief architects of his anti-Jewish campaign to the room and told them that this was a sign for all times. He opened the doors with a flourish and strode into the room. He stopped short and stood there with his mouth agape. The beautiful visage of his face had been totally destroyed! The sculpture had been torn apart and stuck to one of the black walls where it now formed strange words. Hazim's blood ran hot with anger and a maniacal desire to do the same to whoever ruined his pride and joy.

Roaring in his anger he yelled, "I will very slowly kill the people that did this!" Hazim couldn't read the words formed in gold and never stopped to realize that the hidden floodlights were still pointed at the gold even though the wall was dozens of feet from their previous locations. Turning to his followers he said in a low voice, "What do the words say?" There was a touch of insanity in his eyes and none of the others wanted to set him off or there could be a bloodbath with them supplying the blood.

Hamad El-Hallie had been a spy in Israel for a dozen years and managed to pass as an Israeli because he had grown up on the outskirts of the Gaza Strip and had worked in the Israeli community. His command of Hebrew was excellent. His knowledge of the Jewish/Christian Bible was very good and he had no problem either reading the words or interpreting them. He wasn't worried about Hazim killing him because he also knew the history behind the words and it didn't offer him a future either.

He looked directly at Hazim, his dark brown eyes looking black in the dim room. "The words are in Hebrew, the Jewish language. They say, *"God says your reign is ended, your life is forfeit, your rule has been handed to the people."* The last words there, *"Ad Khan, Charon af Hashem, gam HaEish"* means your fate is sufficient for the burning wrath of God, because your destination is the Lake of Fire."

Hazim wanted to snort in derision or laugh at the supposed message but a fear washed over him that left him mute.

Thirty minutes earlier in Jordan, Kazim Nabech knew that the Jews had less time than anyone thought. In fact, now that the programmer had set the targeting for ten major Jewish cities into the missiles and carefully tested them to assure they would not miss, Kazim knew that his ancestral enemies were out of time.

Feeling a vague concern about being stopped again before he could strike Israel, he hastened to have his troops move the two launchers out into the open and raise the missiles to launch position. He had the Russian technicians verify that the sequence was ready and the liquid fuel was completely loaded into the missile's bellies. After he had what the Americans called a "green board" he grinned widely and with little pomp or ceremony he pushed the two launch buttons on the portable control panel.

He was a quarter mile away from the launches as both missiles climbed rapidly away on towers of flame. It would only take them six minutes to reach their target release areas and then the warheads and fake warheads would disperse. In less than three minutes after that Israel would become no more than a tragic memory for the world.

In Tel Aviv, Washington, the Kremlin, and in the defense centers around the world, sirens sounded and klaxons blared the warnings of missile launches.

The tracks of the missiles indicated that they were launched from Jordan and their trajectories were short, not intercontinental, but definitely arcing over towards the Middle East.

In Hazim's plush underground bunker one of his technicians ran into the room with a frantic look on his face. "Master! Two missiles have been launched from Jordan and their computed track has them coming here! What are we to do?"

Hazim suddenly grinned and laughed maniacally, "Nothing!" He shouted. "We can do nothing!

The missiles followed their programming exactly as they were designed and at the proper moment the warheads were released among the fake warheads to confuse interception. The older Russian design was more than effective as a weapon of mass destruction. The warheads rained down on the selected targets at supersonic speeds and at the altitude of four hundred feet over the targets they detonated. Hundreds of Megatons of nuclear blast, heat, and radiation pulverized the targets. The surrounding terrain was leveled and the destruction was more than complete.

Everyone watching the missile strikes by satellite or spy craft felt a deep sense of horror and regret that mankind could bring such misery on its own species.

The list of cities that had been obliterated was being shown on the big screens in NORAD's headquarters buried in Cheyenne Mountain near Colorado Springs, Colorado in the USA. An unknown feed from that broadcast was also being shown in the Fortress by Charlie Wu.

Even though they had such a sense of concern for Israel and sadness for David and Sarah the team held each other's hands and stood before Yahveh in commitment to His will. As the destroyed targets were listed the Crossfire Team stood stunned as they saw the information on the aircraft carrier in the Med.

No one was more surprised than Kazim Nabech. He looked at the information mounting up on the video screen in front of him with dread and ice filling up his soul. He thought, "This can't be! I checked the targeting and it was for the cities in Israel, not Iran! This is impossible!"

It dawned on him that the God of the Jews was real and had used him as the tool of revenge against the people that hated God's people. He stiffly turned and walked outside only to hear, "What have you done?" screamed in shrill tones by Hamid Ridha. He turned to look at the smaller man and noticed he had a really large handgun in his small fist. The brief thought flew through Kazim's mind that the combination looked ridiculous and humorous at the same time.

But it didn't make him smile. He was still attempting to understand the enormity of his actions. "No! Not his actions, but the actions of the Jew's God".

He realized that Hamid was probably going to kill him but that didn't bother him too much. He was already dead to himself. Everything he had professed, everything he had spent his life on, was chaos and backwards. He looked at Hamid as he said, "Don't you think you need to use two hands on a gun that big?"

The little man's face got even a shade deeper than before as he took aim, one-handedly, and cleanly shot Kazim through the heart. It was a big gun and the one shot ended the life of Kazim Nabech. He fell to the ground already dead. His last thought was that this was a much nicer death than he deserved or would eventually get. He then found himself standing before Yahshua for judgment and now understood that his death was simply a precursor of the hell he was going to receive, forever.

Hamid stared at his old friend and mentor and realized that he, Hamid, did not have any future either. He put the hot muzzle of the gun under his chin and pulled the trigger again.

CHAPTER FIFTEEN

It took less than two hours of mixed grief and curiosity over the devastation in Iran, before the other Arab nations began calling for a retaliatory strike against Israel.

The curiosity was because none of the Iranian cities had been destroyed, just part of the remote desert. The entire ten MIRVed warheads in each of the missiles had fallen together on two remote parts of the Iranian desert. Why they had been directed there wasn't known or understood by most people. The activists and radicals did notice that they had lost all communication with the leaders of both their crusades to destroy Israel and the entire country.

In the last minute before the warheads struck, Malik Hazim had run down to the control center in his plush bunker and he watched as its electronics worked perfectly. He now had no doubt at all about the missile targets. He realized with horror that they were directed at his hidden base and the country's nuclear site. His last thought before the fireballs blew through his supposedly impregnable hidden base was that Israel had somehow found him and someone would have to pay for that.

The intelligence centers around the world were also mystified as to why the missiles hit where they did until the word flew through their organizations about the hidden bases from a suddenly remorse terrorist in Iran who wanted protection for his information. Chairman of the Joint Chiefs of Staff, General Miles noted that even though Iran's leader had actually fooled all the intelligence networks, he forgot that God sees everything. "All things that are hidden will be revealed."

Strangely enough, it was China that tried to redirect the hatred from Israel to the Arab Strike Force. The Chinese Premier tersely spoke through all of the communications medias and was covered by all broadcast sites even Al Jazeera. He reminded everyone that the missiles had been stolen from Russia by the ASF and the missiles had been launched from Jordan by the ASF, not from or by Israel. He made it perfectly clear that to attack Israel for this disaster would only set the entire Middle East on fire which would be ruinous.

Russia was not silent about the attack. They floated the theory that it was Israeli agents that had brought about the theft of their missiles using the ASF as a scapegoat. The Jewish state had probably commandeered the base in Jordan to deflect the blame for the attack from Israel. The whole world knew Israel had to eliminate Iran's nuclear capability to prevent the Iranian government from fulfilling their open threat to destroy the Jews.

Russia reminded the world that they had a peace pact with Iran and now considered themselves at war with Israel for the missile attack. Russia did not want to use nuclear weapons on Israel because it would totally destroy Israel and secretly because they coveted the Israeli warm water ports for themselves.

The Chinese Premier reminded the world and especially the Arab countries that the west, led by the United States would back Israel. Interestingly enough, the U.S. didn't jump into the propaganda war even though they knew the weapons had been taken by the Jihadist warriors of the ASF.

To emphasize the Chinese position on the matter, the Premier advised everyone that if Russia or the Arab world used this event as a reason to attack Israel then China would be on Israel's side and the Chinese weren't noted for being reluctant to eradicate their enemies. That should have taken the fire out of the anti-Jewish talk and shut up most of the people advocating attacking the Jewish state. But, a demonic delusion, allowed by God, was ruling the Middle East countries and most ignored the Chinese ultimatum.

Russia started massing their army and negotiating with other nations for an all-out attack on Israel.

Jordan announced that they had found the launch site of the missiles totally abandoned except for the missile launchers and two corpses. They denounced the people responsible for using their land to launch the missiles without their knowledge or approval. Jordan rejected any notion that they were complicit in the operation on any terms.

The argument the extremists employed was, "Why would the ASF strike the desert of Iran? It doesn't make any sense! Each country was suspicious of each other and still thought secretly that somehow, Israel was the cause of the death and destruction."

God's wrath over the attempted strike against His children continued to play out that day. In the desert of Iran a third hidden military base launched thirty fighter-bomber jets against Amman, Jordan in response to the missile attack.

Jordan's Air Force intercepted the Iranian force and shot down most of the attackers. Three of them got through the blockade and dropped their bomb loads on Amman. Hundreds of people were killed and hundreds more injured. Amman retaliated against the Iranian base but lost most of their aircraft to defensive missiles. In response to their mutual defense pact with Jordan, Libya launched a tactical nuclear tipped cruise missile that reached and obliterated the Iranian base. An Iranian submarine torpedoed and sank a Libyan-flagged container ship carrying relief supplies to Africa in retaliation for the missile attack.

Very quickly sides were being drawn up in what could be an all Arab against Arab showdown. That worked directly into the plans that Russia had for attacking Israel. The European countries were in great turmoil due to their large and growing Muslim populations that were demonstrating against everyone and bringing industry to a shuttering halt. The sudden conflicts also brought the OPEC oil process to a halt which affected the whole world.

The United States, already crippled by economic woes, was concerned that it would be dragged into another major middle-eastern war. The country had suffered a major loss of confidence by investors and the stock market dropped dramatically, again. The elections were now tipped heavily against the conservatives. It looked like the liberal candidate and his party would win next month. Robert Stokely had been the Liberal VP candidate until his running mate, the Presidential candidate, had been assassinated three months before. But, the country's mood was rapidly becoming isolationist. The liberal party saw their chance to move the country towards a socialist state where the administration would run all aspects of everyone's lives.

Even so, America and the world powers tried to calm down the hostilities but their efforts were largely being ignored by all sides. Large armies were being massed on the border of each country and threats were flying as the world teetered on the brink of all-out war. The rhetoric became militaristic and demanding. The dark clouds of a third world war were gathering everywhere.

Since the United Nations had collapsed during the poisonings of Israel and America the major body attempting to coordinate national interests was the European Union since it comprised a large number of countries. A peace envoy was sent to the Middle East to attempt to calm things down. The European Commission sent their Italian Commissioner, Marco Marino to Saudi Arabia as a first stop. Marco had been born in Turkey but had moved to Italy with his family years before.

Impressing the Saudis with his commanding presence and clear logic he got their complete cooperation and their temporary but unilateral standing down of their military forces. In a whirlwind of activity Marco visited each of the major Arab nations in an attempt to convince them to also back away from their aggressions.

At this perilous time in history Russia saw its chance to take over Israel and much of the Middle East oil slipping away. So the Russian Premier orchestrated a major Muslim assault against Israel. While Russia itself merely sent hundreds of their "advisors" to choreograph and coordinate the Muslim assault they could deny that they, Russia, had attacked Israel. They of course would send in rescue teams to help Israel after the attack. Those teams would consolidate Russia's control. The Arab armies measured over one hundred thousand troops using Russian tanks, arms, and field tactical nuclear weapons. These troops came from the countries that despised the tiny nation of Israel and had vowed to erase it from the Middle East, these countries were Iran, Syria, Azerbaijan, Armenia, Georgia, Chechnya, Kazakhstan, Kyrgyzstan, Uzbekistan, and Turkestan and Turkey.

China and the U.S. raised strident calls in the world stage for the Arab confederation to withdraw and threatened dire results; they were ignored as feeble and ineffectual by the attacking countries.

As the confederation armies reached the border of Israel and began their assault into the mountains of Israel, a 9.8 earthquake struck the region and the land suffered such an upheaval that mountains crumbled and the land shook so violently that thousands of troops were lost, crushed or dropped into bottomless chasms.

As the troops regrouped after the earthquake a strange phenomenon occurred. Dozens of dust dervishes which looked just like faint, miniature funnel clouds, moved through the assembly areas of the troops. Men swatted them away and kicked at the spinning clouds where they stirred up the dust on the ground. There was an immense rumble in the sky and each one of the dervishes quickly thickened and grew immensely in power. Before anyone could comprehend what was happening there were dozens of violent tornado funnels weaving around each other and throwing men, tanks, anything they struck, into the air and destroying them. Many more thousands of troops died from these freak storms.

Deceived by a powerful spirit sent by God, the Muslim and Arab armies each wanted to lead the attack on Israelis while they still had any troops. Each of them would not allow another group to assume control. Eventually they turned on each other. Tactical nuclear weapons which had been supplied by the Russians and meant to be used on Israel killed thousands of the Arabian army personnel.

Seeing the devastation and lack of coordination on the part of the attacking armies and to prevent the conquest of the Middle East by the Arab confederation, the combined air forces of Israel, China, and America picked this time to strike massively against the troops from the sky.

Advanced stealth aircraft from all three nations rained low-yield nuclear bombs onto the remaining confederation troops. This sudden invisible air attack against the already disarrayed armies completely demoralized the remaining army units on the plains before the mountains of Israel. Fleeing the Israeli army and death from above, the remaining survivors fled from the field of battle and headed back to their homeland by any means they could find.

CHAPTER SIXTEEN

After the hostilities ended, Marco Marino moved quickly between the Middle East countries to prevent any more violence. He succeeded because he was able to show them that their fears were now groundless and that he would work fairly and equally with each country to resolve their complaints and concerns. The major turning point in his ascension was his declaration that he had personally brought about the end of invasion and it was through his negotiations that peace was restored to the region and war avoided. He took complete credit for routing the Russian confederation and preventing the destruction of Israel. The world press was more than glad to trumpet his great achievements in ending World War III.

After that, wherever he went peace followed. In less than three days he had calmed the Middle East and was recognized as the international representative to the Arab world in its dealings with the European Union and the rest of the world in general. To consolidate his dealings with the Middle East Marco returned to the EU and made a strong argument for an expanded world union that would include all of the Arab states and those in Africa with the EU to form the largest and most powerful union in the world. Israel would not agree to join such a union in fear that their tiny nation would quickly be swallowed up by their much larger neighbors.

Based on his popularity throughout the world, the EU realized that their union would suffer greatly and possibly collapse unless they embraced Marco's ideas and they agreed with conditions. The first condition was that the new Arab nations would be associate members and not voting members as things were too unwieldy at present. They had just managed to reduce the number of true managing nations from twenty to ten. The second condition was that Marco would have control of the newly expanded union. The other leaders ceded much of their control and power over to the new union and Marco Marino.

Marino was unanimously selected as the President of the new group which was known in the west as the One World Government. Other countries clamored to be included in the new trading and cooperative giant so as to not be left out.

Seeing the writing on the wall, so to speak, the American Congress took up the discussion of joining Marco's enterprise to prevent the U.S. from becoming the rest of the world against America. On top of his support of the new American Union of Canada, the U.S., and Mexico, the new Liberal Presidential candidate, Robert Stokely, greatly encouraged their efforts and urged quick passage of a bill allowing the U.S. to join the new One World Government. Those in the know realized that joining the new world government would balance out the twenty trillion-dollar debt that the U.S. had created during the last twenty-seven years.

Many in the U.S. worried about such a move and none more so than the Christian community which recognized the signs as Biblical Prophecy of the Anti-Christ and the end times. Christians world-wide who studied Biblical Prophecy realized that the one-world-government was going to happen but were trying to slow the slide of replacement of the American sovereignty and control of the country to the OWG. They brought lawsuits to prevent the government from ceding control to Marco Marino.

The ACLU quickly brought legal countercharges against this "religious" intrusion by Christians into state affairs as illegal per "Separation of Church and State".

While the people bought guns and ammo by the droves, the new liberal government group which was virtually assured of being ushered into power rushed pell-mell to get several bills through Congress for the new President to sign as soon as he was sworn in next January. Unknown to the Congress or the people of America, the new President-elect had already committed to sign treaties with several foreign countries that would first limit and eventually eliminate the rights of Americans to own or bear arms. While this was an end-around effort to subvert the Second Amendment of the Constitution of the United States, the new President felt it was in the best interest to remove weapons from the masses. His best interests that is, as he eyed his new leadership role in the coming one world government.

Lame duck President Bollen was steadfast in his rejection of the efforts to pass the One World Government bill but was ineffectual as the liberal press did what they could to ignore his cries for sanity and they effectively isolated the remnants of his Presidency. The already left-leaning Congress blocked any efforts he made to prevent the decline of American sovereignty. The liberal media trumpeted the EU efforts to finally bring peace to the planet, which they pointed out was an effort unlike previous administrations, especially the present one.

Marco Marino had stopped the conflict, dispelled the dark clouds of war, and had stabilized the situation. To keep it that way he recommended two goals to be accomplished. The first was to go to Israel and negotiate a seven-year peace accord. The second was more far-reaching. He recommended that a new system of control for world commerce be considered. Computers were so much in control of the world's commerce at this point Marco felt that they could be used to give true equality and fairness to every member of the human race.

Since the US had replaced gold with the Federal Reserve Note of the United States as the world's monetary standard, it was easy for the world to replace that with a totally computer controlled standard because a major threat loomed in the form of the theft of personal wealth. To prevent crime and the usurpation of the individual's wealth, Marco Marino recommended that an implanted computer chip would completely prevent identity theft.

That idea was universally accepted in the spiritual darkness of Europe and ways to accomplish such a process were tasked to be accomplished by the middle of the next year. To quiet dissenters and those that said they would refuse such a "mark", the new OWG made it clear that if a person did not have the chip they couldn't buy or sell anything and would eventually not be allowed to own anything, like property, or homes. Any property they already owned would be forfeited and given to the state to use as they saw fit.

The brilliance of such concepts swept the poor people of the third world countries and then the Middle East, with the exception of Israel and Christian communities around the world. China and the Russians both rejected such a concept and would not accept any of the requirements. But, the tide of popular opinion was being organized to recognize these as obstructionists and standing in the way of world peace by the EU and the OWG.

In an effort to prevent national polarization and a new possibility of war, Marco Marino recommended that the rest of the world ignore these complainers and concentrate on creating the greatest era of peace the world has ever seen.

A major movement began throughout Europe to recommend that Marco be the leader of the new OWG. There were few to stand in his way and quietly, behind the scenes he took steps to see that anyone who stood in his way would soon be silenced. But, his time had not yet come.

CHAPTER SEVENTEEN

The Crossfire Team returned home to their Fortress headquarters in the mountains west of Denver, Colorado and after resting and recovering from their efforts, Mark and Sarah set up intense training routines for all of the team on a rotation basis through the gun range and the gym. The core team continued to monitor the hectic pace of events in the world at large.

There was no mistaking the signs of the times and the rise of the prophesied Anti-Christ in the person of Marco Marino. The hugely popular world movement toward mandatory acceptance of the "Mark of the Beast" was troubling as was the sweeping abandonment of long held American ideals by the new left-leaning government-to-be which was poised to sweep the elections in November.

Jack got a call from President Bollen requesting permission for a state visit by himself and some of his selected personnel to the Fortress in two days. Jack was more than willing to receive the man that had been the team's friend and staunch backer for the last four years.

Laura interrupted Mark's training to drive everyone to work hard on cleaning everything and making the place presentable. Jack called a meeting the evening before the visit to set forth the Crossfire Team's positions concerning world events and the pending transition of the American government.

Everyone, including the warriors of the SOG and the part time members assembled in the huge living room of the Fortress. Laura checked the roll call to ensure that everyone was there. The list included, Jack Malone and herself, Mark and Sarah Connelly, David Zahavy and Alexis Hutton, Mike White and Su Li, Sensei Jim Grady, Carol Moffet, Steve and Larry Malone, Stan and Debbie Hargrove, Charlie and Linda Wu, Victor Chamberlain, Bob Wexler, Carol Nolan, Judah Maritz and Aaron Jacobson, and the entire twenty-five-member Crossfire Sensitive Operations Group (SOG). The team's pastor, Tim Carson was unable to attend due to a major two-day service for his flock to address the concerns caused by world affairs.

Jack stood at the front of the assembly and welcomed each and every one of the team. As he was speaking, Carol Moffet moved over to sit by Laura. Laura put her arm around Carol's shoulders and smiled at her. Carol asked in a low voice, "Laura, I've been here such a short time I really don't know most of the people here or their roles with the team. Could you help me?"

Laura nodded and studied the team as her mind cataloged the people there and their involvement in the team's efforts.

"Jack and I were called by God to stand for Him four years ago in a men's store in Denver". She compared Jack's present appearance to that time. "Jack is still a six-foot, four-inch tall hunk as far as I am concerned. His blonde hair has thinned and he keeps it trimmed short as is necessary by our combat lifestyle. If anything, I think his gray-green eyes are more penetrating than before and his body has bulked out in his chest and arms. I was in love with him then and I know I love him more today, especially his faithful service and love for the Lord."

Thinking of herself it startled Laura to realize that she had aged somewhat over the last four years herself. She smiled at Carol. "I like to think that the last four years have been beneficial to me because I certainly get plenty of exercise. I've, hopefully, matured somewhat. I've gotten used to keeping my hair cut short for the same practical reasons that Jack does. Jack tells me that my eyes have a more serious look than in the past. As long as he still finds me attractive, even in fatigues, I'm happy. I'm blessed by the special gift which Yahveh has anointed me, the golden armor and the gleaming sword of the word that shines with the light of Yahveh's esteem. As you know when the enemy appears and I am praying in the spirit, the armor and sword will appear and allow me to do combat with the demons." Laura thought back on some of those combats and shivered.

"Just recently, as the number of demonic violations has risen and they have begun to take my capabilities into their attacks, Sarah has also been given the golden armor and sword of Yahveh. The two of us make an awesome team of spiritual warriors.

Looking at Mark Connelly and his wife Sarah, Laura said, "I love Mark and Sarah as our truest friends and because they are both true believers who we can always count on to stand with us through anything."

Mark has been with us from the beginning of our trials, even before the team became a team. He has lost some of his youthful playfulness but has gained so much more as he has matured into a thoughtful and effective warrior. He is the leader of our combat efforts because, as a retired U.S. Navy SEAL he has the most combat experience."

Laura smiled at Mark as he looked at her with a question concerning her talking about him. Laura nodded to the warrior who nodded back and went back to listening to Jack. Laura continued, "As you can see, Mark is a couple of inches shorter than Jack and is a strong, solid man. He outweighs Jack by about forty pounds of muscle mass and is a tireless fighter who gives his all. I really appreciate his devotion to Yahveh and to his duty. His career in the SEALs as a team leader gave him the training we needed to lead the Team when combat is needed. He and Jack make a great duo as leaders for the team."

Both women studied Sarah for a few seconds. "Sarah is slightly shorter than I am at six foot. Sarah also has been with us from the start. Her confidence is based on years of spy craft as a Mossad field operative. A thorough professional in the spy business she brought a great deal of depth to our operation. She told me that after watching Yahveh and Yahshua work through us she began to doubt her Jewish upbringing. When her mission control officer, and good friend, David Zahavy was killed in Tel Aviv, defending both Sarah and myself, Sarah pleaded with us to help her save him as he died. God moved and Yahshua restored David to life. This one event impacted her so deeply she gave her heart to Yahshua."

Carol nodded her agreement, "I remember when she saved me at GTherm and I was so impressed by both of you and Alexis. What gives you the strength to stand up like the men in battle?"

Laura smiled broadly, "Our love and confidence in Yahshua and Yahveh. I assure you I wouldn't be doing this if it wasn't His will for me to do it. It's not in my nature to desire the death of others. But, Yahveh has given me not only peace but the desire in following His will." Laura was quiet for a few seconds. She looked Carol in the eyes. "When He empowers me to do combat with demons and His righteous anger fills me I. . . I sometimes wonder if anything in this world is safe from me."

Laura smiled again. "Sarah and I have become best friends. Sarah fell in love with and married Mark after the terrorist situation in Israel. Sarah left the Mossad to become Mark's anti-terrorist business partner and became the fourth core member of the team." Laura remembered that was over three years ago.

Laura sighed and then continued her description of the assembled team members for Carol.

She pointed out David Zahavy. "That man had his life changed radically when Yahshua brought him back to life after he was killed in Tel Aviv. His meeting the Son of God changed him from the Jewish man he had been into a born-again Christian sort of like Saint Paul of the Bible." Laura laughed, "Somehow, actually meeting your Savior tends to give one a clearer view of things."

"David was a field controller and team leader of the Israeli Mossad, which is the premier intelligence operation in that country. He worked with the Crossfire team as needed with the Mossad's blessings. He joined us last year after being forced to leave the Mossad by bad politics and pressure from Omicron. His depth of knowledge and tactics is immense and his contributions to the team are highly valued. David's wife left him when he left the Mossad and she took his two children. But, she left primarily because he had become a Christian which clashed with her steadfast belief in Judaism. David misses his kids but knows that they were much safer considering his new role with the Crossfire Team.

Laura looked directly at Carol, "I like the fact that David brought a class element to the team with his precision in everything he does. He thinks three times and acts once. He is the fifth oldest member of the team being in his late thirties. Only Steve and Larry Malone, Sensei Jim Grady, and Mike White are older. David keeps in excellent physical condition by exercise and diet. It's that good physical condition that lets him keep up with the younger team members in the field. You'll notice he always dresses for success and is immaculate in his taste and his choice of clothing."

Carol studied the older man carefully.

Laura saw Carol nodding her head in agreement. "Unless, of course, he is at war when he will get just as dirty as any of the other team members. You will find that he is always ready to lend a hand to anyone and he makes sure that nobody is ever left behind, period." She grinned, "Especially Alexis."

Indicating the blonde beauty relaxing next to David, "Alexis Hutton is a new member of the team. She has a background in the secret woman's cadre of the U.S. Army Rangers. This gave her the training and toughness to keep up to the team's combat requirements. She refined her skills in the field of spy work with the National Clandestine Service. This made her even more effective for our team. Her looks belie her capabilities, she is very skilled at hand-to-hand combat, all forms of weapons, communications, and especially good at infiltrating an enemy camp, army, or country."

Shifting Carol's view to the other side of the room she pointed out a tall military man. "Mike White was recently a Colonel in the U.S. Air Force and is the newest member of the team. In the four years of our existence he has flown us on many missions through the worst conditions and fire fights we've had. His service was as a pilot on loan from the Air Force by order of the President and the Chairman of the Joint Chiefs of Staff."

Laura indicated the young Asian woman next to Mike. "During the challenge in Zyngola our transportation became more important and more frequent. At that time Yahveh brought Su Li into our lives. Mike White campaigned the administration for permission to train her. She is an expatriate Chinese, now an American citizen. Mike was given permission to use Air Force resources and he trained her to fly leading edge fighter aircraft and helicopters. Lately, as the number of missions has continued to increase so much, Jack and Mark offered Mike a position with our team. Mike is in his thirties and correctly sees a dim future for the military under the looming liberal government. He accepted the position and brings a ton of experience and knowledge with him. He is one of the top pilots we've ever seen."

Laura picked up her glass and sipped on some water. "At the young age of seventeen Su Li learned to use the exceptional talent God gave her for flying. Her parents had been CIA spies and were captured and killed during interrogation. She sold everything and wandered until she met a Chinese smuggler named Thor. He was handsome and rich and they became a couple. Thor saw her potential and had her trained as a pilot for his operation. When she wanted to learn to fly helicopters he sponsored her there also. After he was killed by the Chinese military, Su Li left China and worked as a pilot for hire. Hired by the Mossad for clandestine missions, she flew us everywhere in our Zyngola missions. These flights brought her up on the Zyngolan radar and she had to escape. We took her with us as we infiltrated Zyngola. She was such an exceptional pilot we asked her to join the team, which she did."

Jack concluded his opening remarks and asked Laura to lead the team in a prayer for guidance and understanding. Laura led the prayer and then grabbed four people to help bring refreshments for everyone.

CHAPTER EIGHTEEN

Laura sat down again, caught her breath, and was about to resume her description of the various members of the team for Carol when Jim Grady walked over with a couple of questions. Laura answered them for him and he thanked her.

As the Sensei walked back to his seat Laura smiled at Carol, "Sensei Jim Grady has been with the team from the beginning in Denver. Although he looks a lot like a bear of a man you'll notice that he moves with consummate grace and lightness. He is at least a ninth degree Master in two martial arts and was both Jack and Mark's teacher while they were training with him at slightly different times. He probably weighs two hundred and forty pounds but still is very trim. He brings wisdom and talent to the team and has survived a lot of combat helping the team on missions. He counts honor as most important. That is a trait he learned during his training in China. He is a very gentle man with exceptional talent. After he experienced an attack by a demon and was saved by Yahshua at the very beginning of the team's existence he has become a solid believer and has dedicated his life to follow the Son of God."

Laura looked at Carol. "Now, since you were gifted with the ability to see the multidimensional world of spirits and humans in the Heavenlies you have also become an invaluable member of the team. I believe that your extensive training in the interpretation of the "grid" of events, past, present, and possibly future, is a wonderful gift from Yahveh for equalization of the Crossfire Team to counter the increasing incursion of the enemy into the human realm. Being a health and fitness advocate who takes their own advice you have been taking lessons from Jack in martial arts. Mark is training you in combat and weapons, and from David Zahavy in world politics and counter terrorism. Does that pretty well describe you?"

81

Carol made a small face and nodded her agreement. "You forgot to mention I'm beautiful too." She laughed in agreement with Laura.

Laura pointed out Steve and Larry Malone. "That is Jack's father and uncle. Steve's inventions, as refined by his brother were the original products produced by Jack's private company. As his father, Steve is responsible for Jack's love of martial arts. His advice is very helpful in keeping Jack, and myself, in balance and keeps us aimed at Yahveh rather than this world."

Laura pointed out Steve's older brother, Larry. He's three years Steve's senior. Larry's expertise was in electronics until he became an ordained Pastor. He is based out of a very unique church in the Rocky Mountains which was built using some of our technology, especially the Viewports."

Laura pointed to a couple standing to one side of Mark and talking to him. "Notice the well-built guy with Jack? He looks very serious which gives him a wise and authoritarian look. Notice the slim woman standing next to him who looks like a quiet housewife with brown hair and a petite figure?

"That's Stan and Debbie Hargrove. They became team members after helping to rescue Jack from an Anti-Christian "temple". Stan has a great deal of field experience and leadership and was a Captain on the Salt Lake Police Department. He became unpopular with his Chief of Police when he helped rescue Jack from an organization that had a great, but unsavory influence on the department. Asked to be part of Mark's anti-terrorist company, he has since become an important member of the team as has his wife, Debbie."

Laura chuckled quietly. "Stan was quite surprised to find out in the Oval Office that his quiet, unassuming wife had a history as a hunter/killer sniper for the federal government." Laura laughed, "Up to that point he hadn't had a clue about her secret life in their eight years of marriage. She wasn't allowed to tell him about it until the President authorized, no, actually ordered her, to tell him."

"Debbie was a government contract sniper for twelve years. She is combat trained, and has taken lives in the course of performing her duty for her country. I think Stan has come to appreciate her apparent softness while admiring her hidden toughness. He told me that he loved her and had ever since he'd met her ten years ago. He said that Debbie's strong faith in Christ had intrigued him and his faith had been reinforced greatly when she helped him when he ran into a demon in an attempt to save a young girl."

Laura indicated the Oriental couple quietly sitting across the room from them. "Charlie and Linda Wu are another unique husband and wife package that has been with the Crossfire Team since its inception. Five years ago both Charlie and Linda, were top spies for the Chinese Internal Security forces. Sort of a combination of our CIA and FBI. On a mission they had encountered Christianity in a dying man and had determined to find out about his faith. They became Christians themselves and outlaws therefore in China. They left China for asylum in the United States. They knew of Sensei Grady and through him they signed on to work with the team at the beginning of their adventures. Charlie's expertise with computer systems and the intimate knowledge of the world's networks of spy organizations is very helpful to us and eventually, led him to run the computer center here at the fortress."

Charlie saw they looking at him and he smiled and waved. Laura waved back and turned to Carol. "Charlie is an asset in the areas of spying, combat, and intelligence gathering. We rely on both him and Linda every day."

"I think that Linda Wu is a beautiful lady with a determined mind that isn't to be denied. She compliments Charlie in the areas of spying, intelligence gathering and computer operation. You will notice that she prefers to stay in the background and let Charlie be the front man. But, don't every cross swords with her. She's a very competent warrior who trains with the men."

Laura indicated a tall, good-looking, African-American man. "Victor Chamberlain is one of the richest men in the world. He became a Christian and a sponsor after the team rescued him on his own island and saved him from death. Victor is well respected wherever he goes. His fortunes have increased greatly from his food processing empire after he became a Christian and started to provide tens of millions of dollars of relief for starving nations monthly. He finances things like the two aircraft we have and major acquisitions as needed. Victor is one of the nicest men you'll ever meet."

"The older gentleman Victor is talking to is Bob Wexler. Bob has been Jack's civilian partner in Jack's company, Technology Alternatives. Their primary business is the refinement and manufacturing of Steve Malone's inventions such as the LifeCape, the Viewport window system, and the field generator. Bob tends to stay with the business and avoid the combat missions if possible. He's already done his time in the military and felt he was a little too old to be crossing swords with bad guys. His role with the team is one of support and coordination between Jack and TA."

Laura tipped her head to indicate a pretty woman standing near them. "That is Carol Nolan; she is an agent with the Colorado Bureau of Investigation. She is really sharp and has great contacts in law enforcement in Colorado. She was rescued by the fledgling Crossfire Team when it first started. She had been undercover and had been captured by Don Miland, a local crime lord in Denver. He was torturing her when Jack, Mark, and Sensei Grady raided his mansion. Carol has worked with the team on several missions and serves as the coordinator between the CBI and the team."

"The two young men talking to Mike White right now are Judah Maritz and Aaron Jacobson, Judah is on the left. They are two ex-Mossad agents that left the company and their native country to follow David Zahavy to the United States and the Crossfire Team. Their contributions have been excellent in the area of spy skills and interrogation capabilities. They are working with Charlie Wu primarily in investigation and mission parameters."

Laura indicated the large group of military types scattered throughout the crowd. "The other people here are members of the Crossfire Sensitive Operations Group, or simply, the SOG. They are the majority of the military SOG that Yahveh had gathered to assist the Crossfire Team in several major missions. They are all rock-solid Christians and very accomplished in their chosen fields which include psychology, biomedical, and life sciences as well as combat."

Laura completed her inventory just as Jack opened the session by calling everyone's attention to some serious comments. "Team, be aware that we are rapidly approaching the end times, the Tribulation period, and the return of our Savior. The events I have listed for you indicate that there is a possible Anti-Christ at work as I speak to you. The man I'm speaking about is Marco Marino and he is one of the leaders of the EU. He is attempting to bring a strictly Muslim peace to the Middle East and has become a popular leader in the Muslim countries as well as Europe. Rumor has it that many of the EU leaders may have ceded their control to him as of two days ago."

CHAPTER NINETEEN

Don Tobert of the SOG held up his hand and was recognized by Jack. "Sir, doesn't the Rapture have to happen before the man of perdition is revealed?"

Laura's heavenly training opened up in her mind a new area that had been hidden until then. She stood up and asked to respond to the question. Jack deferred to her.

Laura turned to the rest of the team. "It is true that before the man that will be known as the Anti-Christ is revealed several events have to happen according to Biblical prophecy. First, the war that just happened had to occur. In the Bible this was prophesied as the war of Gog and Magog which pitted many of the Muslim armies under Russian army leadership against Israel. As we saw last week, God will come against the invaders Himself and destroy them. Ezekiel, Verses 19-20, say that there will be an earthquake so great that people all over the world will tremble. In the ensuing chaos, nations will begin to turn on each other. The confusion will lead to the largest case of death by friendly fire ever seen.

Verse 22 of Ezekiel tells us that there will be plagues, torrents of rain, hailstones, and burning sulfur. Just as God destroyed Sodom and Gomorrah, he will destroy these invading forces. Once again, God will make it known to all the nations that He is the Lord. He will give the nations proof that He is the Holy One in Israel. As anyone who has read and believed the prophesies of the Bible know, God, Himself, stopped those armies of two to three hundred thousand from the north from actually succeeding in invading Israel. But, as you are reading in the news, that attack helped propel the Anti-Christ into prominence. He took credit for stopping the assault on the Jewish nation. "

"During the days of terror just after the nuclear attack on Iran, the people of Israel secretly completed the third temple. This is the one after the original one built by Solomon and the second one built by Herod several thousand years ago. This temple and the startup of the sacrifices were also predicted by Biblical prophecy."

"Unknown to the world in general, the Jewish faithful began performing the morning and evening sacrifices of animals for the first time since the Diaspora of the Jews to other nations and the total destruction of the second temple. Without Christ, who they do not accept as Savior, their only hope is that the sacrificial blood of animals will cleanse their sins before God. You can see that this is extremely important to them to remove their sins."

"To prevent another such attack on Israel, Marco Marino has announced that he will sign a treaty between the EU and Israel. This treaty will state that the European Union will protect Israel for the next seven years. These seven years represent the seventieth week of Biblical prophesies in Daniel."

Laura sighed, "The world will cry peace, peace in our time, But, it will be a false peace and the Anti-Christ will bring on God's wrath which is known as the Tribulation as described in the book of Revelation in the Bible. Everyone will know it was a false peace after the first three and one-half years when the Anti-Christ breaks that peace accord by personally stopping the restored sacrifices and he blasphemies by defiling the new temple and setting himself up as god."

She shook her head. "The Tribulations will be a horrible time that will see the death of over three billion human beings or, roughly half the population of the world."

She smiled at the somber people before her. "But, there is hope. The Rapture, or the calling forth of Christ's people who love Him, will happen after the treaty is made. When the church is brought out of the world the Spirit of Yahveh, commonly referred to as the Holy Spirit, can concentrate on Israel, leaving the remainder of the earth open to the Anti-Christ. The spirit of the Anti-Christ is presently being held back by the Holy Spirit and the prayers of the saints until the end of the age of the Gentiles and the Anti-Christ cannot truly begin his conquest of the Earth until the saints have been raptured off of the earth."

Alexis stood up and asked, "Laura, I thought that the battle of Gog and Magog was the battle of Armageddon. Aren't they one and the same?"

Laura shook her head again. "No, the battle of Armageddon is the final battle of the war that starts with the battle of Gog and Magog. These are two great major wars that will serve to glorify the Father. These are also the two of the wars the Bible tells us will precede the return of Yahshua and His Saints to planet Earth when he will set up His thousand-year reign as King of Kings and Lord of Lords."

"Armageddon has been written about so much and so often, and has been the focus of so many books and motion pictures, that it has by now become a universal symbol of mass destruction and catastrophe. It will involve millions of soldiers who will come into the Middle East to destroy Israel at the end of the Tribulation period as well as the millions of soldiers of the Anti-Christ's armies who are there to repel them."

"The War of Gog and Magog has received much less attention. Yet, in its own way, it was almost as decisive in the scenario of these Last Days as its better known counterpart, Armageddon". In the Bible the "Battle of Gog and Magog", the battle which just occurred, is described in Ezekiel Chapter 38, verses 1 through 9. Those prophecies are described in these words--" *And the word of Jehovah came unto me, saying, Son of man, set thy face toward Gog, of the land of Magog, the prince of Rosh, Meshach, and Tubal, and prophesy against him, and say, Thus saith the Lord Jehovah: Behold, I am against thee, O Gog, prince of Rosh, Meshach, and Tubal: and I will turn thee about, and put hooks into thy jaws, and I will bring thee forth, and all thine army, horses and horsemen, all of them clothed in full armor, a great company with buckler and shield, all of them handling swords; Persia, Cush, and Put with them, all of them with shield and helmet; Gomer, and all his hordes; the house of Togarmah in the uttermost parts of the north, and all his hordes; even many peoples with thee.*"

"*Be thou prepared, yea, prepare thyself, thou, and all thy companies that are assembled unto thee, and be thou a guard unto them. After many days thou shalt be visited: in the latter years thou shalt come into the land that is brought back from the sword, that is gathered out of many peoples, upon the mountains of Israel, which have been a continual waste; but it is brought forth out of the peoples, and they shall dwell securely, all of them. And thou shalt ascend, thou shalt come like a storm, thou shalt be like a cloud to cover the land, thou, and all thy hordes, and many peoples with thee."*

Laura continued her answer, "Using the names by which these nations were known during Biblical times, today we know these countries as Iran, Iraq, Libya, Ethiopia, Egypt, Turkey and the Moslem Republics known as Magog. These countries formed a confederation to invade Israel and the Middle East, for the specific purpose of conquering the Jews and destroying their country. Theirs was a religious crusade, or Jihad, with the sole motive of proving that the prophet Mohammed and his god Allah are superior to Moses and his God Yahveh. "

Waving her hand to the north Laura expounded on her information. "Russia directed this invasion of Moslem nations. Now it was assumed that after the western invasion of Iraq that it would not be included in the Moslem nations of the war of Gog and Magog, because Iraq had become fully self-governing and made peace with Israel. But, as we saw last week, the radicals in Iraq rallied thousands of dissidents to join the march on Israel. They lost the battle along with the other nations."

Laura continued, "There is a certain degree of geo-political logic to bolster the fact that Russia has for many years coveted a warm water port in the Middle East. It has been determined that Russia wanted to also take over the oil wells of the Arabian Peninsula. Then, in one stroke the Russian Bear would regain her status as a world superpower to which the western world must plead on bended knees for the energy needs so vital to modern industrialized economies. To facilitate this power grab, the past and present President of Russia arranged his own coronation by rewording their constitution to allow him to rule again for twelve years. As a former leader of the USSR's KGB he is very deceptive and does not plan to give up the leadership in his lifetime."

She nodded to Jack and sat down.

CHAPTER TWENTY

Jack smiled at the rest of the team. "Well, that pretty well sums up our job if the Rapture is going to happen in the next few weeks. If Marco Marino is the future anti-Christ then events are proceeding at this moment for him to assume control of the European Union and the majority of the area around the Med. Israel has opted out to not join his little band of One Worlders and probably won't, even if America does."

Jack stood there in thought. He looked at the core members of the team and asked, "What, if anything, should we do in the immediate future to prepare for these events other than just expect them?"

Mark smiled at Jack's loss of direction. "I believe that Yahveh has been using us almost non-stop as His hands on Earth for the last few years and He will tell us what to do in the future. All we can do is pray, practice, train, and be as righteous as possible so that we are indeed included in the Rapture when it occurs."

There was a chorus of agreement on that point.

Lilly McDermott was one of the PsyOps ex-Air Force officers who had been led of Yahveh to join the original SOG and later when the government distanced itself from the team she had followed His lead to resign her commission and join the Crossfire Team. She had listened to the discussions and had agreed that she wanted to be included in the Rapture when it occurred. She sat to one side of the group so that she could see them all and evaluate the statements as they were made. She realized that it was her psychological training that made her test everything against that training. She had never been with such a unified group in her life. She thought she had in college but after graduation everyone dispersed and the friendships ended. It probably was the shared danger and mission-specific cooperation that brought these people together but she realized that it was also their mutual faith in Jesus Christ or Yahshua that melded the team together so well.

She closed her eyes to thank the Savior for leading her to this time and place which reinforced her faith at every turn and mission. As she prayed she sensed a presence in her mind. She had felt the presence of the Lord many times and was humbled that He would consider her worth the time. She relaxed in the feeling and in her mind's eye she saw a light that grew brighter until everything else faded into the far background. She recognized Caleb as the warrior angel she had seen before.

Caleb stared at her for a few seconds and then asked her the most important question in her life. "Lilly, you have dedicated your life to the Savior and have obeyed His requests. You are worthy of being called to heaven in what you call the Rapture. To not be here during the Tribulations is a worthwhile goal. At the same time the Savior needs warriors such as you and the rest of the Crossfire Team to stay on Earth for a while longer to do His will and to protect the innocent and those marked for service. It is completely your choice. You have free will and the Savior will think no less of you if you choose to join Him when the church is called. How say you Lilly?"

The shock of knowing that she was found acceptable was enough to make her knees weak but to be allowed to choose how to serve her Savior was an honor beyond words. She mentally asked Caleb a question. "If I choose to stay behind to do the Savior's work on Earth, when will I join Him?"

Caleb smiled at her in her mind. "The Savior will welcome you whenever you have the opportunity. If you battle to the end of the first half of the last week, He will draw you to Himself then."

Lilly read between the lines as was her normal testing of spoken statements. What the angel had just told her was that her place in heaven was assured over the first three and one-half years of the false peace treaty that would happen after the Rapture. Of course that was only true if she remained faithful and righteous until she died or was called. There was still some performance anxiety. It was also assured if she should die in battle or for any other reason before then she would go to heaven. She searched her heart for the proper answer. Her whole being had always been one of service to the Savior and she already knew how she would choose. "Caleb, I will stay on Earth to do the will of the Savior for as long as I can."

Caleb nodded his understanding of her sacrifice. "I can tell you that Yahshua is very proud of you and will never leave you or forsake you. Go in Yahveh's will." The angel faded from her mind and she spent a while longer singing a song of praise to the Savior of her love for Him. She opened her eyes and came back to a very somber group.

Laura stood up and got everyone's attention. "I am guessing that we all got the same choice from Caleb. There is no shame in not staying and actually that might be considered the far saner option. Can I see a show of hands of those choosing to remain?

There was no hesitation as all forty-five team members raised their hands. Tears rolled freely down Laura's cheeks as she acknowledged the willingness of everyone of this great group of people to sacrifice a guaranteed free ride for another three and half years of battle against hell itself. All she could say was, "Thank you". She turned to Jack and said, "All members choose to fight for Yahveh and our Savior through the first half of the final week."

Jack had to scrub his face to remove his tears. He stood up and thanked each and every one of the team. Then he dropped an additional bomb on the group. "Caleb also told me that we are moving our base of operations. We will be leaving this Fortress in two weeks' time."

That caused a stir of questions but he held up his hand to silence them. "I don't have all the particulars as yet but I do know that we are relocating to Israel. Caleb advised me that the climate here will not be conducive to our brand of service for Yahveh. The new administration will do everything in its power to remove our mandate and protection so that we don't embarrass them with the new One World Government."

"The Presidential orders that established the preserve around the Fortress and the troops training here will be reversed and our actions will be curtailed completely if we remain here. Now, before every one of you asks what type of accommodations we will have, I don't know as yet. I do know that the Father will arrange what we need to do his service. I will let all of you know when I know. For now, after the President's visit tomorrow I want each of you to start packing your personal items and Laura, Charlie, Linda, and I will arrange for the team's things such as the weapons, supplies, furniture, and things like the computer center to be transported. We will receive an invitation from the Israeli government and the Mossad to relocate to their nation within the week."

Jack brought the meeting to a close and sat down with Laura. He looked deeply into her eyes and found the assurance he needed that she was completely agreeable with the need to stay on Earth and move across the world. Jack put his arms around her and hugged her tightly. "Oh lady, what have we gotten ourselves into this time?"

She didn't respond but just hugged the love of her life more tightly.

Jack became aware that there several people waiting to talk to him so he released his hold on Laura, kissed her on the forehead, and turned to the team members. He immediately recognized the problems the move would cause for Sensei Grady with his students based in Denver. He also expected that Carol Nolan and Bob Wexler would want to stay in Colorado for their lives were centered there. Victor Chamberlain was not bothered by the change in addresses for the team as he was based on his island and could work anywhere in the world. Jack was a little surprised when his father and uncle told him that they would go with the team to Israel. His Uncle Larry had groomed his youth pastor to take over for him during the last two years. His dad and step-mother were free and clear of any constrictions such as mortgages or children and wanted to go in support of the team in any way they could. After seeing the commitment of his dad and his uncle for the Lord and the team, Jack realized he had teared up again.

Steve and Larry talked and said that it would take them at least six months before they could make the move due to disposal of land and property as well as other family members to talk to and convince this was the right thing.

CHAPTER TWENTY-ONE

The next morning Jack had the entire team in their dress uniforms assembled at attention in the garage when President Bollen and General Miles, exited the official limousine. While technically not in service to the government of the United States most of the troops had been soldiers, sailors, or Marines and they all saluted the Commander in Chief and General Miles. The President returned the salute and stopped to say a word to the assembled team.

"I want to thank each and every one of you for receiving us this way. This country can never repay you for your efforts on its behalf over the last few years. I can also guarantee you that if the liberal administration wins the election and has its way, you will lose any recognition you did receive. But, all that aside, I want to tell you that I, and General Miles, have nothing but the highest regards for your efforts and your service to the United States of America. I am proud to have been your Commander in Chief and will definitely include you in my memoirs in the warmest of terms. Thank you all."

He stood back and saluted them again, which they all returned. Then Jack dismissed the troops and escorted the two men and their Secret Service bodyguards to the living room.

After some refreshments and drinks were served and the guests were comfortable, Mark asked General Miles about the two nuclear strikes on Iran and any further information about the targets.

General Miles shook his head. "We will probably never know exactly what used to be in those two huge craters in the Iranian desert but we do know that Malik Hazim has not been heard from since then. Also, several dozens of his chief policy personnel are also missing. Iran simply says that the missiles struck the wrong places and there is nothing to worry about. The NSA has ensured us that there have been no communications from the Hazim administration or the man himself on any communications media since the strike. Personally, I think Yahveh wiped his whole regime off the face of the earth and ditto for their nuclear facilities. The whole fuel processing thing has been abandoned or shut down. You're going to have to draw your own conclusions because all the Intel houses are drawing a blank."

Jack looked at the President, "Sir, would you like to explain this state visit?"

President Bollen smiled and nodded his head for a few seconds and then looked directly at Jack. "You know that in a few months I will be a regular citizen again. I won't have any power or control over the country's affairs nor the military. Both Howard here and I will be out of work. What with the incoming administration vowing to undo everything we have accomplished in supporting your team and our military advances we have decided to save what we can so that the heathens don't waste the efforts of so many brave men and women and the investments involved."

The President waved his hand at the General. Howard Miles stood up and addressed the assembled core team. "Jack, I told both you and Mark about eighteen months ago about the probability of just such an administration that would be in opposition to our efforts. I had a leading that we needed to secure a future for the Crossfire Team after we leave office. After talking to the President, who concurred with me all the way, I took his advice, which has always been your advice also, and started praying for a solution to accomplish our aims. You have to understand that it needs to be legal and it can't permit successive administrations from undoing it. After quite a bit of prayer and fasting for two weeks Yahveh gave me a brilliant answer. I explained it to the President and he again agreed. He also insisted that we keep it absolutely secret. That was a tall order but we managed to work it out using the black ops project system."

General Miles stopped and looked over the group in front of him. "I have to admit that I have kept everything secret from you and your team also. But, I did that more out of a sense of humor than one of secrecy. You remember Major Gary Danning?"

Everyone nodded or said "yes" in response. General Miles smiled, "I thought you would. At any rate, a year and a half ago, based on the idea that Yahveh gave me I commissioned Major Danning and his crews to build you a new Fortress. I was working on faith here and it required a lot of other people and regimes to agree, but they did, because Yahveh is behind it."

General Miles looked around at the team members and nodded. "I am fairly certain that Yahveh has let you know that the Crossfire Team is moving to Israel very soon. Am I right?"

Jack nodded his agreement.

General Miles smiled, "That is good because that is where your new base has been built. We asked Major Danning to do what he did here only better. I think you will agree when you get a look at the new "Fortress". One of the problems we encountered was that most of the mountains near Jerusalem and Tel Aviv are held in reverence by many of the Israelis. To build a base for an American Team, even one as popular as yours is in Israel, would set off a major storm of protests and legal challenges. So we went a different direction. Our NSA contacts used their expertise in conjunction with the new advanced LANDSAT satellites and were able to locate an equally unassailable place for your base." He took a DVD out of an envelope and asked Mark to bring it up on the 70" flat screen TV behind them.

After it was ready he activated the DVD and was satisfied with the gasps he heard behind him. The panoramic view of the new Crossfire base was more than amazing and fairly breathtaking.

The General smiled at the assembled group. "This, my friends, is a masterwork by Gary Danning. Let me explain one thing at a time. First the location is a geological bubble in the earth's crust that is over one-half mile below the sea bed surface which is actually granite bed-rock with an additional three hundred feet of water above the sea bed directly over the base. The location is very secret but within the legal three-mile limit of Israel."

He activated a second view. "Using the terra forming science that we have been developing for future Moon and Mars colonies we were able to create a small world for the team to operate from. While we do use wave-power machines to generate electricity for the base, the majority of the working power is from three fifty-thousand Megawatt nuclear generators located near the base but remote enough to protect the base from radiation or melt downs."

The General changed the view to that of an immense park with grass and trees and a stream wandering through the park. It looked like a beautiful day anywhere in the world with the sun shining and some far-away clouds in the sky. "Notice that this is a fresh air open park. You're probably going to ask how we can do that over a half of mile below the surface of the sea. Well, it is a prototype, but it seems to work very well. The sun emits all the correct wavelengths and sufficient heat to keep the vegetation happy and growing. We did transplant the vegetation from the surface rather than attempt to recreate it."

He changed the view to a diagram of the park, sky, and sun. "As you can see, the "sun" is nuclear powered, and rightly so since the real sun is a nuclear furnace. The "sun" in the base rises in the east and travels over a precise path to set in the west every day at the appropriate time of the year. It is based on the time in Israel so that it isn't jarring to one who goes out or comes in. If the real Sun is at high noon over Israel, then the base "sun" is also at high noon. It is almost as if you went indoors and had a huge atrium. There are also some major air handling centers to keep everything fresh and breathable."

Mark asked, "What are the physical dimensions of the base?"

"Four miles in length, one-half mile in height at the base location and one and one-half miles in width, not including the power stations outside of that."

Jack shook his head, "Why so big? Cleaning a place that big will take a lot of effort." That got a lot of laughs from the members of the crew that had just spent time cleaning the current fortress for this visit.

The President added a comment, "It's that big because you have to have a one-mile runway for the combat and experimental aircraft to land and take off."

Su Li laughed out loud, "Gentlemen, please enlighten us as to how you are planning to have these jet aircraft get into air or land on the landing strip with all that earth and water above it?"

A new voice joined the assembly from behind the Crossfire Team members. "You'll love it, Su Li." Major Gary Danning walked up and waved to everyone. He saluted the President who casually returned the salute.

Gary was a good-looking officer in his early thirties with brown hair and eyes. It looked like the serious mien, normally required for military staff ranks, was hard put to keep his infectious smile in control. He grinned at Su Li and Mike White and had the General bring up another graphic on the TV screen. It was a side view of the "bubble" he had terra formed. "If you notice the actual living space of the base is roughly a one-half mile cube. On the surface of the base there are the daily activity functions including the replacement for your terrarium in the Fortress here. There are six additional levels going down that we will discuss in greater detail later."

He indicated the southern end of the "bubble" and pointed out the details. "If you'll notice the cavity isn't all level. We took advantage of the upward incline on the southern end to create a flight corridor for your aircraft. After lifting off of the runway your aircraft will be controlled by a sophisticated computer that will direct the aircraft through the flight corridor. At the surface the water shallows to less than fifty feet. We have "helped" the Israeli Infrastructure Committee in the creation of several small, uninhabited islands or actually, isles. This has been done primarily as a feasibility study concerning the creation of artificial islands to relieve the population pressure on Tel Aviv. These test islands have been created out of waste rock from the desert and are in place for a five-year review of how they affect the tides and currents near the Israeli coast. The southernmost and largest of these islands has a rocky southern exposure of over one hundred and forty feet in height."

He had a picture and a diagram of the island shown. "After the island stabilized last year we undercut the center part of the lower eighty feet of the seaward side of the southern face of the island. It looks like the sea shaped the opening. The undercut goes back almost one hundred feet. It is sixty feet high by two hundred feet wide and is secured by a special artificial wall at the back of this cave. If you took a small boat and some good lights with you, all you would see is more of the rock surface extending from the top of the cave to below the water line. If you happened to be looking when an aircraft is coming in, which you wouldn't be allowed to do, you would see the "wall" rise upward in less than thirty seconds. The thirty-foot-thick wall is backed by a security structure of granite and steel that is six times as hard to breech as one of the gates leading into the Fortress here."

He had another view replace the view of the false "wall". "After the security structure is raised you see that the floor of the flight corridor drops away for another two hundred feet. This allows the flight corridor to be a slanted flight way that is two hundred feet wide, two hundred and fifty feet high, and over two miles long. The corridor flight electronics will center the aircraft in this space until it enters into the actual base area where the pilot will have the full air space to fly in as needed."

Gary turned to the assembled people. "This construction was completely approved by the Mossad and secretly by the Kinnesit because it is in their best interest as you will see."

Su Li cocked her head to one side. "So Major Danning, we fly down to sea level and into a cave with a removable wall at the back and then we fly down a tunnel. Admittedly a big tunnel, but, never the less, a tunnel. Then we come into the base area and land normally. It doesn't look too tough except, what if we have high winds or storm conditions at the entry point?"

Gary nodded while smiling. "Just to set your expectations correctly, we've made over fifty transits of the tunnel so far, both in and out, and have had no problems." Gary grabbed an open seat and sat down.

Mark stood up and asked, "General Miles, what other accesses are there to the base? I doubt that you would leave us just the one which could be bombed out of existence fairly easily." Mark sat back down and awaited the answer.

The General nodded his head. "As usual, you've hit upon the weakest link in the flight arrangement. I can assure you though, that access will be very aggressively defended by both ourselves and the Israelis and that it would take more than ten cruise missiles to sufficiently damage the flight corridor opening. But, to answer your other question, there are other access points. There are four additional vehicle and personnel entrances to the base. All of them exit on Israeli soil and at places that are under control of the Mossad or the IDF. None are naked to observation as they enter or exit inside buildings that camouflage their real nature."

CHAPTER TWENTY-TWO

Major Danning took over the description of the base at that point. "As you can see in this drawing that once you are in the base containment area the normal airbase operations and material handling is done on the sub-world surface just as those services are handled on the surface. The Crossfire Team's real operations are three levels below the surface area inside the base. Your combat operations, war room, meeting rooms, and daily functions for the team will be handled on level three."

Gary indicated the next level. "Level four will provide the individual suites for all members and the recreation facilities. Each suite will have its own laundry and storage areas for personal requirements. Level five will contain the workout facilities, shooting range, bowling alley, entertainment facilities, and another small atrium for rest and contemplation. Thanks again to General Malone's ingenious "viewports" we have a wide variety of vistas for each of the rooms."

"Level six is cold and dry storage for food, weapons, ammo, etc. All of this is completely stocked at present." Gary had the General show the next slide. "Notice that your computer facilities are larger and better cooled. This is for the new generation of computing which we worked out with Charlie and Linda Wu. Victor Chamberlain personally funded a good part of this whole arrangement. The part that is that wasn't covered by the black ops funds."

The next slide showed a satellite view of the area of the hidden base. "We managed to upgrade an obsolete K-11 Keyhole satellite that SpaceOps has written off as no longer usable. Fortunately, it is in a geosynchronous orbit over the base." Gary smiled, "You have no idea the strings we had to pull to get a shuttle to visit this satellite and provide the upgrades. NASA is still trying to figure out where the orders came for that one." He showed a picture of the satellite. You have the latest software and hardware which is good because we don't know when we will be able upgrade anything in the foreseeable future. You will be able to track, identify, and have targeting information on anything in the area."

Mike White raised his hand. "Gary, are each of the suites equipped with a suitable number of scuba tanks and suits for the occupants in the event the sea leaks in?"

Gary shook his head, "No. If the sea gets in you will already have wings because everyone would be way past saving. The only thing that would cause that type of leak would be a pair of one-hundred Megaton nuclear weapons and if that happens a leak won't matter."

Laura smiled a small smile. "If the Anti-Christ's army wants to take us out we will already be in his gun sights by being close to Israel anyway."

Jack nodded, "True, but the Anti-Christ isn't going to make Jerusalem his base until the second half of the final week of Daniel's prophesy."

Jack was about to ask a question of General Miles when his cell phone vibrated on the "urgent" setting. Pulling the phone off his belt he got up and walked away from the group so as to not disturb the presentation. "Jack Malone" he responded.

"Mr. Malone? This is Bill in ComSec; I've got a priority call for you from a Mrs. Frank Mullins. She insisted I contact you immediately and implied that you would want to hear from her. Should I patch her through?"

Jack thought about the last time the team and the Mullins were together in the Philippine Islands and the deadly battles that had resulted. "It's all right Bill, hook me up."

Frank Mullins had been very helpful in hearing from Yahveh when they had been on an operation in England and Jack already had a strong feeling that this was not going to be a social call. Andrea Mullin's voice was urgent when she started speaking. "Jack. This is Andrea Mullins. I had to call you because my husband is a hard-headed man who can do the wrong thing trying to do the right thing!"

Jack understood that, he'd had similar experiences and according to Laura, he could be hardheaded also. "What's Frank gone and done now Andrea?"

Andrea Mullins sighed and then spoke rapidly. "We got a call from an Evangelist, Karl Wilmette, who's working with the remote native tribes in the mountains of Peru.

He's been working with a primitive tribe called the Utukz who have had very little contact with modern civilization. He called us yesterday and was very agitated because of what he found on his latest visit to the tribe. It's unclear to me as to what he found because he talked to Frank mostly and Frank got all upset. He related a tale about aliens and strange lights in the deep jungles in the mountains near where the tribe lives. Apparently several of the tribe went to look at the strange goings on and only one made it back. The poor fellow was dying of either advanced old age or many diseases and he told an incoherent story about "others". Others is their word for anyone different than themselves. Apparently, Karl went to the Utukz tribe and came back with stories of aliens. Frank said that God told him they were demons. My dear husband rushed out of here this morning to go to Lima and meet with Karl Wilmette. I know Frank well enough that he will go up in the mountains and get himself killed. Can you do anything to stop him?"

Jack thought about the logistics of the request while balancing it against the impending move to Israel. "Andrea, I'll have to call you back in a little bit. I need to see what we can do. Don't worry about it though. We can get to Peru a lot faster than Frank can if it can be done at all."

Andrea thanked him for considering it and said she'd wait for his call.

Jack hung up and went back to the meeting. The rest had decided to have another informal break while they discussed the move and the new base.

Jack got Mark and Laura's attention and grabbed Sarah by the neck as they walked to a quiet area away from the crowd. David and Alexis saw the gathering and came over and joined them. Jack summed up his conversation with Andrea Mullins and her request for help. He suggested they pray as a team for guidance and then decide what they should do. The six of them held hands and closed their eyes.

Jack started out the prayer with, "Heavenly Father, your love and mercies are boundless and we praise your name for the work we can do for the Kingdom in your Son's name. We seek your guidance about Frank Mullins and the problems in Peru and if we should undertake a rescue mission as requested by Andrea Mullins." Jack knew that Yahveh knew everything about the situation before they asked but he also knew that they had to pray specifically about their plea before Yahveh.

Laura picked up the prayer. "Father, our desire is to serve you and if this is Kingdom business then we want your direction concerning our part and your permission to do it. Frank is a friend and an ally of the team and we want to help him if possible. We seek Your will".

No words and no angels were forthcoming but all four of the members felt an urgency and a blessing from Yahveh for their involvement in the matter. Laura suddenly felt the need to talk to Carol Moffet about the situation.

They ended the prayer and looked at each other. Laura said, "I get the leading that we are to help Frank. I've got to talk to Carol about this."

She walked over to find Carol already at work on the problem. The white diamonds on her head and throat were blazing white and she had fallen to her knees with her hands raised, palm up, at her sides. The President and his crew were staring at her but the rest of the team had become accustomed to her sudden bouts of "work" and just gave her room.

Laura moved over by the President and explained the situation. "Carol is in communication on the spiritual plane right now. Jack got a call seeking help with some strange happenings in Peru and we started praying about our involvement. I was led to talk it over with Carol but Yahveh got there first."

The President had seen Laura in her armor and had felt the hand of God on these people and felt no doubt about their connection to the God he served too.

Carol relaxed suddenly and the white diamonds faded from view. She smiled and opened her eyes. Spotting Laura she climbed to her feet and tipped her head to the right to indicate she wanted to speak to Laura privately. Laura smiled at the President and General Miles and walked over to meet the young woman.

Carol shook her head slightly. "I never become accustomed to my sudden involvement in the heavenly realms. One second I'm talking to someone and the next I'm there and seeing thousands, if not millions, of ongoing time lines representing future plans, desires, and actualities for mankind. It's so awesome it takes my breath away every time."

She looked at Laura speculatively. "You do realize you activate my function every time you pray for guidance concerning the team?"

Laura's training by Hugo, much of which was hidden in her mind until the right time, opened up a small section of information. "Yes, I do realize that, and that is the way it is supposed to happen. God had you in mind to do this long before we met you." Laura smiled at her. "You are a powerful link in his Kingdom purposes for us all. We really do appreciate you and your anointing."

Carol smiled back at the older woman. "Laura, you have no idea how humbling it is to just have the chance to help you and the team. I love it! Anyway, Frank was right; there is demonic activity near the Utukz tribal home. Frank's involvement provides Yahveh with the right to connect us and the rationale to get involved even though the enemy has requested complete isolation of our team from this operation. God honored that request as long as no one else asked for our help. The enemy's request is very odd. It's almost as if they were trying to get our attention. Hmmm."

She thought for a second, "Do you understand the rules that I have to work with concerning this information?"

Laura made a small wave of her hand, "Somewhat but nothing definitive, why?"

Carol sighed, "I'm bound by Yahveh not to reveal hidden things unless you are already aware of them or at least have some knowledge of them before I speak of them. Yahveh couldn't involve the team in this matter because He had granted the privacy of events to the issue."

Carol smiled broadly. "But, He didn't violate the terms because the Evangelist called the Pastor. Then, when Frank took off to solve the problem by himself, it was sufficient for Andrea to call Jack. Jack's interest allowed me to see the "hidden" plan of the enemy. I still can't tell you much because you don't know the questions to ask yet. But, you will. This all has to unfold at Yahveh's timing. Again, there is great danger and a critical need for action by the team. I can tell you that you've run up against this type of demonic countdown before and, I was right about their request to isolate the team from this activity. That was simply a ruse. They want the team there. Call me when you understand more about what's going on in the mountains of Peru."

CHAPTER TWENTY-THREE

Laura repeated what Carol had told her to Jack, Mark, and Sarah.

Jack nodded, "We got the leading to get involved from Yahveh when we prayed about our direction. We need to start a planning session immediately and get Su Li to prep one of the Shrews with a flight plan to Lima" Jack frowned. "I'll go explain to the President why we have to cut short our reception of his visit."

Jack walked over to the President who was enjoying talking to Carol and Alexis while they were waiting for Jack. "Mr. President, I have to apologize in advance for this but, we have an urgent demonic intrusion that Yahveh wants us to attend to in Peru. We all really appreciate your efforts on our part by setting up the new base in Israel and hope that you and yours can join us after the inauguration."

The President nodded his understanding of their situation and suggested that they take Major Danning with them so that he could continue to fill them in on the new base while they were in flight. Then he took Jack to one side and said quietly, "I am going to take my extended family on a well-earned vacation after I leave office. I will contact you when our group reaches Israel."

Jack smiled, "We would be delighted Mr. President. Please extend our offer to General Miles if you would."

The President shook Jack's hand. "You can tell him yourself. He's already asked to accompany you on whatever mission you have going. Truthfully, he is unofficially out of a job already. The incoming administration already has their transition team in his office to prepare for the handoff after the election. While this is unprecedented by a candidate that hasn't won the election as yet it seems he has the control to do it. They are so sure of themselves and I can't find anyone that will gainsay anything he wants to do. Anyway, General Miles can't do anything without their tacit approval so he plans to continue being away from the office for the next three months until the inauguration makes it official. Is it all right if he sits in on this one?"

Jack nodded his approval, "We would be grateful for his insight and his experience."

Mark had listened to the exchange and asked, "Didn't General Miles have a tour of command that included Peru for a while?"

The President nodded, "Yes, he did. All right, I have to attend to the election and the aftermath in Washington and I might as well get after it. I understand that Marco Marino is making a highly publicized trip to Israel on behalf of Turkey and the EU. We think he is going to offer to protect Israel for the next seven years and will sign a peace accord with them. Reminds me of the Bible and a certain world dictator. The president looked at Jack, "Make sure you're prayed up. A pleasure seeing you all again and we look forward to having more time together in the near future." The President shook Jack's hand again and started to turn away. Turning back he smiled, "Of course, if the Rapture happens I expect to see you in heaven." The President turned and headed for the elevators followed by his Secret Service people.

General Miles walked over to Jack as he watched the President leave. "I guess you're going to be saddled with this old warhorse for a while. That all right with you?" He carefully watched Jack's reaction in his body language and facial expression.

Jack smiled and put his hand on the General's shoulder. "We would be honored to have a fellow warrior with your qualifications assisting us on this. I understand you have some knowledge of Peru and its inhabitants."

Across the room Mark was telling Sarah. "Get the core team together in the war room and have Mike White accompany Su Li in the Shrew. I think we will need all the hands we can get this time."

Sarah grinned, "Here we go again."

Mark leaned over and kissed her. "I love you. No other gal I know would look forward to battling demons as if it was a fun job."

Sarah grinned and took off to kick things into gear.

Jack walked over to Steve and Larry. "Well guys, we have to go on a mission so how would you like to help Charlie and Linda Wu coordinate the move to Israel?'

Larry looked at Steve, who nodded, and then back at Jack. "Anything we can do to help, we will."

Jack got Charlie and Linda together with his dad and uncle and then headed for the war room. Laura asked Gary Danning to accompany her and led him to the war room. Jack steered General Miles in the same direction.

The core team of Jack, Laura, Mark, Sarah, David, and Alexis sat down in their individual positions and turned their consoles on. Jack showed Major Danning and General Miles to open work stations and showed them how to work the console.

Laura started out with the date and the number Charlie's computers just gave to the new mission. She then did a roll call and turned things over to Jack. Jack repeated the original request and the results of their prayers and Carol's inputs. He then introduced General Miles and Major Danning as Mission Specialists. General Miles spoke into the record that for the time of the mission he would defer to General Connelly on things military and to General Malone on mission requirements. He did this to remove any hesitation due to his position or rank in the midst of action or combat. Gary repeated his information and concurred with General Miles as to the team's authority in this matter.

Jack called Charlie Wu into the conference and asked him to use all assets available to detail the area in question as to demonic activity or military operations. He then asked General Miles to detail what he could about the target country and location.

Calling up a map of Peru on his console, the General threw it up on the big screen above the end of the console table. He cleared his throat and began.

"Ancient Peru was the seat of several prominent Andean civilizations, most notably that of the Incas whose empire was captured by the Spanish conquistadors in 1533. Peruvian independence was declared in 1821, and remaining Spanish forces defeated in 1824. After a dozen years of military rule, Peru returned to democratic leadership in 1980, but experienced economic problems and the growth of a violent insurgency. The presidential election of 2006 saw the return of Alan Garcia Perez who, after a disappointing presidential term from 1985 to 1990, returned to the presidency with promises to improve social conditions and maintain fiscal responsibility.

Peru's location is in Western South America, bordering the South Pacific Ocean, between Chile and Ecuador It has an area totaling 1,285,220 sq. km with 1.28 million sq. km of that land and with 5,220 sq. km of water. The entire country is slightly smaller than Alaska. The country has a coastline of over 2,400 km and the country claims a territorial sea out to 200 nautical miles."

The General took a drink of water. "The country's population is slightly over twenty-nine million as of the last estimate. There are several major infectious diseases with a very high degree of risk. These are: food or waterborne diseases: bacterial, hepatitis A, and typhoid fever. Vector borne diseases are: dengue fever, malaria, Oroya fever, and yellow fever. The official languages are Spanish and Quechua. Unofficially there is Aymara, and a large number of minor Amazonian languages. To determine the time difference use UTC-5 which is the same time as Washington, DC during Standard Time." The General finished his high level description of the Peruvian country.

Mark said, "I think we need to get to Peru in time to head off Frank and find out from him what the local situation is in the jungle."

Jack handed out the usual assignments with Mark taking the lead for military strategy, Laura and Sarah for demonic combat with David, Alexis, and himself as support and control. General Miles and Gary Danning would be observers or military support as needed. Jack looked around the table and said, "Let's go."

As the others left to set up for the trip, General Miles put his hand on Jack's arm and stopped him. "Just a question. You are preparing for this operation in exclusion to anything else. Why are this single pastor and his situation so important to the team?"

Jack realized that as the team matured they had begun to take mental shortcuts which new people, such as General Miles, wouldn't have. "Sir, I'm sorry but due to repetition we have normal operational shortcuts that most people aren't in on or aware of. Let me explain. We don't have an agenda or plans as such. We are operating strictly as servants to Yahveh. Regardless of the importance the world would place on what we do, we pray, and the leading from Yahveh is our guidance. This is backed by input from Carol and her interpretation of the multidimensional grid, or potential events she can see in the Heavenlies. I can't tell you why Frank Mullin's trip to Peru is more important than other things. At least, not yet. But it is the leading of Yahveh that we confront this demonic activity with all the resources we have. Does that clear up your concern?"

Howard Miles smiled, "Positively. I can understand following orders, especially the Lord's orders. You'll have to forgive me for being so "in the world" but that's been my battlefield for so long it will take me a little time to reorganize my thinking to a multi-world map which includes the spiritual world."

Jack nodded, "Yes sir, it takes everyone a while to understand that the spiritual dimension is much more real than this stage we are on."

The two men continued to talk as they headed for the armory to get their gear for the trip.

CHAPTER TWENTY-FOUR

During the first part of the flight Jack watched and listened as the seven other people brainstormed the mission based on the minimal information they had so far. It was an excellent example of highly trained professionals bouncing concepts off of the other talent available to refine their ideas or eliminate them completely. There were no ego trips, no agendas, and no rivalries.

Jack summed up the best concepts, logged them into his iPad and suggested that everyone get some sleep as it may the only chance they get for a while.

Everyone grabbed pillows and blankets and settled down in their individual seats that converted into beds as the lights were reduced to a low level. Jack checked on the piloting duo and found them deep in conversation about flight characteristics and combat capabilities compared to a wide variety of other aircraft, fixed wing and rotary. He suggested they spell each other and get some rest themselves.

Climbing into his seat bed he found that being six-foot, four-inches tall has some drawbacks as his feet hung uncomfortably off the end of the chair. As he tried to get comfortable he felt his feet being supported and looked down. Laura had seen his discomfort and came over and extended the foot rest so that it accommodated his greater length. He wasn't aware that it could do that.

As she climbed back into her bed he reached out and took her hand. "Thanks."

She leaned over and kissed him on the cheek. "Good night, love"

The plane fell quiet as the assembled crew drifted off. That was, it was quiet until General Miles began to snore, loudly. After a few minutes of the racket Jack heard somebody, probably Mark, rack a slide on a handgun, chambering a round. The concept of shooting the General because he snored was so outrageous that Jack laughed out loud. His laughter was echoed by most of the others until it ran its course.

112

General Miles woke up and said, "What's that all about?"

Sarah, in the seat next to the General suggested he roll over because he was snoring. He said, "Oh." and rolled over. A few minutes later the sound of a safety being set almost started the laughter again.

Jack fell asleep praying that he could walk blameless before Yahveh in love. It concerned him that he was a soldier for Yahshua and taking life had to have some negative consequences even if he was doing what Yahveh told him to do. He was thinking about King David, who was not allowed to build the temple for God's name because he had blood on his hands.

While the passengers were trying to find sleep, the flight crew continued in earnest conversation on the flight deck.

Mike White set the controls on autopilot and relaxed back in his seat. This aircraft had a really comprehensive autopilot. It could detect, avoid, and even enter into combat with other aircraft all on its own. It was freaky weird in that it was almost human. Actually, Mike really liked the aircraft and all its advanced features. He turned to Su Li, the command pilot for this flight, and asked her a pointed question. "Su Li, I have a concern about your combat piloting capability. Care to discuss it with me?"

Su Li digested the comment and turned it over in her mind several times before answering. "Sure, what's up Mike?"

Mike smiled, "I will tell you that I have never seen, let alone trained, a better natural combat pilot than you. Your gut instincts far exceed the requirements for creative combat and is a match to those of some of our top U.S. Air Force pilots. It's just that you work outside the box so well that it seems like you're writing the next generation book on combat. What do you attribute that to?"

Su Li thought for a minute. "I guess I would have to thank my father for his brains and gall, to be a CIA spy in China for example. I'd also have to thank my mother for her advice to not accept stereotypes and be all that I could be in everything I do. Lastly I think my time with Thor was very helpful to my designing my own path, especially with aircraft. That was because he didn't have a design cell in his brain about aircraft. He was just bold and knew I could do things he couldn't and he accepted me and encouraged me. That concept still runs in my piloting thanks to you and your training. I'll take the best that has been designed and see if I can't find a way to extend the envelope in any way I can. Actually, it's freedom within strict boundaries. I can't try anything that will defy reasonable combat flying, but I can make what is acceptable, better."

Mike was nodding with her description. That was how he had perceived her capabilities. "I do have a concern though. Now, I'm not being sexist but I am worried that, as a woman, hormonal or emotional issues could affect your decisions under stress. They are normal forces that women face and men don't. If you were thrown into combat at a bad time hormonally or emotionally, would you be able to set your emotions aside and tend to business or would it cloud your judgment and possibly drive you to make a bad decision?"

Su Li thought long and hard about how to answer her teacher. "I can't promise that something won't throw me off, but I have exercised combat at a critical time emotionally and was ice cold on my flying. I'm referring to the time the Chinese Navy killed Thor and I came back and blew their boat to bits from a helicopter. I remember thinking at the time that it was pure revenge but it didn't matter because I was a trained and competent pilot that functioned without feelings when I decided to destroy the boat. All that emotion didn't matter in the need to fly right and do the right thing at the right time. I'll tell you what, you set up a simulation and see if you can rattle me so that my flying is affected. If you can, then we'll know if there is a possible problem. Of course, I may just kill you afterward because you irritated me."

Mike thought about that for a while. "Okay. I'm going to assume your flying will not be affected by your emotions or hormones." Mike grinned and added, "Even if you are a girl."

Su Li turned her head to look at her trainer and smiled a smile that Mike didn't like at all. He was well aware of her capabilities for combat other than as a pilot and he knew he just didn't measure up in that area. Then she laughed at the stricken look on his face. "Don't fret Mr. White, the team still needs you and I expect to learn a great deal more from you in the future."

They both fell quiet and watched the vault of heaven as their plane cut through the moonlit night air in supercruise. It was a world only pilots see and it was spectacular. Both of them thanked God silently for the honor of seeing it.

Several hours later, Jack woke up to the delicious smell of breakfast and the aroma of coffee being brewed. Sitting up he saw Laura and Alexis working in the small galley along with David and General Miles.

CHAPTER TWENTY-FIVE

After landing at Aeropuerto Internacional Jorge Chávez in Lima, Peru, Su Li moved the Shrew into a private hanger. Jack and Mark, still dressed in civilian clothing, caught a ride to the main terminal. Checking the arrival of Frank's flight, they found they still had twenty minutes until the plane landed. Mark thought for a second, "Bet you a meal that Frank didn't think to bring any real luggage."

Jack grinned, "You're on. Let's get one now and I'll buy. If I'm right, you owe me."

Since they still had at least a half hour for Frank to land, disembark, and clear customs they ate slowly and discussed what Carol could have meant when she told Laura that they had run into this type of demonic activity before.

Mark considered that and shrugged. "The demon game plan is to kill, steal, and destroy so it can't be too original, can it?"

Jack eyed his friend closely. "Are you getting blasé? We don't have the smallest idea of what God can do and you know Satan copies His stuff. So, yeah, it could be an original copy of something we haven't seen before."

Mark watched the people passing by. "Hmmm, that is a good point. We will need to have some serious prayer before we go against this new batch of critters."

As they cleaned up their table and were leaving the food court, Jack's phone chirped and he answered it. He was pretty sure it would be Laura wondering what was taking so long. So, he was surprised to hear Carol's voice on the other end. "Hi Carol, what do you need?"

Carol Moffet sounded almost out of breath. "Jack, listen carefully to me. A few minutes ago I was given a word for you, especially Laura and Sarah, from the Lord. "Beware the slithers.""

Jack stopped walking and asked, "What are the slithers?"

Carol's reply didn't help. "I don't know but you need to pray carefully about this. I heard this from Hugo."

"All right Carol, we'll look into that, thanks, bye."

Mark was about to ask about the call when he spotted Frank steaming through the crowd like a cruise ship through day sailors. He obviously had an urgency to solve his friend's problem in the mountains. Moving to intercept him Mark said, "Well, look who's here. Hello Frank."

Frank at first didn't recognize Mark and attempted to slip around him in his rush. Mark took a solid stance and put out his arm to block Frank's path.

Frank frowned and then realized who they were. "Oh, hi guys, what are you doing in Peru?"

Jack put himself behind Frank somewhat to block the rush of humanity past him and give him a little room. "We are doing Yahveh's work. He told us to come here and work with you to solve your mountain problem."

Frank could be hardheaded but he wasn't stupid. "Andrea put you up to this didn't she?"

Jack smiled, "Well, she did ask us to help you but it was Yahveh that insisted."

Frank sighed deeply, "Okay, I admit I could use some help this time. But, I didn't want to bother your team because you're involved in bigger things. It will be good to have two more bodies with the experience in dealing with demons on this though. Where's your luggage? I left in such a hurry I didn't take time to pack."

Jack saw the grin on Mark's face along with the little, "I told you so" look.

Jack took Frank's arm and led him out of the crowd and back towards the way they had come into the terminal. "We've got a private hanger where we can do some planning. Why don't you wait until we get there to explain what you know?"

The three men grabbed a ride back to the hanger with a luggage handler and walked into the Shrew with Frank in tow. Frank's eyes widened when he saw all the people sitting at the planning table. "Oh my stars, you brought everybody."

Jack introduced Frank around and then had him sit down and describe the problem as he knew of it.

Frank started off telling about an old friend and evangelist, Karl Wilmette. "He's been working with the remote native tribes in the mountain area around Pucallpa.

He's been working with a primitive tribe called the Utukz that live much deeper into the jungle in the Andes Mountains. These natives have had very little contact with civilization. Karl called us two days ago and was very agitated after his latest visit to the tribe. He told me a tale about aliens and strange lights in the deep jungles near where the tribe lives. Several of the tribe went to look at the strange going's on and only one made it back alive, sort of alive. The young fellow was dying of knife wounds and he told an incoherent story about "others". Others is their word for anyone different than themselves. God told me they were demons. What I didn't tell Andrea because she'd get upset was that the other men were killed by what the dying man told Karl were whirling Kashees, or knives. He was very clear on this point; they were balls of knife blades whirling rapidly in all directions. He said these balls of flying blades horribly sliced the other men to death in seconds."

Jack shook his head and asked, "What were you planning to do about this?"

Frank shrugged his shoulders. "I don't really know. I do know positively that Yahveh told me to get down here as fast as I could.

Laura had been praying as she listened to the Pastor. "I think that Frank and Andrea were God's way of putting us on notice to be here also. Not belittling your role Frank, I see it as a necessary and intricate part of God's plan. You need our combat capabilities and we need your rapport with the natives so that we can accomplish Yahveh's work. I smell a demonic rat in the works though. These whirling knives in the man's story concern me."

Jack broke in, "Carol called me at the airport and said that the team, but, especially you and Sarah, need to beware of the slithers and that it came from Hugo."

Laura looked at Sarah and became very serious. "This may be a demonic response to our upping the ante with two swords people. She was referring to Sarah's also becoming a golden warrior to fight alongside herself.

Jack suggested that they should pray in unison to see what the warning was about.

CHAPTER TWENTY-SIX

The entire assembly bowed their heads and prayed for wisdom and guidance. Jack felt the usual heaviness that indicated to him that the Holy Spirit was present and pressing down on them. As he prayed everything around him became quiet. He felt a sense of pleasantness and harmony and he opened his eyes to see Hugo standing in front of him in an area that was beautiful but not detailed. It was sort of like being in a cloud.

Looking to his left he wasn't surprised to see Laura, Sarah, and Mark. What did surprise him was that standing to his right were Su Li, David and Alexis. He looked back at Hugo.

Somehow Hugo didn't look as much as a wise sage as he had before. He was spryer and more youthful and had a small grin on his face. "Hello Hugo" Jack said.

Hugo looked at all six of them and opened his hands to include them all. "Welcome to Hugo's workshop. You have all been selected by Yahveh to receive some advanced training that you will need. This is in direct response to your prayers to Yahveh so that you can do His will."

Laura asked, "What type of training will this be, Hugo?"

Hugo laughed heartily. "The type you desperately want Laura. Combat sword training."

David commented, "Oh joy."

Hugo came closer to the group. "Understand this. You have been chosen to be Yahveh's answer to Satan allowing his demons to make their incursions into your dimension, especially when they use methods and techniques that normally don't exist in your world."

"Originally, these demons were stalemated by Laura's anointing and fierce combat to stop the ones that gained legal access but were assisting ones that were not on Earth legally. The demons in your dimension legally can't be killed by bullets because that is their nature and when they are legally in the human dimension they keep their nature. The one's that aren't supposed to be there don't have that protection and can be done away with by any means."

Hugo looked at Laura. "Laura became very powerful in stopping the legal ones. So much so, that they started attempting to overload her capability. That is when Sarah was also anointed with the armor and sword of God, thereby doubling the team's capability to defeat legal demonic incursions that are simply a front for other demons that enter illegally."

He shook his head, "The enemy has decided to up the ante unilaterally this time and has created a unique group of demons specifically appointed to destroy Laura and Sarah. They are called the "Slithers" and they are the elite among their evil brothers in capability, especially with a sword. Remember these demons were once God's warriors and were specifically designed to be the best in sword combat."

Mark asked, "Why do they still use swords? Why don't they use high tech weapons like assault rifles and lasers on us?"

Hugo nodded his head, "A very good observation and question Mark. The reason is that Satan and his demons are incapable of creating anything new or maintaining it. Again, this is in their nature. I am not capable of creating anything either, but I am a servant of the most high and He is the creator of the universe. Still he doesn't extend that capability to the enemy. That is why they still rely on the fang, claw, and edged weapons. Oh, they can get their human slaves to use high-tech devices such as guns, lasers, and bombs. But, they themselves aren't capable of that sort of mischief. That is why we are going to have this little training session."

A sword appeared in Hugo's right hand. "You seven will all be anointed to combat the legal enemy, which will include the Slithers, with edged weapons, primarily this sword."

Mark asked, "I'm not normally a swords person and how will we compete with this "whirling ball of blades" that killed the natives in Peru?"

Hugo studied Mark for a few seconds. "To your first point, you are not a "swords person" because you've never trained with one. You will be an excellent and talented warrior with the sword just as you are with your other weapons. To your second point, again the enemy is once again misusing their authority and Yahveh will not tolerate it anymore. The "whirling ball of blades" you are referring to is simply a time technique that I will teach you. Essentially, it is normal swordplay but at an accelerated rate. You will be able to match, and even exceed their speed so that it will seem like a normal battle to you and your enemy. Although it will seem like two whirling balls of blades to anyone else."

Laura felt a great sadness in her heart and tears came to her eyes. "Oh, those poor natives that were killed that way."

Hugo looked at Laura and a wave of peace flooded her whole being. "Laura, your compassion is admirable but, they all knew the Lord and dying in their innocent curiosity as believers they were with Yahshua before they realized what was about to happen. They are exalting God in great happiness right now. Don't let your heart be troubled by things that have to happen. Even Yahveh knew the enemy would take these lives since the beginning of time. The Lord allows it because it is necessary at this time. Remember, very soon, He will wipe away all tears and there will be no more pain or sorrow. Your mission is to take this unauthorized advantage away from them in such a manner that they will not attempt to do it again."

Hugo looked at all seven warriors and looked very somber. "Yahveh has tried each of you and found you willing and capable to do this work of His. He has honed your team as a gleaming blade and will now empower you to rise up and smite the enemy and drive them back wherever they try to impose Satan's will upon the innocent of the world. You will be tried as never before and not all may survive until the Lord calls your team home."

Hugo smiled, a facial feature that had become more natural for him since meeting this particular group of people. "Do not be saddened by this and remember that your efforts will influence many to come to the Lord who would never have considered it before. Through you they will see Yahveh as the righteous judge and the most awesome warrior in the universe. Thousands of souls turned from their false idol in Zyngola after the challenge between Zultar and Yahveh. Children in that land now secretly wear white and stand firm in a faith they would never have known of if you hadn't stood firm to do His will at that time."

Hugo waved his hand and swords appeared in each of the team's hands. "Let's begin with the basics. Humble yourself Jack, you will learn much more than you learned from your Sensei on Earth."

The practices moved quickly to more advanced techniques that amazed all of the team but especially Jack Malone. Yet, at the same time it all came together with such logic and synergy that Jack's skills jumped levels in the first two sessions.

None of the members lacked in physical coordination and the lessons were not only learned but ingrained in muscle memories for all time. Simply gripping the hilt of the sword placed the entire lexicon of swordplay in their minds. Jack inquired of Hugo, "Couldn't you have simply placed this information in our minds without the physical training?"

Hugo smiled at Jack's naivety. "Yes, but then you would fail in combat because you would not be confident that what you know is correct. This practice will give you the memory of everything you are learning in the positive memory of success. You really need this."

Jack bowed his head in humbleness. "I apologize for questioning your reasoning Hugo."

Hugo put his hand on Jack's shoulder. Jack felt a jolt of something like electrical power jolt through him from the anointing the angel carried. "One of the things that make you a great warrior is your understanding. Never, ever, stop asking questions that bother you. No one but Yahveh and Yahshua are infallible, not even an angel. Like you all, Caleb, Rose, and I are but servants of the Most High."

The lessons advanced and Hugo introduced time compression control so that the warriors could meet the enemy's high speed attacks. To accelerate to that level the warriors simply had to change the prayers they were praying when they were doing combat against the demons. The prayer included the plea to Yahveh to allow them to match the enemy's attacks. Hugo had each one of them practice it before the others many times until it became like a learned response to ask Yahveh for the ability to do it.

Jack couldn't estimate how many hours, or possibly days they had been training. He wasn't tired and they weren't hungry or sleepy which obviously was because they were in the spirit but somehow also here physically. Hugo pronounced all seven of them proficient and then threw them a curve.

He asked Alexis and Mark to come forward. After they were there he had them face each other. "I want you two to battle with your best efforts to destroy the other. You will not, of course, be allowed to injure each other. But, this will give you one-on-one practice. All right, begin."

Jack watched as Alexis took the aggressor role and attacked Mark. Mark parried her attacks and then attacked back. Several times during the match one and then the other went to high speed. After five minutes Hugo brought the match to an end. "All right, stop and step back." Hugo's words carried authority and the combatants did as they were told.

Two by two in many combinations the members of the team tried their best to best each other. Most duels came to a draw like that of Mark and Alexis. In some areas one person out thought the other and won a match. After that Hugo had several people attack one person to train them to combat multiple attackers. After the contests were done Hugo commended them all as being the best he had ever trained while they were still human. "Remember, you are Yahveh's hands on Earth. He will have your back."

Jack found himself still praying with the others on the aircraft. He saw the other five look around and then go back to praising Yahveh.

When the prayer ended, General Miles looked at the group and asked, "Well, do we have an answer to these slithers?"

Jack grinned, "Yes, we do."

CHAPTER TWENTY-SEVEN

After Jack explained what had happened to seven of their members in the few moments of prayer, there was silence. Realizing that the three men that had not accompanied the seven of them might feel left out, Jack earnestly prayed that Yahveh would give him the words to make the team whole again. What he got in answer awed him mentally. He had to go over it twice before he was sure he understood what it implied.

He took a deep breath. "The assignments for you three gentlemen are even more important than sword fighting in combating the enemy."

That got the attention of everyone on the plane. Jack marshaled his facts and looked at David first. "David, the Lord wants you to handle all non-legal demonic activity even though you have been trained and equipped for swordsmanship. This will include demons that have entered our dimension without God's permission and all humans involved in any attack. Let's be clear about this. You will have our backs, all of our backs because many times the six of us will be battling against the legal demonic entries which will take all of our concentration. Yahveh let me see that the enemy plans to throw Slithers and other demons against us to overwhelm us while attempting to flank us with sufficient illegal demonic and human hordes to strike at us while we are engaged in the main battle. You, and in this case, Mike White and Major Danning will have to bring sufficient firepower against these forces to prevent them from killing us."

David sat there for a few seconds assimilating the challenge that faced him. "I don't understand something and perhaps you could explain it. There are demons that have applied for God's permission to enter our dimension and are granted that permission. Yet, I thought it was God's law or rule that they shouldn't do that. How do they get permission?"

Laura had another piece of her training become open to her. She looked her husband for permission to intercede and Jack nodded at her. "David, there have always been specific times when demons have had permission to enter the human dimension for their evil purposes. But the permission only allows for specific actions and they must perform within those limitations. For example, if they could not get unlimited permission to attack the Crossfire Team they could possibly get permission to attack, say, Jack. Since God grants this permission based on performance it will automatically expire if the demon attacks you. These demons are here legally, like the Slithers have requested specific permission to attack members of the Crossfire Team. That's why they can't be hurt by bullets, because they have the right to be here and carry their natural or innate defensive capabilities with them. But, that permission is granted with the counterbalancing permission for the Crossfire Team to defend itself against such attack. That is why several of us have been given the ability to repel such an attack, and if we are skillful enough, destroy the Slithers."

David slowly nodded his head in understanding.

Laura continued her comments. "Satan chafes under the need to clear his attack with God because that makes him subservient and he doesn't feel he is less than equal to God. Even though Christ defeated him at the cross he is rebellious and that leads to his ordering illegal entry into our dimension by demons without God's permission. These are the primary reason this team was created and anointed to cancel out these egregious acts. Now, there are several differences between legal and illegal demonic presences in our dimension. Illegal demons are not capable of bringing their normal natures with them. That makes them vulnerable to gunfire and explosions and that is where you come in at this time. You are so very good with weapons and explosives according to Sarah and there will probably be multitudes of illegal demons for every one that is here legally. Yahveh wants you to be the executioner of any illegal demonic or demonically controlled human forces wherever we meet them." Laura nodded her head to allow Jack to resume his assignments.

Jack looked at David, Mike, and Gary. "Normally I would put the SOG members under your command and you would, hopefully, have sufficient force to subdue the hordes

I expect we will be subjected to here in Peru. Unfortunately, they aren't here. So to solve this problem right now this effort must be handled by you three alone. One or more of us will try to stay and assist you and likewise to defend you against any legal demons that try to take you out to free up their illegal brothers."

David had been calculating the odds and already planning his actions. "Thank you, Laura and Jack for the honor of this assignment. Of course through Yahshua I thank Yahveh for everything. I think we will be able to execute our assignment, don't you guys?"

Mike White had worked with the Crossfire Team for years and simply smiled and sat quietly. Gary wasn't as confident as David or Mike and deferred to David's greater field experience. "Whatever you say, boss."

Jack grinned at the Major's comment. "I guess this is probably a little more action than you expected, right Gary?"

Gary Danning nodded, but added, "I...Well, I...Yes, yes it is and I welcome it."

Jack nodded, "Good man."

Jack then turned to the General. "General Miles, your assignment is to be the Crossfire Team's liaison to the Peruvian forces, native and governmental, if any. Work with Frank Mullins and his contacts to arrange for extraction of native personnel that could get hurt, women and children for example, the sick, the lame, etc. Also recruit any able-bodied men that can be educated enough to support David. Illegal demons can be killed by spears and arrows too."

Jack sat back and looked at the troops. "I think that this combat will probably lead to the fiercest battles we have ever faced because Satan has targeted us and he will pull out all the stops to eliminate us. He has apparently requested permission to do exactly that. I suggest that we draw his forces into a trap and turn the tables on them. Are there any other suggestions?"

Laura stood up. "Yahveh wants me to make it perfectly clear to everyone that Satan himself cannot be attacked or killed even if he would make an appearance. He has scripture to fulfill and we are not his destiny. I am fairly certain that none of us will face him one-on-one or even be anywhere near him. But, just in case you do have such a shot, do not take it. It won't work and your pride at making such an attempt will be a sin against us with Yahveh."

Laura thought for a few seconds while she prayed for the right words. "I want to remind each of us that we must do the will of Yahveh and do nothing for ourselves. Remember in the Word in Joshua 7 what happened when Achor son of Carmi of the tribe of Judah, took some of the things devoted to the Lord for destruction. And the anger of the Lord burned against Israel. If just one of us sins against the Lord, we will all face the anger of the Lord."

That sober comment made them all realize the burden they had to carry.

Mark and Sarah then made operational suggestions which were accepted into the planning. Finally, everyone prayed for Yahveh's grace and mercy on them and their ability to fulfill His will.

Frank and the General left to secure transportation to the village. David and his team headed out to secure sufficient heavy weapons to support the rest of the team. Jack had the others put on their body armor and gathered their weapons to do a scouting job.

CHAPTER TWENTY-EIGHT

After leaving the plane and securing a vehicle, David had Gary Danning drive the three-man team a few hundred feet away from the hanger and then stop. Punching in a unique code into his cell phone David listened for a few seconds and hung up and waited. His cell phone rang and he answered it in Hebrew. The conversation took less than two minutes and David hung up with a smile on his face.

Mike White asked him, "Shall we see what the Peruvian military can provide us?"

David shook his head. "No, the required paperwork and clearances would take months before we could get a grenade. Drive over to the restaurant here on the airport."

Gary did as he was directed but was concerned about their apparent lack of progress.

David got out and Gary asked, "Are we meeting a contact here?"

David laughed, "No, we're going to eat lunch. Come on."

David handled two more phone calls in Hebrew during their meal which took almost an hour. Gary was chaffing at the delay which was leaving him confused and exasperated. "Why aren't we searching out the things we're supposed to be getting?"

Realizing his partner had never worked with the team before and apparently had also never worked in the black ops world; David leaned over and told him. "There are different ways to accomplish our goal than our begging the Peruvian military for help or supplies. I've contacted my old company, the Israeli Mossad, and called in three or four favors. The Mossad is favorably disposed to helping the Crossfire Team because we have saved the Jewish homeland from destruction several times in the last several years. They are sending us a care package." He looked at his watch. "Which should be here in about thirty minutes?"

Somewhat placated but still uncertain, Gary wondered about the "care package" but was smart enough to not question David's capabilities so he held his silence. Several minutes later, Mark Connelly walked into the restaurant and sat down at the table. He nodded to Gary and Mike.

Twenty-five minutes later David's phone rang again. David listened and said one word in Hebrew and hung up. He put money on the table to cover their meal and they left the restaurant and drove back to the hanger with the Shrew in it. An Israeli C130 pulled up to the main hanger doors which David had a ground crew open so that the transport plane could pull into the hanger.

After the engines were shut down and the hanger doors closed the large ramp on the back of the C130 was lowered and five Israeli special ops soldiers descended and met with David. The Israelis used the Peruvian forklifts to move seventy-four massive crates out of the aircraft and stacked them next to the Shrew. David signed some paperwork and got a plane tug to come and back the C130 out of the hanger. A few minutes later the engines revved up and the plane taxied away as the hanger doors were closed again.

David looked at his paperwork as Mark Connelly walked up and looked at him with one eyebrow raised. David pointed to one crate and grabbed a pry bar. All four men worked to open the huge wooden container. When the end of the crate was opened Gary Danning whistled.

David walked into the crate and started up the vehicle located inside the crate. He carefully drove it out into the hanger.

Mark was impressed by the small vehicle. It was a multipurpose, tracked assault mini-tank with the latest attack capabilities. It had a turret with a Vulcan 20mm explosive projectile cannon and two independently targeted mini-guns that could be controlled by computer to search out and destroy pre-defined targets at a high rate of fire. These were chambered in 5.56 MM like the M-16 rifle. There were two of the vehicles in the crate. Each little tank was operated by one person. The tanks were named "Rolling Death" in Hebrew.

As David climbed out of the little tank, Mark asked what was in the other crates. David showed him the paperwork and both of Mark's eyebrows rose. "What will this cost us?"

David laughed, "When your lives depend on our backup, cost is no factor."

Mike White stared into the crate and asked, "What do I get to drive?"

David had them all attack a second crate. When it was open Mike smiled, "I have heard of these but never thought I'd get to see one let alone pilot one. Cool."

Mark got an aircraft tug and used a chain to slide the skid out of the crate. Sitting on the skid was an oddly sleek arrangement that looked like a small helicopter and at the same time a tiny jet plane, and paradoxically, a missile platform. He looked at David for an explanation.

David smiled broadly. "This is the Israeli version of the American drone aircraft, the Reaper."

Mark looked the machine over and saw extreme lethality in a nice package. He looked up and said, "Gary, Mike, I hope you guys know how to read and speak Hebrew because it looks like the controls are labeled that way."

David shook his head and reached into the missile platform. He powered it up and typed in a set of commands and then shut it down. "Look again."

Mark looked and everything was in English. "I'd like to know how you do that."

David smiled, "So would everybody else."

CHAPTER TWENTY-NINE

After praying for protection and guidance the two men and four women went out and boarded a borrowed USAF Blackhawk helicopter.

Su Li used the GPS coordinates they had been given by Frank to fly to the village in the mountains. She located a nearby clearing and set the aircraft down.

Jack told everyone to leave their weapons on the chopper. He then led the small team to the village and was met by the leader of the people at the edge of the clearing in which sat a collection of huts. Jack stopped and nodded his head to the elderly man whose hair was completely white. "We are friends of Frank Mullins and have come to see if we can help you with the problem in the hills."

The wizened little man studied the assembly for a few seconds and noted that they weren't carrying any weapons. He spoke in halting English. "We are happy you have come to help us friends of Frank Mullins. You are welcome to our village. Since you have no guns how can you help us?"

Jack smiled internally which didn't show on his face. He thought, "This man is unusual as he doesn't hem and haw but comes directly to the point." Jack responded to the question. "We come as warriors of Yahveh to confront the enemy. Our weapons are spiritual and are available as needed. We are not here today to engage in combat but to scout out the enemy and their place here in the mountains."

The leader, who had been given the name "Joe" for unexplained reasons, evaluated the group and while he was obviously unsure he was concerned. "Some of our best warriors also went scouting this enemy and are no longer with us. I would not like the same thing to happen to you." He seemed to look inwardly at something. "Also, your interest in these evil forces could bring them down on my people."

Jack nodded his head slowly. "There is that possibility. Frank will be here soon and will offer sanctuary to you and your people for the time of battles. Our wish is to return your land to you as it was before, without the threat. We want to thank you for your concern and we will be careful."

Jack determined where the young men of the tribe were slaughtered and the Crossfire Team members headed that way. As Hugo had trained them they walked in the spirit, silently praying praise and worship to Yahveh and Yahshua. This way they were prepared in the event of a sudden attack.

Laura walked along with Jack as Sarah did with Mark. The women's previous experience had apparently heightened their sensitivity to demonic activity and made them naturals for going first.

In less than twenty minutes the team members reached the killing grounds as described by Joe. They spread out and investigated the signs of the attacks and deaths. The villagers had been allowed to retrieve the bodies for burial but there were pools of dried blood and bits and pieces of the young men that had been hacked to death.

Alexis and Sarah were studying the ground at the point of attacks. They looked at each other and Sarah nodded to Alexis. They walked over to Jack and Laura. Sarah waved her hand to indicate the battleground. "The only tracks or footprints belonged to the young men and the natives that retrieved their bodies. The Slithers left no signs of their presence. Does that mean that they weren't fighting from a ground based formation?"

Jack was inclined to agree with that logic. "I think you are right. So, if they don't come on the ground are they floating like Rose does?"

Laura asked, "How does that alter our combat against them? Or, does it?"

Jack thought about that and decided to pray for wisdom.

Laura rotated to her left. "We've got company from the tree line uphill."

The team followed their plan and four of them faced the tree line while the other two covered their backs and sides.

While no physical presence appeared a voice was heard. "Be gone or die."

Jack signaled the others to back away and retreat. They kept their formation as they moved back downhill.

After they reached the village they told the chief they would be back soon. A few minutes later they were airborne and headed back to the city on the Blackhawk.

Mark put on his headset and keyed the intercom. "Jack, why did we back down and run?"

Jack studied his friend for a few seconds. "Because we didn't come to do battle. We don't have the backup we would need if they came at us hard. All the hardware that David acquired was still back at the base. But the main reason was that I got a leading to leave. There's something very wrong with this setup and we need to understand it before we get killed by being misled."

Laura shook her head. "We know that Yahveh wanted us to take on this demonic attack and stop it. What is different now?"

Jack thought back and said, "I'm positive that we are supposed to do battle with the demons in the jungle. But, when we were challenged by the voice, I got a small revelation that this is only part of what we need to be doing. I know that this mission brought us here and we need to defeat these demons, but, I'm not sure it's the main battle. Or, to put it another way I think this is a deliberate attempt to make us focus here and to destroy us if they can, yet, at the same time we're being diverted from another major effort the enemy doesn't want us to know about. I really need to pray and fast about this."

Laura nodded her agreement. "I'll join you."

After the Blackhawk helicopter landed at their base, Jack and Laura secluded themselves in the back cabin on the Shrew and sought the Lord throughout the day and into the night. Jack's heart was troubled and he read many passages in the Bible seeking enlightenment. As he waited on the Lord he stopped thinking about the factors involved and simply joined in with Laura in praising the Father and the Son.

CHAPTER THIRTY

As the morning light began to color the inside of the hanger Jack sighed and held up his hands. "I feel the closeness and the love of the Lord but I haven't gotten a leading regarding other efforts we should be aware of yet."

Laura watched Jack for a minute and then said, "I just wonder if this is a case of Yahveh telling us to do something and we missed it. If He's already told us he shouldn't need to tell us again and probably will not."

Jack thought back over the last several days trying to see if they had received any instruction other than what they were doing. He looked at Laura and shrugged his shoulders.

Laura had been doing the same thing by recalling everything about this mission and a thought came to mind. "Jack, do you remember Carol saying something like, *"I can tell you that you've run up against this type of demoniccountdownbefore."*? I know we've fought demons in the jungle before but I don't know that this is what Carol meant."

As she said "...this kind of demonic countdown", Jack remembered another countdown with demons. "Hmmmm, yes. This could be something that we've run into before. I need to call Charlie."

Two minutes later Charlie Wu listened to Jack describe their dilemma and his idea as to a possible solution. "I don't know of anything like that, but I'll see if I can detect anything similar."

Jack felt an easing in the pressure on his spirit. "Okay, Charlie's on it so we can concentrate on this action. They walked out into the main cabin and asked Mark for a status update.

Mark sat back in the plush seat and smiled. "Well, while you kids have been napping we have moved all of David's toys to the site, removed the villagers, recruited eight of the younger men, got permission from the Peruvian government to enter into combat with demonic forces as needed. We've also got eyes in the sky on the area and an update from heaven central as to angelic backup. How about you?"

Jack nodded his head in regards to the excellent advancements made by Mark and the others. "We've got a priority one search being handled by Charlie in determining another action we may need to attend to.

Mark hauled out a map of the mountainous area where the village was and indicated the site of the massacre. "If you look around the area there is no staging area they could work out of if this were a normal attack in the human dimension. Obviously it's not normal. They must be striking out of their dimension directly into ours. I've told David about Charlie's solution to the portals we dealt with in Colorado that time. He'll be ready if that is the case."

Su Li called from the cockpit where she was running some tests. "Jack, Carol is on the line for you."

Jack punched in the aft phone on speaker. "Carol, this is Jack. I have you on speaker phone."

Carol sighed, "Good. This is for all of you. I believe that you need to be at the same field that the villagers were attacked around four p.m. your time tomorrow. The Heavenlies show that the demonic forces are gathering for a major assault on the area at that time."

Jack looked at the others at the table. "Okay Carol, we'll be ready. I also have a leading that there is another demonic activity we are supposed to be dealing with that's not here. Is that accurate?"

"That's right Jack. Do you know what type of activity it is that you need to attend to?"

Jack took a deep breath, "I'm assuming that it will be along the lines of the Siberian lab we assaulted to stop the nuclear amplification of a demonic portal.?"

Carol's voice was less stressed than a minute ago. "Yes Jack that is the other half of this problem that faces you. You have the battle there in Peru and need to stop the other activity before it goes critical."

Jack smiled a frosty smile. "Can you tell us where it is at?"

Carol paused for a few seconds. "No, I can't tell you because I don't know. I see the danger and the urgency but I don't see location information. I fear for the team because both of these demonic assaults are huge in their plans in an attempt to disrupt God's end time timeline."

Jack laughed, "As if Satan could derail God's plans. Is there anything else you can tell us?"

"No, Jack, which is all I can tell you right now. But, be aware that God's plans will proceed but if you fail it could change the timing and bring about the loss of millions of people that would be saved otherwise. I can't tell you the amount of responsibility that Yahveh is placing on the Crossfire Team and how His Kingdom needs you to be victorious. There are literally millions of potential losses for believers and therefore wins for the demonic if you fail on either one of these tasks. Obviously, that is the very reason they have arranged these two, simultaneous events. They believe that you will fail on one or the other. My spirit cries at the tasks laid out before you this time. I love all of you and I want you to come back in victory. Talk to you later.

"Bye Carol", Jack broke the connection and looked at Mark. "I hope Charlie is better than Carol for directions."

Mark had been praying during the talk with Carol and had come to a decision. "Guys, we need to split our forces to meet both of these attacks by the enemy. Carol is right; their timing is set to have both events come to a head at the same time. My recommendation is that Jack and Laura take Su Li and Mike in the Shrew and meet the SOG near whatever location Charlie determines the other event is going to occur. That will give you three swords and a lot of firepower to back you up. Sarah, Alexis, and I will deal with this battle along with David and Gary Danning. We'll just have to forego the aerial part of our plans down here."

Jack considered Mark's plan and couldn't see any better way to handle the dual attacks. "Okay, but two problems come to mind. First, the government is not inclined to give us military assistance so how do we get the SOG to join us somewhere in the world? Second, if you remember our last assault on the lab in Siberia we lost four out of five of us and if the Lord hadn't cancelled the whole event after we destroyed the portal, we'd be dead now."

Mark nodded his head. "True, but this time perhaps you won't be going up against the cream of the SPETSNAZ forces. At the lab in Siberia we were up against the

"Vympel" which was formerly an elite cold war-era KGB sabotage and assassination unit. It is now a counter-terrorist and counter-sabotage unit. But, unlike the Russian "Alpha" units, which learn how to storm airplanes and buses, the Vympel units are Russia's last defense against possible terrorist acts involving nuclear plants, hydroelectric dams, and other industrial complexes. The troops we faced in Siberia are experts in eighteen special disciplines among which are extensive marksmanship and martial arts training. I doubt that you'll run into an equivalent force. God willing that is."

Then Mark smiled, "As to your first point I think I have some contacts with the CIA who will be able to arrange transportation for the SOG without having to inform the new to-be-government which doesn't much like the CIA. Give me a location as soon as you know where you're going."

Mike spoke up. "I've still got some high level contacts with the Air Force and can probably arrange for our refueling needs as soon as we know where we're headed. The General I'm thinking about owes the Crossfire Team big time."

CHAPTER THIRTY-ONE

As the team split up, Mark and his team moved out of the Shrew and into a USAF mobile command center. Su Li and Mike White had already prepared the Shrew for takeoff and in less than thirty minutes the "corporate" jet had quietly winged it way off of the runway. After reaching a sufficient distance from the Peru airport Su Li brought the Shrew up to military air lanes and entered into supercruise to conserve fuel and manage Mach three flight. She headed west across the Pacific toward Asia as the most likely location of a new nuclear-powered demonic portal.

Jack relaxed in the comfortable seat as he went over the optional possibilities. He discarded Russia or China as probable sites because of the previous efforts in Siberia. Those two atheistic countries would have clamped down on their nuclear facilities after the assault on the lab in Russia. But, there were other newly empowered nuclear nations and that is why he picked their general direction. Prayer had not revealed a leading so he used the brains God had given him to make realistic projections.

His cell phone rang and he saw it was Charlie back in the Fortress. The thought ran through his mind that Charlie was probably in the middle of packing up the computer lab for the move to Israel and this request probably came at a bad time.

"Yes, Charlie. What have you got?"

Charlie's voice came through clear and static free which meant it was being relayed through the receivers on the Shrew. "Jack, I'm fairly certain I have what you need. Radiation searches didn't reveal anything new, but when I had Crayton run a search for demonic activity similar to that at the Siberian lab I got a definite hit. I'll give you the coordinates in a second but it is in Pakistan on the Indus River, seventy miles southwest of Islamabad. You should head in that direction as soon as you can. The readings of demonic activity are very high."

Jack told Charlie, "Thanks buddy; we're already headed that way. Send the coordinates to my phone and get me an update on the area and what type of governmental reception we might encounter."

Jack had a second thought on Charlie's report. "Hey, Charlie, how can Crayton use the demonic levels at Siberia? When Yahveh reset that time to the original onset of the portal, I thought all recordings or findings vanished as far as the infestation of demons. It never happened so how does your computer have anything to match with new readings?"

Charlie chuckled, "I knew I liked you as a leader Jack. And the answer is, "I don't know. I suppose God knew we would need this today and left the demonic monitoring information in the computer. The only other answer would be that God missed something and I rather doubt that."

After he hung up Jack told the others in the group Charlie's information and gave the coordinates to Su Li and also to Mike White to arrange for refueling during their transoceanic flight. He then called Mark and set up the SOG flight from Israel to Pakistan. Mark told him that the SOG was already on its way to the airport to meet the CIA plane.

Charlie's information on the location in Pakistan showed up on Jack's phone and he routed it to the on-board printer. He got the crew together including Mike White.

"According to this information, the location of the demonic bee's nest, as Charlie calls it, is in Pakistan, roughly 90 km SE of Islamabad. It's about 20 klicks NE of Chakwel City. Chakwel City is about ten miles in area in the Dhanni region of the Pothohar Plateau."

Jack continued, "Fortunately the area we are focused on is about eight miles away from that city up in the mountainous region of the Margla Hills. The site is supposedly connected to the Swedish Institute of Technology but, according to the CIA, the institute doesn't know anything about the site."

Jack looked at the other people at the table. "The government of Pakistan is not favorably inclined to allow foreign aggression on their soil. Being Muslim I doubt that they will want any Christian warriors on their soil either. Since God has tasked us with this matter we must attempt to penetrate their airspace undetected, land, destroy this new portal completely, and exfiltrate without being seen or stopped." Sighing a big sigh Jack added "I wish we had the X-76 for this trip."

Mike thought about that statement and punched in a preset number on his cell phone. Figuring hours and timing he sketched out a plan before the phone was answered. He got up and walked to the back of the plane and talked to his contact. He got the approval he needed and made the decision himself. Thanking his contact, he walked back to the table and sat down. Jack looked up to see a big smile on his face.

Mike waved his right hand in the air, "Well, if "Ma" Li and I can push this bucket of bolts hard enough to reach the Bagram airbase in Afghanistan before dawn there tomorrow we will have the X-76."

Jack grinned back at the pilot. "I knew there was a reason we wanted you to join the team."

Laura touched Jack's arm. "Is there room in the X-76 for the SOG as well as us?"

Jack nodded. "I think so. If I remember it correctly it will hold up to 45 passengers. That should be sufficient for the manpower but we will have to bring all our weapons with us so it could be a little crowded."

Thinking back in time Jack was elated. The leading-edge fast mover would greatly enhance their chances of not being detected in or out. "All right, let's start planning for our assault. Laura, get everything we can from Charlie and make sure he can watch over us during the assault. Now that there are three of us to do battle with the legal demonic personnel we could have an edge since I doubt they know about my and Su Li's talents."

Turning to the pilot he said, "Mike, I can't give you a mini-chopper but I can give you an automatic .50 caliber sniper rifle so you can act as our high watch."

Mike grinned and nodded his acceptance of the assignment.

Laura turned back to the discussion after talking to Charlie. "He'll be able to give us his undivided attention during our incursion into Pakistan but he'll be split between us and Mark's team during our assault which the enemy has nicely timed to coincide with Peru's major battle."

Jack thought about that for a few seconds and then grinned. "Ask Charlie how he's going to accomplish both tasks simultaneously while at the same time he is coordinating the move of the computer center from Colorado to Israel."

Laura laughed, "He's way ahead of us. He's already got the Cray computers set up in Israel and he is working remotely. He did say that he will slave his oversight to your handheld viewer so that if he's distracted you can catch any important changes. He also said to tell you that the Fortress is ninety-nine percent empty and cleaned up."

Jack thought back over their home for the last year. "That is a great place and I hate to see it just sit there empty."

Laura shook her head, "You didn't hear? Gary Danning has leased it out to the army special forces as a training facility and headquarters. Since the government didn't pay for it and it is in the military's hands the new administration will leave it alone. Especially since we are not working out of there anymore.

Jack thought about it and grinned. "I bet we could get it back if we had a more "friendly" administration in office, like next term."

Laura smiled a small smile and sobered him up with, "There probably isn't that much time left."

CHAPTER THIRTY-TWO

As Jack's team flew through the sky towards Pakistan, Mark and his team moved their equipment to the location of the assault field in Peru. Mark set the two tank units thirty degrees to the side of the center of the expected battle and fifty feet behind the front lines. Having prayed for heavenly protection to prevent the enemy from determining what they were up to, Mark called a last team meeting just before four o'clock.

Smiling at them he joked, "This is not a pep talk. We know the odds and the difference between the five of us and the untold numbers of them. Just be aware that they will come out anywhere and can attack from your rear as easily as from the front. David, Gary, if you're not sure the demon you're facing is here legally or not, shoot it anyway to find out. Alexis will stay with you guys in the event they send a legal demon that can't be taken out by gunfire. Just make every one of your shells, missiles, and shots count."

Leaving Alexis with the backup group Mark walked up to where Sarah was standing looking at the empty meadow.

Putting his arm around his wife's shoulders he pulled her to him and when she turned to look at him he kissed her on the lips. "Just know I will always love you." Mark's sober sincerity touched her heart. She bent her head and put her forehead on his. "I do know that my love. Forever."

Suddenly she pulled away from Mark's embrace and turned to face the meadow. She started to pray and her golden armor and the sword of faith flared into bright existence as the first demons stepped out of the spiritual dimension and into the human dimension.

Mark shouldered his M-8 and put two rounds into both of the demons rushing at them with ebony swords held on high. The bullets had no effect on the demons and Sarah stood forth to do battle. Mark held off maximizing the surprise his new anointing would have for the enemy.

Sarah side-stepped the demon coming at her by dodging to her left and outside the path of its charge. She brought her sword to waist level and thrust it through the right side of the demon as it passed. Looking surprised the demon dissolved into a black mist of smoke that continued to flow past Sarah.

The second demon ignored Mark for the more important danger of the light in Sarah. Sliding to a halt it quickly swung its sword at Sarah's middle but missed by three inches due to the physics of his sudden stop and Sarah's continued movement. Sarah spun around to her left and chopped her sword downward catching the sword hand of the demon. Losing his sword the demon reached out a large black hand and grabbed Sarah's sword arm to immobilize her sword.

Sarah had excelled at the sword training that Hugo had given them and could see the move coming. As the demon grabbed her right arm she flipped the sword to her left hand hacked down on the demon's right shoulder. Slightly off target she actually sliced through the right side of the demon's head and into the torso. The bright, white-hot heat of Yahveh's esteem flowing off of the sword sliced through the demon as if it were made of black whipped cream. The demon faded into black smoke with a wimpier.

Eight more demons entered the human dimension and headed for the two humans. The lead two started spinning into what did look like a whirling ball of knives.

Mark dropped his M-8 since he was fairly sure the high-speed demons couldn't use that talent here unless they were here legally. As Sarah waited for the first two to reach her before matching their speed, Mark started to pray and gleaming bright silver armor covered him and he held a sword the match to the one in Sarah's hands.

As the high-speed "Slithers" came near enough, both Sarah and Mark matched the speeds and the four came together in what seemed normal speed to them. Mark's training had been honed to his advantages. Mass plus heavily muscled arms gave him the ability to bash through the enemy's swordplay rather than parry and thrust which are not normal in Katana swordplay. He used that ability to the maximum as he put all his power into his first downward stroke to the demon on the right.

Mark's training and newly acquired muscle memory allowed him to confidently pull the katana-style sword from its sheath, and hold the sword in front of him like a bat with his dominant right hand at the very top of the handle, directly below the hilt and his left hand approximately 3 inches below that grasping the sword firmly.

As the demon swung its black sword in a diagonal cross cut from Mark's left to his right he stepped back to cause the cut to miss his body. As the demon raised his sword to block a downward cut, Mark raised the sword directly above his right shoulder and swung it in a long swooping arc. He kept the blade perfectly vertical and didn't tilt the blade to either side.

As he swung the sword forward and down at the demon he accelerated the blade tip speed by pushing forward with his right hand and pulling backward with his left had to "snap" the sword through its final few inches of the swing

The power of the stroke caused his gleaming sword to snap the black sword of the enemy demon and cut through the chest of the demon cleaving it in half.

Sarah's talent was misdirection and guile. She feinted a stroke but spun to her right and flexed down at the knees at the same time. The demon didn't fall for the feint but swung a horizontal strike to catch the woman as she spun. As Sarah came out of her spin the enemy sword passed just above the crest of her helmet and her sword cut the demon off at the upper thigh level.

As both of the "Slithers" became greasy smoke, the Connellys came out of the time-managed high speed and found themselves standing side by side in a high-guard position with their swords over their right shoulders. Four of the new demons advanced on them and went into high speed. Mark and Sarah matched them and charged into the foursome to do battle.

Carefully watching the sides of the ensuing swordsmanship, David detected the shimmering distortion on both sides of the battle. Dozens of demons poured out of the rifts.

Using his optical sights David opened up on the demons with a 5.56mm mini-gun. Eight hundred rounds per minute tore into the new ranks and tore them apart. Mark had been right, the pinscher movement used illegal demons to overwhelm the fighters. On the other side of the battle Gary Danning was doing the same on the right side.

Alexis waited patiently for the sure-to-come legal demons to stop the slaughter of the illegal demons. Sometimes David and Gary couldn't see the newly emerging demons for all the slimy black smoke from the recently deceased ones.

The numbers were increasing but the backup team was holding its own when a blast slammed into the armor on David's mini-tank. Alexis' armor flared into existence as she ran around behind David's tank to her left. She saw a second RPG fired at David's tank and deflected it with her sword upward where it exploded harmlessly.

Shaken up but not hurt by the blast, David devoted a second mini-gun to the area from which the RPG round had been fired. Shredding jungle and people the firestorm mowed down the area.

Alexis raced back around the tank to find a sleek black demon advancing on Gary's tank. She ran towards the demon and yelled at it. "Hey, slime ball, play with somebody on your level."

The demon whirled around and suddenly spun into high-speed. Alexis didn't pause but went into high speed as she ran. The demon wasn't prepared for this and Alexis was able to simply run him through as she reached him. The evil was palatable in his eyes as his demonic body faded from view.

Alexis dropped back into normal speed and she back-pedaled to her mid position between the mini-tanks which were still butchering anything that came out of the side rifts and fighting to their sides with humans under the demon's control.

Mark and Sarah continued to battle the legal demons at the point of the spear position and were slowly becoming overwhelmed by sheer numbers. Mark called David on the battle comm and told him to see if the missiles would close the three portals.

Fighting on two fronts wasn't easy but the additional requirements didn't take much extra effort since he had marked the positions of the rifts as they opened. Selecting, arming, and firing the three Hellfire missiles was the work of three keystrokes. The missiles roared away from the mini-tank and flashed into the main and two side rifts. Three blinding explosions closed the rifts and cut down the number of targets. But it didn't eliminate the enemy's efforts because the demons could still come through, only one at a time, but almost anywhere they choose.

CHAPTER THIRTY-THREE

Under cover of the predawn darkness the Shrew and the X-76 landed at the Bagram Air Force base in Afghanistan. Both planes taxied to a large, isolated hanger which hid the transfer of all personnel except for Su Li from one plane to the other.

Mike's foresight had strategically placed fuel trucks in the hanger to refuel both aircraft. The Air Force crews raced to complete their tasks before dawn lit up the sky.

The SOG had flown in from Israel on a MATS flight on a C5A Starlifter an hour before the planes had landed. Jack had them quickly load their equipment and find seats on the X-76.

Conveniently, all airport lights, with the exception of the runway lights, had gone out just before the X-76 had landed and didn't come back on until after both planes took off again.

The predawn lightness to the east was just beginning to brighten that part of the sky and the X-76 stayed low to the ground for a brief time to prevent exposing a silhouette to any people up at that hour. Su Li openly headed the Shrew back toward Peru.

As the newly refueled autonomous aircraft began the short flight to their destination in Pakistan, Jack's phone rang. He saw it was Charlie on the display. "Yeah, Charlie. What do you have?"

"Bad news Jack. I repositioned one of the new Overlord military satellites over the position of the demonic activity in Pakistan and got a bit of a shock. The source is directly in the middle of a major terrorist training camp that is bustling with activity and probably several hundred Jihadists training to kill Americans. It's going to be a little hard to insert, fight, and leave without someone noticing you and calling for Pakistani backup of the military type."

Jack took a big breath and sighed. "Yeah, it's never easy, is it? Of course you wouldn't expect the "illegal, terroristic, jihadists" to want to call the Pakistani military to their base, but who knows who's behind whom over there."

Telling Charlie he would call him back, Jack hung up. As he considered the possibilities his phone chimed to tell him he had a data file. Calling it up he stared at the pictures Charlie had sent him. It resembled an anthill even this early in the morning. A tagged area in red was the location of the demonic signals. It was a major area, an underground structure two hundred feet on each side. Several tiers of guard posts were visible that completely surrounded the activity site. Jack sighed again.

Calling the troops attention, he showed them the information on a large display screen on the bulkhead behind the cockpit. He asked for ideas or comments on how to storm and destroy the place. The best one came from one of the ex-USAF Psych Team. Brittney Demars pointed at the screen display and asked why they couldn't just drop a JDAM 2000-pound bomb on the area and solve the entire situation without having to fight their way in or out.

Jack nodded, "Yes Ma'am, I'd love to do that but unfortunately, the X-76 doesn't carry any munitions like that."

She nodded her head in response. "Yes Sir, but, isn't this close to a war zone? Don't they have an extra bomb they could drop here considering that this camp is preparing troops which will probably attack our troops in Afghanistan?"

All the CIA comments concerning American attacks across the border into Pakistan flew through Jack's mind. The administration in Washington was absolutely against any attacks by the U.S. forces in Afghanistan on Pakistani targets. The Afghans were walking a very fine line between harboring terrorists and not alienating their large Muslim population and meeting the U.S. rules on the war on terror. Washington didn't want to throw the limited cooperation that Pakistan provided under the bus by taking out the Pakistani enclaves. One very sticky wicket for the politicos and the military.

Jack looked at Mike White. "Any favors you could bring in here?"

Mike shook his head.

Jack realized he was sighing too much and didn't do that again.

Laura tapped him on the arm. "Anything that General Miles could help us with?"

Jack doubted that the lame duck Joint Chief of Staff could get anything done through channels but, one never knew. "I'll call him."

General Miles answered on the first ring. Jack explained the problem and the need for help. General Miles asked for the exact GPS coordinates and said he would call them back.

Five minutes later the phone rang and General Miles said to stay completely out of the area of the terrorists' camp for about twenty minutes. He then hung up.

Jack relayed the information to the team and to the controllers for the X-76 so that it would accommodate the delay without exposing them. The computers running the aircraft brought the craft down in an open area at the edge of a cliff on top of a small mesa that Jack thought was far too small for it to fit into, but it did. The screen showed a clear line of sight to the area of the terrorist's camp about thirty miles away and several hundred feet lower than their landing site.

As they waited to see what the General had managed to arrange Laura said quietly to Jack. "Don't you think that we should come up with a name for this plane? X-76 seems so, cold and impersonal."

Jack thought about it for a few seconds, "Okay, let's call it the "Sneaky Pete".

Laura shook her head, "Not classy enough. Since it is only our nickname for it, how about "Otto"?

Jack liked it. "Otto it is."

Jack went back to watching the distant base and was impressed by the clarity of the optics. The heat waves coming off of the sun baked ground didn't distort the picture and even at the distance they were at the magnified picture was crystal clear.

Jack's phone rang. As he heard General Miles' voice say, "Wait for it", Otto lifted off the ground into a hover. It quickly moved itself to an area behind the peak of the mountain it had been sitting on. Otto had switched from direct vision to the satellite view when suddenly the screen blanked out. The view returned and a ground shock wave could be seen travelling outward from the monstrous epicenter of what had to be a nuclear explosion. Jack was shocked, "General, did you just nuke Pakistan?"

General Miles was very calm. "No Jack, we used a MOP bunker-buster, a thirty-thousand-pound bomb, sort of what you requested. Since we are dealing with less than professional nuclear technicians, both human and demonic, and a fairly unsophisticated and new nuclear stockpile, I was afraid that the explosion might set off whatever nuclear source your demons were using."

General Miles chuckled. "That explosion will have all the signatures of a Pakistani bomb and I've been told the site is well known as a terrorist training camp in the intelligence world. The only conclusion to be drawn will be that the terrorists accidently set off a bomb they had stolen from the Pakistani government. Since we used a B-2 stealth bomber at thirty-five thousand feet to deliver the bomb and you are in the X-76, there will be no trace that we were there or were even slightly involved in the explosion."

Jack understood the situation but the revelation brought him another question. "General, how is that you were able to acquire a B-2 and a Massive Ordinance Penetrator on such short notice?"

General Miles' wry answer was immediate. "Let's just say that another target will have to wait a while to be tended to." The General sounded like the military leader he was. "I think your job there is done son, and we could certainly use your additional firepower back here as soon as you can get here."

Jack thanked the General for his timely assistance and hung up the phone.

Jack realized that Otto had anticipated the explosion and had moved so that the blast effects and direct radiation, if any, wouldn't impact it. Jack also noted that the EMP hadn't affected the electronics of the plane at all.

He kept watching the satellite view as the strong ground winds blew the airborne debris and smoke away from the blast site. The view was still unclear but definitely showed a major new canyon where the camp had been that was probably five hundred feet deep or deeper.

Mike White pointed out that the area was riddled with faults and caves and the explosion probably collapsed the entire camp into the deeps of the earth. "Sort of like an early version of hell for the jihadists."

Charlie called in and said that the computers registered none of the original demonic activity remaining. He rationalized that the bomb caused the nuclear source to detonate which eliminated the trans-dimensional portal and stopped the invasion on that end. He also wasn't able to detect any life forms within two miles of the epicenter and that the radiation levels were extremely lethal in that range.

Jack told Otto's controllers to take them to Peru as quickly as possible. When they noted that they couldn't arrange to sneak the plane into the Peruvian airports and that would violate their security, Jack reminded them that they were going to land in the mountains far away from any observation.

CHAPTER THIRTY-FOUR

As Mark watched the missiles close the portals he saw the enemy changing their tactics. Every one of the demons coming through in front of them was a "Slither" expert swordsman and their numbers were increasing every time he or Sarah eliminated one, two more appeared to attack them.

He was now at high speed and fighting two demons at once. The black blades came at him from every conceivable angle. He relaxed into his training as he had learned from Hugo. The angelic instruction was very comprehensive and he noticed that when a particular thrust, lunge, or slash was directed at him, he knew instinctively what would follow and he could prepare for it. It quickly became second nature muscle memory. He saw that Sarah was dealing with three at once. Even with their skill the odds were quickly tipping in favor of the enemy.

Alexis told David and Gary, "I've got to help them." She ran forward and engaged two of the demons that were attacking Sarah. Her appearance caught them off guard and she was able to eliminate both of them in seconds. As she reoriented towards the front, two more demons attacked her and another one attacked Sarah. Alexis heard Sarah mutter, "At least only so many can attack at once."

A demon appeared near David's tank and ran at him. David strafed it with the miniguns only to see it have no effect. David told the three warriors up front that he had a problem with a legal demon. But none of the three could break free to help him since to do so would be fatal in their present dance of death.

David saw the demon almost on top of him and he hit one switch which fired a missile directly at the demon. The huge explosion didn't kill the demon but it did blast it backwards twenty yards. That was time enough for David to exit the minitank and to start praying. His silver armor and the sword and shield appeared as the demon raced back to his position. David stepped to his right to avoid the direct attack and caught the demon off guard. David slashed downward with his sword and cut the shoulder and right arm off of the demon that caused it to dissolve into greasy black smoke.

A second demon started to attack David as three more illegal demons came out of the left hand riff. The minitank was on automatic and it strafed the three illegal demons with the 5.56 mm rounds and blew them away. David heard a word from God and spoke to the new demon in front of him. "The Lord Yahshua rebuke you and sends you to the pit."

The demon stopped and blinked once and suddenly shot straight up in the air and disappeared. David spoke into his battle comm, "Pray for God's protection Gary!" But there was no answer. David glanced over to see Gary's tank turned on its side and blasted open. He couldn't see anyone in it.

David's armor vanished as he switched his comm to Mark, "They've got Gary!"

Mark's stamina was ebbing by the constant battles and he was sure the two women felt the same. When he heard David's call about Gary some personal pride wall collapsed and a holy anger arose in him like he had never experienced. These enemies of God were not going to win this battle. He felt energized and began to wade through the "Slithers" like they were cardboard figures. Suddenly there were no more to fight and he dropped to normal speed and looked at Sarah. She too had returned to normal and looked spent. But, the battlefield was empty and the enemy had retreated.

Mark looked around and saw David standing next to Gary's overturned tank. David reported quickly, "He's not here, he's gone." Mark looked around and then at Sarah, "Where's Alexis?"

It took less than three seconds to see that she was also gone, presumably taken by the enemy.

Sarah looked stricken, "What do we do?"

Mark was at a loss. "We won the battle but at what cost?" He pulled out his cell phone and called Laura.

After explaining what had happened Mark pleaded with her to give them some direction to go after Gary and Alexis and bring them back.

153

Laura felt the loss and Mark's pain at the same time. She prayed for the words and felt led to tell him, "Secure the area and withdraw to the village. I need to pray about this and see what Yahveh wants us to do."

Mark sighed, "Of course you do. I'm sorry I'm as lost as a goose about this and I'm worried about David losing both Gary and, especially Alexis at the same time. I don't know if he'll be rational."

Laura was working off of her gut feelings at this point. "David will be fine and we'll be back there in less than two hours. Stay alert at the village in case the demons decide to strike you there. God is with you Mark, keep your faith in his love and stay strong."

Mark looked at the sadness and pain on his wife's face and told her that Laura wasn't worried. That seemed to give her hope which seemed to lighten the load on her a great deal. He wondered if he felt the same way.

David had retreated to his minitank and drove up to the two warriors. Jumping out he shook his head, "The whole left side of Gary's tank is ripped open and there's no sign of Gary. At least there's no body and no sign of blood anywhere."

Mark looked back at the field with misgivings. He said in a quiet voice. "Have I led them to their deaths?"

Sarah walked over with her armor disappearing as she walked. Mark's armor had faded after the enemy disappeared. She took Mark into her arms and hugged him. "Yahveh said to stop them. You were obedient and succeeded. The capture of Gary and Alexis came as no surprise to Him. I believe He is waiting to see if we will rise up in our faith and seek His help to rescue them."

Mark's flesh reared its practical head. "You know they could be dead by now."

"David seeking the best outcome in that case quoted, "To die is to be with the Lord."

CHAPTER THIRTY-FIVE

The darkness gibbered with fear and vile threats like a living nightmare. Alexis took a deep breath to settle her pulse rate down. She had been furiously fighting alongside Mark and Sarah when everything went dark and her armor and sword disappeared. She was still in the dark but could hear strange and ugly noises near her and around her. Her military training had included several intensive sequences of fighting while blindfolded to teach her to use her other senses in the event she couldn't see. So she dropped back into her Army Ranger role and stopped moving. She let her hearing and skin touch senses provide her with information on her surroundings. She was definitely in an enclosed space which she could tell by the echoes coming quickly from all directions. The space she was in was hot and wet and stunk like an unholy garbage pit. Which she decided was probably where she was.

She knew intuitively that the demons had somehow drawn her into their rift or portal and she was on their spiritual side of the dimensional barrier. Her normally ebullient spirit drove her thinking and she realized that being on the spiritual side got her closer to the Lord and might possibly give her some additional advantages she didn't have in the human world. Of course she didn't have a clue as to what those advantages might be as yet.

She identified at least three other beings or entities near her. One was on the ground level and was moaning. The other two were shuffling around to her right. She rotated toward where she thought they were and relaxed and waited. She was rewarded by a slowly increasing illumination in the red range. She could make out two demons, both bigger than her and a crumpled figure on the floor in the gloom. She took a step toward the fallen one and saw it was human.

One of the demons had a spear or long thin sword and it prodded the prone figure which gasped and cried out. Alexis identified the voice as that of Gary Danning. She stepped closer to him and spoke quietly. "Gary, this is Alexis, can you hear me?"

Gary's voice was weak but audible. "Hey pretty girl, what waterfront dive did we get ourselves into here?" Alexis could hear pain in his words.

"How bad are you hurt?"

Gary was silent for a few seconds. "I think I have a broken right arm and a broken right leg. I'm pretty sure they hit my tank with an RPG and it took out the left side The force of the blast threw me against the other bulkhead and that's where I broke everything."

One of the demons stepped forward and pushed Alexis back from Gary and kicked the man who cried out in pain.

Alexis started praying in tongues under her breath and took a step forward and returned the shove and then rotated to her left and used her right leg to side-kick the demon. It was caught by surprise and fell backwards to the floor. Alexis stepped over the prone form on the floor and put herself between the demons and Gary.

The second demon roared and came at Alexis like a freight train. She side stepped to her left and side kicked this demon. It was like kicking a wall. The demon reached out with its right arm and back handed Alexis in the face. She saw the move and went with it so that there was minimal damage to her head. The first demon was back on its feet and grabbed her by the front of her combat fatigues. He yanked her upward and towards himself. Alexis relaxed and let the powerful pull launch her upwards.

As she flew above the demon she tucked herself into a ball so that she came down behind the demon and landed on her feet. She rotated back toward the demon as it turned around. Alexis then used a front snap-kick to the demon's jaw hard enough to break the jaw, knock out several black teeth and launch the ugly critter in a backwards arc to land hard on his back. Unfortunately he also landed on Gary's legs which brought a scream from him.

The second demon was getting ready to charge her again and he wouldn't make the same mistakes his partner committed. A thought came to her and Alexis started praising the Lord in a loud voice. "Oh Yahshua, give me your strength in this abominable domain. Rise up your power to overcome these pitiful creatures and to find freedom for your brother and sister. I am the servant of the Most High God and I do not bow to these or their ilk. Empower me to bring your righteousness into this place and allow your angels to deal with our enemies. You defeated their master at the cross and I stand on that victory. Show them your power Lord; show them your esteem that they want to sully."

As she praised and prayed it was if she was filling up with light and it began to burst from her being in all directions. It was a pure white light that was blindingly bright in the Stygian gloom. The demons scurried away from the light and fled for their lives. A rumbling roar vibrated the room they were in and suddenly the entire roof and front wall were ripped away. Bright, white light flooded into the room and the biggest angel Alexis ever saw bent down and carefully picked up Gary and Alexis. There was a soundless explosion the darkness disappeared and then they were wrapped in a silken embrace that was so comfortable Alexis almost fainted. She found the strength to thank Yahshua from the bottom of her heart for their rescue from the demons of darkness. Then she relaxed and lost consciousness.

Alexis came to her senses lying on her back on tough grass in the dark of night. There was no sign of the angel or the demons. It was warm and humid but in a normal way. She realized that she was close to where she had been when the demons captured her earlier.

She heard a cough and got to her feet. By the dim starlight she saw a form on the ground and she went to it. It was Gary and he was groaning. Alexis felt around but she had lost her light and her comm gear. She kneeled down and put her hand on Gary's shoulder. "Do you feel strong enough for me to carry you back to the village?"

Gary groggily looked around in the dark. "Is that where we are? Wait one." She saw him moving around and then he moaned again. "Actually, I doubt that I could stand it. Maybe you should get some help, you know, something with wheels or wings."

Alexis sat down on the ground. "Will you be safe to stay here alone?"

Gary's voice was edged in pain. "What? I only have a broken arm and leg, right? I will be as quiet as a mouse. Just make it as quick as you can, please. The pain levels are pretty high and I think that last kick the demon did to me may have broken a rib or two."

Alexis got up and brushed off her pants. "Be very careful. I will only be gone about fifteen minutes . . ."She crouched down near him as two figures came at them in the dark. Alexis stood up and ran towards them. The two natives stopped and held out their spears." Alexis realized who they were and stopped her charge. She held up her hand and said loudly, "Please let Mark Connelly know that we are here and need medical help."

There was no vocal response but the two natives disappeared and in a few minutes' lights started heading their way from the village. Mark and David ran up to where she and Gary were. Alexis told them about Gary's injuries and then grabbed them both in big bear hug. Mark hugged her back and broke away to call for transportation to the village for Gary. In the background they heard Gary say, "Anything but a mini-tank."

After they returned to the village with Gary on a stretcher, they did what they could do to make him comfortable and told him to hang on for the X-76 which should be there in a few minutes. Mark gave him an injection of Morphine to dull the pain and examined his arm, leg, and ribs. Neither of the extremities were compound fractures and none of his ribs were broken. Gary was quiet due to the drug and patted Mark on the hand. "Thanks, I needed that."

Alexis told the others about their ordeal. Gary added that Alexis had done all the fighting, heavy lifting, praying, and praising. Then he went to sleep.

CHAPTER THIRTY-SIX

After Mark finished debriefing Alexis he told her to get some rest while he pondered their next move. His phone chirped and he answered it. "Mark."

Jack's voice was a welcome sound as he asked Mark to provide some lighting for their VTOL landing near the village.

Mark had already positioned David's mini-tank at the end of a level open area exactly for this occasion. He pushed the "LIGHTS" button on the hand-held remote and the wide-angle, high-intensity combat lights on the tank illuminated the entire field. "There you go buddy. Listen, Gary suffered some damage during the fighting and we need to use the X-76 to take him to a hospital where he can get some bones set."

Jack told him, "Wait one."

After a few minutes of silence Jack continued, "Okay, as soon as we deplane, let's get him in here. Laura and I are going to stay with him and the controllers for this Uber jet have cleared us to take him to the USNS Comfort which, thankfully, is not too far from Peru at the present time. We will get there before dawn and the crew has been ordered to ignore us completely except to have a gurney waiting for Gary. He'll get the best treatment possible there. Is he in a lot of pain?"

Mark chuckled, "No, not really, I gave him some Morphine and he's asleep at the moment. He has a lot of pain when not medicated though and he needs fixing as soon as possible."

Jack said, "We're here now."

Mark heard the quiet landing outside and helped move Gary's litter to the plane. After it lifted off and disappeared from view he took the rest of the crew into the hut that had been provided by the villagers. It was a little tight but everyone could hear him.

Mark welcomed the SOG troops to Peru and the jungle battle site. "Guys and gals, I'm glad you're here. We were able to stop the demons on the first contact but I'm sure they'll adapt to our new circumstances and come at us even harder next time. We will have to watch out for couple of new things they did during this battle. One, they used human troops which is not unusual but this time they were equipped with RPGs which knocked out half of our backup capability. The mini-tank Gary was using was hit and suffered a lot of damage. I doubt that we will be able to use it for the next battle. Second, Gary was injured by the explosion and knocked unconscious. Somehow the demons were able to transport him into the demonic realm along with Alexis. I assume they wanted to torture them to determine our strengths and weaknesses. Alexis was able to extract them with the help of an unknown but very large angel."

Mark looked around at the assembled team. "The problem I see with this is that they were able to capture Alexis while she was in full combat with her armor and sword and she doesn't know how. This could lead to more captures like that. We're going to seek the Lord and see what we can do to prevent that or at least what to be aware of if there are any warning signs that accompany that type of operation."

Laura had been praying and stood up. Mark looked at her and nodded. She turned to the assembled team and smiled. "I believe that this new technique of theirs could be turned to an advantage for the good guys, that's us, if we can find a way to create havoc for their operations once they take us there."

Mark thought about that for a minute. "While that sounds good it could backfire on us. If I were controlling the demons, I would have learned to bind up or disable the captives so they can't fight back like Alexis did."

The discussion went on for twenty minutes until Mark added to the guard rotation and told everybody else to get some rest. David had slipped out and gotten two more empty huts for the troops to spread out into for the night. About an hour after they bedded down the X-76 returned and Jack and Laura joined them. Mark brought them up to speed on the local situation and then suggested they try to get some rest in the remaining hours of the morning darkness.

As Jack was attempting to get to sleep he suddenly felt a touch from the Father that brought him to tears. The touch was love and compassion from God that was so wonderful it was overwhelming in its purity and righteousness. The feeling was gone in less than a minute but the afterglow was almost as good.

Jack sat up and prayed his total commitment to Yahveh and Yahshua which included his life and his love. He noticed in the dark that Laura was sitting up also. Glancing around he saw everyone in the hut stirring and sitting up. He looked at his wife and said, "Wow. What was that about?"

His cell phone chirped and he answered it. Charlie Wu's voice was somewhat rattled and Charlie didn't get rattled easily. "Jack, it's happened!"

Jack didn't understand that comment. "What's happened Charlie?"

"The Rapture of the Church, that's what's happened all over the world. At least that's what Crayton says. Crayton estimates that over nine hundred million people who were here last night are no longer on Earth."

Jack was still fuzzy from lack of sleep and asked questioningly, "How can there be only nine hundred million people missing when there are about two billion Christians on the planet presently?"

Charlie chuckled, "According to the computer figures, over seven hundred and fifty million adults and over two hundred million children under the age of accountability which comes up to almost a billion souls that are not here anymore. I am seeing large numbers of accidents involving automobiles, buses, planes, and trains coming in from all countries. This is going to cause havoc everywhere. Just think of the number of pregnant women who are going to wake up no longer pregnant. Whole families are going to be missing their young children. Jack, this is huge."

Jack agreed and thanked Charlie for letting him know what was happening. He also asked Charlie to continue to bring him up to date on new events or announcements by world governments.

Standing up he announced the event to everyone there. "Charlie's computers are reporting a billion people disappearing this morning about an hour ago. The Rapture has taken place and God has taken His church off of the Earth so that it doesn't have to go through the tribulations. There will be difficult times ahead for all people and we need to stay mission-focused to do God's will here on earth. Remember, we only have forty-two months to accomplish everything Yahveh is giving us to do."

Laura was crying softly and Jack went over to her. "What's the problem, honey?"

There was a heavy sadness in Laura's eyes. "I'm thrilled that a billion people were called to heaven. But, that means the other billion Christians and who knows how many other believers have been left here to face the tribulations of God's wrath."

Jack sighed, "It is God's decision in each person's case. You know that He is a loving God that wanted all people to come to Him. I'm sorry about those that didn't go but they still have an opportunity to stand for God and make it to heaven."

Laura nodded her head. "True, but it is still very painful to think of the family members who were left behind."

CHAPTER THIRTY-SEVEN

Alexis stood up in the silent hut. She was obviously shaken by the news of the disappearance of so many people. In her mind she knew that something like this could happen but in her heart she had never expected it to happen. She took a deep breath to settle her nerves. "I'm not sure what you mean by the Rapture's effect on Earth. I am still so new as a believer I haven't studied up on this prophesy."

Jack could see she was upset so he nodded his head. "I know and I'll try to answer it to the best of my ability."

Jack turned to address the twenty people who were only dimly illuminated by several combat lights as more troops and natives crowded into the hut. "To describe the scene in America and around the world; people, young and old, rich and poor, from all different races, and almost every child under the age of accountability just vanished in a single moment of time. Gone. Silently, and without commotion on the part of the ones that went away. Everything that was not part of them, their clothing, jewelry such as rings, glasses, false teeth, contact lenses will probably be lying in a pile where they were when Yahshua told them to "Come up hither". Because the time of day is different around the world at one time, there were many traffic accidents as driverless cars and trucks careened out of control. Pilot-less aircraft probably fell from the skies with disastrous results."

Jack continued, "Many trains, subways and ships probably lost operators. "Utter chaos" doesn't begin to describe it. I will remind you that Yahveh knows the future of everyone and if a crash caused by the Rapture would prevent another person from being saved, it won't happen. God is big enough to handle billions of events or even trillions of events simultaneously. Still, pregnant women would find that their unborn child is gone. And everywhere in the world there will be an eerie emptiness that words cannot describe. Because the Holy Spirit of God has withdrawn from the general world and will focus on Israel.

Everywhere else in the world there will be a sense of evil that won't go away. It will be a sinister presence striking fear into the hearts of men and women who don't have God in their lives."

Alexis nodded her head in understanding. "What about the people called to heaven? What will happen to them physically?"

Laura stood up and answered that question. "The apostle Paul addresses the issue in great detail in First Corinthians chapter 15. What it boils down to is the difference between a physical body and a spiritual body. When Christ was raised He appeared to the disciples behind closed doors, and they didn't unlock the door for Him. At these appearances He invited His friends to touch Him, saying He had a real body, with flesh and bones; He wasn't a ghost. He ate some food in their presence. So it is a real body capable of interacting with the elements of this dimension, yet not constrained by them. Spirit life in its redeemed form will not have the limitations we know and have to live within the here and now. Just because this is beyond our comprehension is not a valid reason to dismiss it as impossible, or even as improbable."

Laura thought for a minute. "There is an inter-dimensional relationship with the spirit world that we, in the human form, are not normally privileged to interact with from this earthly existence. The resurrection changed all that for the believers. How it actually occurred is only a matter of speculation as scripture does not address the details beyond attributing it to Christ's power. Look in Philippians, Chapter 3, and verses20 and21. Our best guess is that physical matter gets transformed into a state of existence which is no longer bound by time. In this state one could be anywhere at any time, without any of the constraints offered by matter that is bound by time. It is also possible that clothing left behind may have signs of burned fibers in areas of skin contact, as in the shroud of Turin. Don't forget the dead in Christ, the ones that died before the Rapture. I'm sure that examination of the graves of deceased believers will show that the remains are gone, further proof of the veracity of the Rapture"

Mark laughed, "Wow! One out of each seven people of the world's population disappears in the blink of an eye.

That's going to rattle a lot of people who deny the reality of Christ or the Father."

Alexis asked one more question. "What do you mean by the "age of accountability"?

Laura smiled. "Every one, as a child, reaches a point in their life, usually around eleven to thirteen years of age, when they understand the difference between good and evil. Once they know the truth then they have the choice to choose God or not."

CHAPTER THIRTY-EIGHT

At 4:00 a.m. Charlie Wu called from the new team headquarters in Israel. Jack had gotten all of three hours' sleep and was a bit groggy. Keying his cell phone, he mumbled, "What's up Charlie?"

Charlie had a very sober tone to his normally quiet voice. Much more so than Jack had ever heard before. It seemed oddly out of place. Events normally didn't faze the Oriental man. "Jack, everything has changed this morning because of the Rapture."

"Jack, literally, roughly a billion living people are missing from the Earth if you count the children. There are estimates that between 155 million and 182 million Americans are gone. That is almost half of the people in the country. You can't believe the rationales of the various talking heads and media pundits about what happened. In their limited world view, it's a race between alien abduction and selective enemy attack. Now after the Rapture there will be no well-known or serious Christian sources available to contradict them. The Christians that were not taken in the Rapture are insisting that it could not have been the Rapture, naturally, because they weren't taken. It's chaos in every sector of business and even the military is in disarray because a significant number of senior and operational officers are gone."

Charlie sighed, "Now to our operations. First, I lost four of my computer center personnel. The others are confused and can't seem to comprehend what has happened. Worldwide it is pretty much business as usual except in Britain, Scotland, Ireland, and some of the other countries with a significant Christian population."

"You probably have a better idea as to our personnel in the SOG or otherwise. I know that President Bollen and his entire family have disappeared and the liberal party is arguing that they should be in charge. Only two of the Supreme Court are gone and the others I worry about."

"I can detect no demonic activity in the mountains of Peru whereas yesterday it was like a beehive. I believe that the destruction of the nuclear portal in Pakistan must have somehow shut down the activity in Peru. On the other hand, it could be the Rapture that caused them to leave Peru at this time. You probably don't realize it because of your focus right now, but, this is the date for the celebration of the Jewish feast of Sukkot or the Feast of Tabernacles. I really don't know what the loss of a billion people from the face of the Earth means for our future operations, probably nothing since we're just following God. I'm going to stream the news feeds I've been watching for a couple of hours this morning. At least they'll be in English so you can understand them."

Jack signed off and set up his laptop computer using his satellite phone for an internet connection. He opened a window on the screen and brought up the streaming application. He clicked on Charlie's website and started reading the articles there.

Mark had listened to Jack's end of the conversation with Charlie. He was able to determine the major points and on a hunch he called several places on his cell phone. While Jack was reading the news reports of the Rapture Mark finished his calls. He got up and walked over to Jack. Sitting down he got Jack's attention.

"I made some calls after you heard from Charlie. President Bolan and his entire family are gone. So is Gary Danning. The hospital is in a state of shock. Many doctors, nurses, and patients disappeared this morning. A nurse answered the phone and went to check on Gary. All she found were his gown, robe, and his bandages. But, General Miles is still here. I talked to him and he told me he was given the alternatives we were given and he decided to stay and fight with us."

Jack shook his head, "Do you think the President knew what was coming?"

Mark thought about that. "Yes, I think he did. Do you remember when he was leaving the Fortress and said something to the effect of being together with us soon? Unless the Rapture happened?"

Jack smiled at his best friend in the world. "I'm glad that Gary is whole and happy with no pain anymore."

Mark grinned back, "Amen".

CHAPTER THIRTY-NINE

After assuring the remaining natives that the demonic force in the jungle was completely gone, Jack seriously stressed the need for the natives left behind after the Rapture to learn to love Jesus on a personal level. Frank gave them a short sermon on forgiveness and salvation in the few years left and he told them that Joe would have wanted them to do that.

Laura motioned to Jack to step to the side with her. She looked around to see if anyone was in earshot and confident that her comments would not be overheard she whispered, "Jack, you know the only way these left-behind natives can make it to heaven is by defying the anti-Christ and being beheaded. It makes me sick that we can't offer them anything more than that."

Jack prayed silently for wisdom and words. Tenderness filled his eyes as he whispered back, "That is what we believe will be required for people that have rejected Jesus before the Rapture. I don't know that these innocent people rejected Him or just weren't fully aware of who He is. They are a primitive people and were just learning about the good news when the Rapture happened. Who are we to say that the Father doesn't have a different path for innocents who may have made the right decision in a short time but were preempted by the suddenness of the Rapture before they fully understood the choice? Yahshua would be aware and so is Yahveh's Holy Spirit. Perhaps we need to pray for their awakening and acceptance."

Laura was about to say something when one of Hugo's teachings that had been hidden from her until this time opened up in her mind. She smiled at Jack and said, "That has already been done by Frank and, yes, there are different paths for those who are innocent but past the age of accountability. You're right that Yahveh and Yahshua have this situation well in hand."

She looked up and saw Frank smiling at her. She knew he was aware of their concern and the solution to that concern. The only way he would know that is if God told him. Laura smiled back and nodded to the pastor.

The team and the SOG finished their good-byes to the natives and Frank, who decided to stay and work with the natives for a time. Boarding the X-76 they lifted off and headed for Israel, a trip of 7,900 miles. The trip, including an in-flight refueling was handled by the autonomous aircraft without incident.

Traveling through eight time zones at 1600 MPH they left Peru at 8 a.m. and arrived at Israel at 9 p.m. the preceding night.

The X-76 flew down to sea level and into the hidden island flight corridor through the earth without a hitch. It entered the cavernous ground level and settled lightly to the ground on the runway. Turning to the right off the runway it continued to taxi until it came to a hanger on which the doors were open. The craft taxied in and shut down. The door opened and the team got its first look at their new quarters in the darkness of the simulated night time.

Jack and Mark studied the layout and were discussing it when a large, electric, lorry entered and pulled up to the aircraft. Charlie Wu jumped out and greeted the team members with gusto. "Wait until you get a look at your new home. It is several steps above what we had at the fortress."

The look of eagerness on his face was unusual. He was normally quiet and composed. Jack grinned at Mark and they got the troops and their weapons onto the lorry and Charlie touched the switch that took it back towards their buildings.

The lorry automatically docked inside the dock area of their surface building. Everyone piled off and got their weapons and packs. Charlie led them to the elevators. He indicated that the SOG should take the two elevators to the right and that the rest of the team take the one to the left. He smiled at the men and women of the SOG. "You will be very pleasantly surprised. There are wrist band devices for each of you in your rooms. After you're settled just tap the dining symbol on the band and it will lead you to the dining room. Let's say, dinner at eleven?"

Laura cocked an eye at Charlie. "You're having too much fun with this. Try to remember, everyone here is armed and pretty tired."

Charlie grinned. "That's okay. It will be worth it when they see their section."

The elevator moved noiselessly in several directions and opened onto a large circular living/reception area on level 4 underground. Laura immediately liked the layout, the lighting, and the color selections. It felt like home to her.

Charlie picked up wrist bands and gave them to each of the team. "Just tap the bedroom symbol and it will guide you to your room."

David strapped on the wrist band. "How does it know who I am and what room is assigned to me?"

Charlie practically beamed. "It is an extension, an interface if you prefer, of the CRAY computers in the ComSec area. When you strap the wrist band on it measures your bio specifics and matches it to your profile on file. It knows everything programmed about you and will watch over you in the event of illness, potential illness, injury, and it will track your movements so that it can foresee what things it has in control for you."

"For example, if you drink a cup of coffee when you rise every day, it will have your coffee waiting when you awake. It's kinda like a valet, butler, maid, personal assistant and bodyguard all in one. You can set parameters to prevent it getting too personal if you want to. It is a waterproof, idiot proof, almost indestructible asset you will learn to really enjoy. It will remind you of scheduled meetings, direct phone, text, email, and video to your location, and wake you when you want it to."

Laura tapped the bed symbol and the small video screen on the band lit up with an arrow pointing behind her. She turned around and the arrow pointed to one of the doorways in the large circular wall about twenty feet away. Grabbing her gear she walked to the door, followed by Jack.

CHAPTER FORTY

His Interest in their new dwelling caught fire in Jack's spirit and he watched as Laura placed her eye up to the ID-sensor group as she placed her right hand on the plate below it. The door gave a solid but muted "thunk", indicating its massiveness as it unlocked and they walked into "their" room.

The doors opened onto an entry hall that was about six feet long and opened up into the sitting room of the suite. Jack noted the signs of the NovaStar defense system in the walls and realized that an intruder who managed to overcome the door would be confronted at this point by a mind-stunning burst of light and sound that equaled a flash-bang grenade. Then they would be assaulted by the SCARE system which would cause an extreme fear to rise up in them until they had to flee. The walls of the hall that hid these defenses were indirectly lit and beautifully wallpapered. The carpet soaked up sound and cushioned the feet in a plush pile in a muted rose tone color.

Stepping into the sitting room presented a large, airy decor. There were windows and glass French doors running from the floor to the ceiling along both sides of the room. The vista either way was stunning. It appeared that the room was situated on the edge of a tall cliff with magnificent views of the Mediterranean Sea on one side and an endless valley that stretched for miles on the other. The lighting for these scenes was coordinated with the time of day for Tel Aviv and therefore the darkness was relieved by a rising half-moon over the sea and on the other side, the sky glow from Tel Aviv. Due to the hour and the coolness of the sea, the French doors facing the sea were open and an occasional, cool breeze flowed through the window bringing the pleasant, salty smell of the sea. It was very restful and soothing. Jack marveled at the smooth integration of his portal technology and something else, probably transmission electronics, in the deep, undersea location of the base.

Laura was very pleased with the sitting room and she went on to open the double doors to the bedroom with anticipation. She was not disappointed. First, the doors opened by themselves by sliding back into the frame of the door. The window scene was repeated in the bedroom as if the sides of their suite were connected and real. The king-size bed was very comfortable with the latest technology on sleep surfaces and tastefully decorated in colors matching the wall decor. The bed sat out from the back wall several feet and there were hidden drawers, seating, and table surfaces artfully placed throughout the large room. The French doors to the sea were open in this room also and the cool, salty aroma wafted around the room and across the bed. She sat on the bed and closed her eyes. The gentle breeze also brought the distant sound of surf as the waves crashed onto the shore. It was so comfortable that she felt that she could have curled up and happily gone to sleep right then.

Jack walked over to one of the two doors in the wall behind the bed. The door opened automatically as he approached it. This was the door to the right of the bed. As he stepped into the room the indirect lighting came on and he was gratified to find a bathing room that included a seven-foot-long bath tub, a heated water-jet whirlpool, a large glass lined shower and several sink areas. Each area had its own direct lighting complimenting the overall indirect lighting for the entire room. There were recessed shelves with towels and wash cloths and supplies like shampoo and soap. There was a faint smell of lilacs and he noticed the addition of a positive ion generator that gave the room a pleasant fresh odor. There were panels in the walls next to each bathing area that were more of the view portals that could be switched to the view the bather desired. There was a large, 52-inch flat-screen television that could be seen from anywhere in the room. The door had closed silently after he'd passed through it.

To his right was another door to the bathroom. Jack went through it to find a huge closet already stocked with clothes of all types, shoes, boots, and accessories. Jack was confident that the clothes were all exactly correct for both Laura and himself. He mused that there were no secrets from the computer anymore. Exiting the far end of the closet he found himself back in the bedroom on the other side of the bed. Laura had fallen back on the bed and watched him upside down as he came back into the room. "I hope the bath and closet are up to these standards." she said as she waved her hand at the bedroom.

Jack nodded, "They didn't miss a beat. You'll be very pleased."

She jumped up and went exploring. Jack looked around and walked back into the sitting room. He noticed a plain wall panel with an additional eye print/handprint panel off the side of the room. He placed his hand on the lower sensor panel and looked into the eye sensor. The door panel slid noiselessly open and Jack walked into their personal war room. Side by side positions gave them access to all they had been used to in the Fortress and more. Jack sat down in the padded seat and brought up the personnel roster. A large screen above his position lit up to show the position of all of the personnel in the base. There were fourteen more people than the team and the SOG combined and he inquired as to the identity and function of these personnel. The screen split as he selected one of the people. On one side was a picture of the man, his vital statistics, his function and his clearances. The man Jack had selected was one of the base support personnel whose major role was supply and preparation on the night shift. His clearances and qualifications were impressive and his record of service was admirable.

After checking several more of the people Jack picked Mark's icon and pushed the comm button. Mark's face appeared and it seemed he was also checking out the business end of his suite. "Hi Jack, I really like the layout of these new digs. I think Sarah is ready to settle down and stay here forever."

Jack laughed, "I know, Laura is giving out the same vibrations but I think we all know that the clock is ticking away our last thirty-six months and we have probably got work waiting for us."

Mark snorted, "Who, other than Yahveh and Yahshua is left on Earth to give us directions? The new U.S. President doesn't want us to exist and that will include the military management such as the JCS and the Generals in the

Pentagon. I doubt that we have any remaining support in the alphabet agencies either."

Jack nodded, "Since the Rapture we will have to rely strictly on heavenly guidance and direction. As to these lush living quarters I doubt that we were chosen to simply relax and be pampered for the next three and a half years. If we had wanted that we should have asked to go in the Rapture instead of volunteering to stay and fight for God."

Mark had sobered up considerably. "You're right enough. I think we can get some Earthly advice and assistance from the Israeli government and the Mossad. Especially since they are our base mates."

Jack thought about that and it troubled him somewhat. "We need to double check everything in prayer."

Mark laughed out loud. "While we're discussing our private wars, why don't you push the large orange button to the left of your keyboard?"

Jack pursed his lips and eyed the switch. Deciding to trust Mark not to mislead him, he reached over with his left hand and punched the button. The room went to a red spectrum and two wall panels opened up on either side of the room. Jack's left eyebrow raised as he inventoried the armory represented there. There were four 6.8 mm M-8s, magazines for each weapon, grenades, knives, harnesses, flash-bangs, and more. Jack whistled, "Are we planning to go to war inside this base?"

Mark nodded, "Just in case we get an intruder or two. By the way, your bracelet also replaces your medallion for the new NovaStar defense system inside this base. The new "improved" version has features that weren't available with the first two editions."

Jack smiled, "Let's make sure everyone reads the new operating manuals so we are up to speed with our weapons."

Jack pushed the orange switch and closed the panels. "We need to get the troops together, but, not until the core team has a chance to pray for Yahveh's will and direction."

Mark nodded, "Sound the alarm Ridley, gather the troops. Into the battle rode the chosen warriors."

Jack shook his head at Mark's whimsy. "I think that we'd better sleep first. It's two o'clock in the morning here and my internal clock is confused."

CHAPTER FORTY-ONE

The next morning, Jack saw that the core team was present and accounted for in the new war room on the combat floor. He looked at Mark and nodded.

Mark stood up and everyone gave him their attention. "Warriors, in the faith I am the least among you. But, even I know that we really need to continue to seek the Father for our direction and His will in these last days, especially in these Last Days." He looked around the room at the sixteen people present. Mark took a mental roll call. He saw Jack and Laura, Sarah, David and Alexis, Stan and Debbie, Su Li and Mike White, Carol, Charlie and Linda Wu, Steve and Larry Malone, Victor Chamberlain, and then he counted himself. He thought "Good people all."

Bowing his head, he led the initial prayer. "Heavenly Father Yahveh, in your Son's name, Yahshua we ask for your guidance and direction so that we can serve you and the Kingdom of God responsibly. Please, grace us with the knowledge of your will in these matters and speak to us now." Everyone sought the Lord individually. After a while Mark looked up and saw he had everyone's attention again.

While nothing of note was reported at the end of the prayer session, Laura had a giddy feeling that something momentous was about to happen. She could feel the power of God in her and all around her.

Jack stood up and was about to release the group, when suddenly everything changed. It seemed like the roof and the floors and sea above them disappeared and they were standing on a cloud in the middle of the air. The cloud extended to the horizon in all directions and there was no sun in the bright blue sky but everything was brightly lit. There was a gentle breeze coming from his left but other than that there were no other sensations. Jack looked around and saw the same view behind him too.

Everyone started talking at the same time and it created a clamor that was just as suddenly stilled when a gold and white figure appeared in their midst. Jack recognized Rose, the angel that had been with them ever since she made herself known to Laura two years earlier.

Rose allowed the calmer gold color to overshadow the fierce white glare and rotated in place studying each of the people standing there. She smiled and her voice rang out clearly. "Welcome warriors. I have been given the task to provide the direction you desire for the present."

She waved her hand and an arc of chairs appeared. She gestured with her head and everyone went to the chairs and sat down. Rose went in front of the group and sat down on nothing. Her eyes were bright blue and had a very penetrating quality.

She smiled at the assembled group again. "The Most High, Yahveh, God of the universe wants me to tell you that he is pleased that you and your fellow warriors offered to continue to battle for His Kingdom for the next season. I too, am glad because I've come to love you all and, to tell you a secret, we angels can use the help.

As you know, the enemy of mankind, Satan, has been taking liberties not permitted in these last days. A unique group of his worshipers has been causing the saints of God trouble for the last several centuries. These are the occultists and, until today, they lived in the shadows and did their evil out of man's sight. With the true believers of Christ gone from the Earth this spawn of Satan feels it is their time. Time for them to come out into the public and show their evil power so that all can see and fear them."

Occultists get their power from Satan himself. They worship the devil and use sorcery to make themselves believe they are in control. Nothing could be farther from the truth. Satan will use these willing tools as he wants to until they are of no further use and then he will take their souls which will end up being tortured in Hades just the same as an innocent but lost non-believer and eventually, Satan and his demons."

Rose's head shook from side to side. "They are fools, but dangerous fools. Satan can fool many people because he can imitate some of God's work, but remember, he is not creative. He can imitate but not originate. While he can lead many astray with fake miracles, a person needs only to see if the work matches up with God's word to see the truth."

Another angel appeared sitting next to Rose. Most of the team recognized him as Hugo, a heavenly teacher of millennia. Rose nodded to Hugo who took over the teaching.

"Hello all of you. I've met most of you before, especially Laura and Carol. Let me describe in your limited dimensions who your enemy is. The word "occult" means: "hidden from view; secret; mysterious." It has been defined in the following ways:"

"First, it means secret, hidden except from those with more than ordinary knowledge. It also means involving the supernatural, occult powers. The occult covers the supernatural, mystical or magical. A person...who studies or practices any form of the "occult sciences", such as divination, magick, mysticism, spiritualism, and so forth, is called an "occultist".

"Although many occult groups do tend to share in common elements of secrecy and exclusiveness among themselves, it is useful to understand that not all groups which may be classed as "occult" are the same. Pagans, contrary to popular belief, do not worship the devil. Indeed, Pagans are people who dismiss God and have a leaning towards nature. They seek to harness the power of nature through various magical rites. They sometimes dabble too far and are enveloped into the dark world of demons."

"Some of the Pagan groups in existence on Earth today include: Druids and Wiccans. Some groups tend to worship a female deity whereas others will worship a male deity of some description. Wiccans normally class themselves as practicing 'white' witchcraft, and say that they do good. However, it must be stressed that white witchcraft can certainly lead a person down the slippery slope towards its black counterpart. The Word of God does not draw a line between white or black witchcraft, but simply warns against practicing "witchcraft" These are not your team's concern."

"Spiritualists are those that attempt to contact the dead. The Word of God explicitly forbids attempted contact with the dead. God's Word states that the dead do not have contact with the living, and that the messages which are meant to come from the dead are actually from deceiving spirits who are familiar with the departed, a "familiar spirit" These are also not your concern at this time."

"Satanism has dabblers, the theatrical, and the professionals. Dabblers and the theatrical Satanist are generally harmless and simply seeking their "place" in the universe rather than seeking the one true God. Lately, some that would have sought out Satanism have instead been lured into becoming home-grown terrorists."

"The most dangerous types of Satanists, however, are "Professional Satanists." These people are highly organized and have operated out of a secretive network of people. Many will meet in Satanist temples which require absolute obedience from those who attend. These people do believe that the Devil really exists as a personal entity. Many of these people are also involved in drug trafficking, child abuse and prostitution."

*Remember, regardless of their devotion or cooperation with demonic forces all of these people are unknowingly getting involved with deceptive and harmful spiritual forces which stand in opposition to Yahshua. "

Hugo looked contemplative for a few seconds. He looked up again, "One of your missions for the next season will be to counter the efforts of these "professional groups" of Satanists because the removal of the saints to heaven has emboldened the enemy and he has assigned legions of demons to these groups to create great fear in the populaces. The majority of the people remaining on the Earth have been systematically brainwashed to believe that Satan is the most powerful force in the world and his demons are unstoppable, implacable, and to be greatly feared, with Satan the most feared as their leader. Modern film and television has fostered this image in a mistaken pursuit of ratings and money. They don't realize that the popularity of the satanic is one of the enemy's long-term plans to enslave the people of the world in fear."

Hugo stood up. "As the demons join their tools to create this fear, your team and others will be the fist of God on a forsaken Earth. Satan knows he is not allowed to use his forces directly against lost humanity. He doesn't care and Yahveh is going to use your capabilities to prevent the enemy's excesses. I wish you all blessings and expect to see you all soon." He vanished from view.

Rose also stood up. "Hugo means that he expects to see each of you when you finally get to heaven, not that you will not succeed in your battles. I know you will be victorious and I will be there too. Your first mission will start in three days and it will be against a group known as "sab'a al-a3la sheitan moodam" in Arabic. It originally meant seven supreme Satanists. The group now numbers in the hundreds and is about to launch an attack on the Western Wall in Jerusalem. Your team needs to eliminate this group before the demons that are now with them make their attack. Ask Carol to define the time lines and secure the location of the targets."

Rose faded from sight but the crew was still in the heavenly setting. Laura suddenly fell to her knees and then prone on her face. The same feeling came over the others and they quickly joined her, face down on the cloud. Peace like a wind blew over them and settled in their spirits and Jack heard the voice of God. *"My children go to this battle in my strength. I will give the enemy into your hands. Destroy them to a person, let none escape. I, the Lord have told you."*

The presence left and the team found themselves back in the war room of the new fortress.

CHAPTER FORTY-TWO

As they began discussing the mission Mark asked Jack, "Why the elaborate presage to an assignment? I mean we've faced worse missions with only a word from an angel. This time we had Rose, Hugo, and a word from Yahveh."

Jack was about to respond when Laura spoke up. "This mission is obviously of more importance to God than we suspect. God doesn't deal in flamboyant gestures; He doesn't have to do that. I think that we should approach this mission with the intensity that we do the worst ones. Remember, just because God says we will be victorious doesn't mean some of us won't be hurt or killed."

Carol stood up and asked to be released to go to her room and pray. Jack nodded and she left.

Jack took a deep breath. He was still amazed by the whole thing, especially the peace he had felt when Yahveh spoke to them. "Mark, David, Sarah. You three find out all you can about this Saba Al-A3La Sheitan Moodam through the Mossad and any contacts of yours that are still on Earth.

Laura, see if any of the alphabet agencies will work with us or at least give us information. I'm going to call Gary Eisenthal and see what he knows about them, if he is still on Earth. Alexis, Stan, Debbie, work your old contacts for any information they might have, especially present locations. Su Li, you and Mike work with Charlie and Linda on drones we can use in the area of Jerusalem. Charlie, also see what the computer world has to tell us. I wouldn't rely too heavily on Wikipedia." Jack got a glare from both of the Orientals on that. "Steve, you and Larry work with Victor on checking our supplies both for here and for mobile service. I think we might need to stock the packs, planes, and mission-specific requirements. I'll give you guys a hand as soon as I'm free. Let's go to work folks, like we are the soon to be King David and we're facing Goliath."

Steve looked at Larry and Victor. "Suppose we need to stock stones and slings?"

Larry raised an eyebrow. "You never know. I know where we can get some in Denver and in Dallas. I don't know about Tel Aviv."

Victor quipped, "Check with Sarah, I'm pretty sure she's used them in the past."

The team scattered to their tasks while Carol was deep in prayer. The white diamonds at her neck and forehead were glowing white hot.

Carol knew the feeling an eagle has as it glides over a forest looking for game. But, as she glided over the time lines and events in the matrix that was all of creation in eleven dimensions she knew her next meal didn't depend on her ability, just the lives of the entire Crossfire Team and the SOG. Oh, it depended as much on their abilities as her investigation, but she was full of happiness and pride for being given the chance to work so closely with God and Heaven.

Her year of practice and effort and the two years of training she had received from Hugo gave her confidence and a sense of mastery that very few, if any, other humans still on Earth ever knew. The lives of many people depended on her investigation and understanding. Lives of people she had come to love and respect with her whole heart. Still, she was filled with peace and confidence that she could do her part correctly and accurately.

Just because the affairs of roughly six billion people, millions upon millions of angels, and a smaller number of demonic spirits were intricately woven in the matrix below her she had become adept at localizing the activity she was asked to look at for the team.

Carol isolated the correct time period, the next week. This alone was a challenge because the angels, demons, God, Yahshua, and Satan were not bound by time or sequence. But, the real world was and that meant that the spiritual forces involved had to adhere to the time on Earth to accomplish their plans. Plus, the enemy and the angelic forces had to have everything they wanted to do approved by God before they could be involved in the human dimension.

Having located the correct time, she set about eliminating any of the several million operations and events along with their time lines that weren't involved with their new enemy, codenamed the SSS, Jerusalem, or the team. That still left several hundred thousand different lines. Then she eliminated all minor plots and events. That winnowed it down to only several dozens. Now came the tricky part. The enemy knew of her and her ability to see their requests and approvals. So, they put in false requests and events to confuse her. Hugo had shown her how to detect a false event or timeline from the real thing and she proceeded to do just that.

Now she only had thirty time lines and maybe fifty-five events that were on the probable axis over the next seven days. She studied the events and where they were on the timeline attempting to understand the strategy they implied. Then she cross referenced those times against the events on other time lines. She was able to discard several more because they were contradictory and didn't work in the overall scheme of time.

Finally, she had a grasp on the enemy's requests and plans. Now, for the really critical part of her job. She arranged the events and time lines in her mind and started praying that God would give her wisdom concerning the events and enough information that she could resolve any hidden agendas.

As she recognized the actual attack plans she felt a sickness envelop her spirit. This could not be allowed to happen.

Several things occurred to her and she noted them and then followed up on the thoughts. One of them took her in a whole new direction of thinking. She followed that strand and realized that the enemy was not aware of the Crossfire Team's involvement in their schemes as yet. "This is good."

Carol prayed her thanks to God. She noticed her spirit had been cleansed of the illness the plot of the enemy had caused. She returned to her room. This was very spacious and comfortable but seemed mundane after her flight over a small part of eternity. The diamonds faded on her head and throat as she stood up and went to find Jack or Mark, or Laura, or Sarah.

CHAPTER FORTY-THREE

Two hours later the core team reassembled in the war room. Jack listened to the various reports and organized the information. Mark, David, and Sarah had a wealth of information about the activities of the SSS from the Mossad and a request that the Israeli group be included in any mission against the group that was planning an attack against their country.

Laura reported that the various agencies in the U.S. were restricted by the administration and couldn't provide info or assistance to the team. Although, Laura indicated that some of the agencies, especially the CIA and the FBI subtly indicated that there would be some buckaroo access set up in the next few days.

Gary Eisenthal didn't have any specifics on the group but had the same background information that the team already had accumulated.

Alexis, Stan, and Debbie came up dry and had nothing to add to the discussion.

Charlie and Linda had a list of drones and sub-miniature drones that they could use over Jerusalem and other parts of Israel. They also reported that they had some ELINT or electronic intelligence inputs from the Mossad that pinpointed the headquarters of the group.

The World Wide Web was close to useless concerning the group and the only information was actually disinformation, probably placed there by the group themselves.

Steve, Larry, and Victor had cataloged the present and needed supplies, weapons, munitions, and the like for all the categories they were tasked to take care of by Jack.

Jack smiled, "Well people, we now know what they are up to, where they are located, and that we must take them down without fail in the next thirty hours. Shall we start surveillance and planning?"

David spoke up, "I suggest we get an operative or a manager from the Mossad in here before we start. This will be on their soil, as are we at present, and I know things will go much more smoothly if we bring them in at this time. They can really help us here and we need to include them."

Jack thought about it and agreed. David made a call and ten minutes later a middle aged man with the name of Parker Abbas was ushered into the war room by Sarah.

Parker Abbas was a trim man with thinning hair and a small Van Dyke beard that was neatly trimmed. He was a cautious man who listened a lot and spoke little. Nothing about the man was memorable which was the mark of a successful spy. He could blend into any crowd and simply disappear.

After being introduced he asked to be read in on the mission. Mark gave him the story from the beginning through the discovery that the Satanists planned to destroy the Western Wall in Jerusalem and waited for his reaction.

Parker took in the tale of God, demons; Satanists and a violent attack on his country with a concern that these imported Americans were attempting to pull his leg to test him. But, he had studied the history of the group and the success they had accumulated too. He looked at the assembled crew and detected no zaniness, nor any strange attitudes. What he saw was a dozen and a half people who were very serious about their "calling" and didn't have a problem with their assignment from God to obliterate an entire group of people.

Parker spoke directly to David in Hebrew. "David, I'm not sure I really understand the religious thing here. Being assigned by YHWH to completely destroy this group without any restrictions? How comfortable are you with the source of this divine instruction?"

David knew Parker very well, in fact had trained him in field work. He also knew how entrenched Parker, like many of the Israelis were in their doubt about direct intervention by the supernatural into human history. He carefully crafted his answer. "Parker, I know what you believe, and I know you're an extremely capable team manager within your normal limits. But, I have been working with, and for, this team for several years. I am not a Farblondzhet (lost, crazy, insane person). In the last year I have battled face to face with demonic forces and that is what this raid is about. These Satanists have been reinforced by actual demons off of the spiritual plane. The enemy's direction is for this group of Satan worshipers to blow up several of the high holy places in Tel Aviv. This is a demonic attack against the heart of our country. I feel strongly that we need coordination with the Mossad. That coordinator needs to be a person who can open his mind to new possibilities and the involvement of the supernatural. Can you do that?"

Parker was very well aware of David Zahavy's records and integrity. "Okay, I will work with you, but, I will keep my eyes open. Okay?

David laughed, "Don't worry, what you'll see will keep your eyes wide open for a long time."

Jack then proceeded to describe the location of the SSS's headquarters and probably their arsenal in Jerusalem. They were located near the wall that was their target. He brought forth the fact that according to Carol the enemy had no clue about the involvement of the Crossfire Team, or for that matter, the Mossad. It would be a real surprise attack. Jack looked at Parker and asked him. "Are you willing to participate in a total slaughter? We are commanded not to leave any survivors according to God."

Parker smiled, "No survivors. Well, that's normal operational tactics for us concerning enemies of the state. I would ask that this operation be done with as little public notice as possible. What manpower or ordinances do you need?"

Jack nodded. "We probably already have that covered thanks to the assistance of the IDF and your organization. The Mossad's involvement in this raid will be cooperation, government approval, and containment of any news to the public. You, on the other hand, will be directly involved as one of the raiders. Unless you want to designate an alternate."

Jack watched the man's face as he contemplated the options and requirements.

Parker nodded, "My organization will take care of the government approval and provide containment. But, I will be a guest at this dance." He was very positive about his involvement.

Jack smiled. "Okay, let's get the surveillance in place and start counting heads for the raid to ensure a total removal of this cancer before tomorrow night."

CHAPTER FORTY-FOUR

As the planning began, Jack asked Sarah to give the group a perspective on the Western Wall that was to be the target for the Satanists.

Sarah used her computer to bring up some three dimensional high-definition views of the wall, the tunnels, and the surrounding area as she described the scenes.

"One of the reasons these Satanist scum have picked this target is that it is one of the remaining, and holiest, parts of the original temple. Jewish males of all ages from young boys to the oldest of grandfathers come here to pray to God. All of their heads are covered with yarmulkes, the skull cap that reminds Jews to be respectful of the presence of God who is always with them."

"To the Israelis this wall is a direct link to God. It is a touchstone to the Jewish faith and history. Abraham was the father of the Hebrew race. He came from Ur of the Chaldees, somewhere in present-day Iraq. The clan then spent 400 years in captivity in Egypt. They came back to the Palestine area, the Promised Land. "

"The ten northern tribes disappeared from the stage of history when taken into captivity by the Assyrians around 720 BC. The two southern tribes later spent 70 years in captivity in Babylonia. Finally, in the 1st century, Rome tired of their intractability and destroyed Jerusalem, forcing many Jews into exile. A second Jewish revolt in the 2nd century extended what has become known as the Diaspora - the exile of Jews from Israel, and the subsequent settling of Jews into practically every land and culture on the planet. "

"At the Western Wall, if you listen you will hear the sound that gives the Wall its other name - the Wailing Wall - the ebb and flow of prayer all around. Men and boys, clustered in groups, some praying collectively from prayer books, some studying the Torah together, others by themselves praying directly against the Wall. Jewish scholars say that when the Temple was destroyed by Romans in 70 AD, God moved his presence from the destroyed Temple to the Western Wall. Jews therefore believe that when they pray at the Western Wall, they are praying as close to the presence of God as possible on this earth. "

"Note that the Western Wall was a retaining wall of the Second Temple, also referred to as Herod's Temple, because megalomaniac Herod, the Great, rebuilt it in the 1st century BC. The First Temple was built by Solomon, a leader of legendary wisdom, back in the glory days of the Kingdom of Israel around 900 BC. This Temple was destroyed by Babylonian invaders under Nebuchadnezzar in the 6th century BC, when most of the Jews from the southern Kingdom of Israel were taken into captivity to Babylon."

"The Second Temple was then erected by Jews returning from the Babylonian exile around 500 BC. It was a much humbler structure than the First, but Herod, himself only half-Jewish, rebuilt it as much as a monument to himself - he was an prolific builder and you can see remains of his vision and ego all over Israel - as a peace offering to the Jewish people he was supposed to be ruling."

"The subterranean excavations that run the full 1500 feet length of the Wall are approached by descending north into an access tunnel adjacent to the Wall. Herod leveled off the top of Mount Moriah to provide a base for the Temple which became known as Temple Mount. Mount Moriah is itself hugely significant to all three monotheistic faiths - Jewish, Christian, and Muslim. It is the site of the near-sacrifice of Abraham's beloved faith child Isaac. You can see why its destruction will be a major blow to the Jews."

"The Wall itself is made of massive, dressed stones with one alone measuring over 40 feet long and approximately 600 tons in weight. Hard to destroy without devastating the entire area. Note that these Satanists don't give any favor to Muslims any more than they do to Jews or Christians."

"The Western Wall, which forms the western support wall of the Muslim-controlled Temple Mount, also exits onto the Via Dolorosa, Christianity's Way of Suffering, which is walked now by pilgrims memorializing the final movements of Christ in route to his death on Golgotha."

Sarah ended her description with a dire warning. "To allow these evil people to destroy the Western Wall would be a staggering blow against all three faiths that would be hard to overcome with the advent of the anti-Christ government and repression of worship for any but that of himself."

Mark asked of nobody in particular, "Just how are they going to destroy such a massive structure without using a nuclear weapon?"

Sarah frowned, "You think too much as an American westerner. These vile people have no concern about collateral damage or massive death of anyone but themselves. Maybe they are planning to use a tactical nuclear warhead. Haven't many of those found their way out of Russia's satellite countries and presumably into the hands of terrorists like these people?"

As if her own thought frightened her, Sarah paled somewhat, "If they were able to get one or more such weapons into the tunnels under the wall and detonate, the collateral damage would be in the thousands of dead and a major destruction of that part of the city."

Jack nodded, "That is probably just the effect they want to achieve."

Mark shook his head, "There are literally hundreds of Israeli Border Guards and police that are constantly on watch for any such attempt. They have the latest in radiation detection and are very strict about anyone getting near the Temple Mount, especially with a bomb or other destructive device. Plus, you've got the Mossad constantly investigating any group that has plans to attack any Israeli site."

Alexis laughed and everyone looked at her. "Mark, I've been trained to circumvent security measures, as has Sarah. Consider a concerted effort by a well-funded group to attack the Temple Mount. They could recruit a scientist that had clearance to study the tunnels under the mount. Using the demonic shielding like they did in the Houston bombing they could get a ten-megaton warhead into the tunnels as scientific equipment. They may have already done that. Or consider an effort to tunnel into the existing tunnel system. Or, a new tunnel that is close to the existing tunnels but easily good enough to detonate a nuclear weapon which would destroy all of the area of the Temple Mount, the Western Wall, and a goodly portion of Jerusalem."

Su Li spoke up, "But, that would destroy their Mosque and kill thousands of Muslims as well as Israelis, wouldn't it?"

Sarah sighed, "That is their goal. They want all religions to fail and the devil to be supreme. They will destroy everyone in the world if they can, just to make sure they kill every Jew or Christian that worship Yahveh God."

Jack started to key in a number on his panel. "We can at least attempt to see if there are any major demonic shielding efforts in that area."

CHAPTER FORTY-FIVE

Sarah had learned a primary lesson about her role in this life. She had lived most of her life as a Jewish believer. Albeit with very limited religious involvement due primarily to her life style in the military and the Mossad. Her conversion to spirit-filled Christianity had been dramatic and impacting on her.

She went to her bedroom in their suite and got on her knees. She worshiped Yahveh and Yahshua and sang of her love for them. Then she lifted a heart-felt prayer for guidance as to her role in preventing this most-heinous of crimes against God. She cried out in fear and desperation for help for the team and the city of Jerusalem. Then she quieted her spirit and waited on God to answer.

She felt a presence and opened her eyes. The angel Rose sat on her bed with her feet tucked under her and the calm golden color predominate. Sarah's heart swelled with hope as she watched Rose smiling at her. This casual position and a sense of camaraderie was something that Sarah had never seen before.

Rose's voice was a mellow contralto that was very pleasant to hear. She looked intently at Sarah. "Your Father in Heaven has heard your plea Sarah. He loves you greatly and admires your dedication and heart for His people. He told me to tell you that He is going to provide your team with a heavenly covering that the enemy cannot penetrate nor will they be able to discern your goals or efforts. As for direction, you are to ask the earthly servants of the enemy what they have planned and determine how to block their efforts in this matter."

Rose's color shifted slightly allowing the powerful fierce whiteness to color the room as she stressed her next comments. "You have to move quickly because there is little time left to stop their efforts. Go with your best guess if you have to, because your best guess is ten times better than most. Remember though, these Satanists are quickly becoming protected and aided by Marco Marino in his ascendancy to world domination. He will rapidly become your biggest problem when he learns of your continued existence. Keep your ears open to world events, especially in the Holy Lands as it will affect your actions in this matter. I have great confidence in the team and in you as a warrior. I will be there with you as will others from the Heavenly Host. Go with a prayer to Yahveh in all things."

Rose held out her hand from which a beautiful, lilac beam of light reached out and bathed Sarah. Rose's voice seemed to vibrate in Sarah's soul. The angel faded from sight as Sarah heard, "May the peace of Yahshua fill you."

Sarah took a deep breath and realized that all of her concerns and worries were insignificant now. She relaxed and ordered her mind to accomplish everything God had given her through the angel.

Getting to her feet she tapped her communicator and asked the core group to assemble in the war room again. Feeling a righteous anger against the Satanists begin to build a fierce determination in her spirit she strode out of the bedroom and toward the war room.

Everyone was waiting for her when she entered. Sarah sat down at her position and started the recording. She quickly explained her prayer and the response she got from Rose. Then she put forth an idea that had been forming in her mind since her angelic meeting. "Rose said that we should "ask" the earthly servants of the enemy what they have planned and determine how to block their efforts in this matter."

She specifically picked out Alexis and David by asking them to consider the espionage aspects of her idea. "What I recommend we do is collar one of the leaders of this cabal and convince him or her that we are demons and we want to determine if they are fully versed in the operation. If they really believe that we are their source of power and are merely checking for thoroughness, then I think we will get the information we need. Of course we will have to cover ourselves by making them forget the meeting and provide a likely reason for the disappearance of this person during our interrogation."

Sarah strongly stressed the very short time they had available to accomplish their goals as Rose had told her.

Jack spoke up. "Why don't you three get together with Judah Maritz and Aaron Jacobson and brainstorm the quickest snatch and drain job you can? The rest of us will see what we can get in the way of information on the latest movements of this group and how we can protect the tunnels in addition to the Mossad and the IDF's efforts."

Everyone turned to their tasks as the trio left the war room and called for Aaron and Judah to join them in the main gathering area. Once the five were seated around a table Sarah outlined the general idea and threw the discussion open for suggestions.

Aaron laughed, "We need Intel on who are the leaders and what their weaknesses are before we can decide on a target. Once we get that then we can intelligently make a choice."

David slid eight folders across the table to Aaron. "These are the suspected leaders of the group. The ones with the red band on their folders are what the Mossad feels are the tactical leadership and would therefore have the best Intel on this operation."

Aaron and Judah quickly scanned the documents and as they closed the last ones they looked at each other and grinned. Aaron slid one folder back to David. "This guy, Ahmad Zuliman, is the best choice because he is local, he is a closet homosexual, and he has a lover that we can use for a cover story. His "lover" is a Mossad informant and will work with us as needed. According to this data they are to meet tonight at Ahmad's home, alone, as usual. Also Ahmad likes to use cocaine which makes him ready-made for some of the psycho drugs we use to interrogate subjects."

Sarah nodded. "All right, let's plan for an interrogation at Ahmad's tonight." She checked her watch. "That gives us less than eight hours to be ready and in place."

David looked a bit pensive. "This is just too easy. I need to call in a favor and find out just how reliable our informant really is under any circumstances. I don't trust people who take money for information and put it to their "friends". Especially gay people who do that because there are too many pressures on them that can be used against them. I'm worried he might be a double, or even a triple, agent."

Sarah knew the drill and David was right. It was a little too easy, convenient, and too readily available for their needs. "Okay, we'll plan on doing the operation with, and without the informant's help. Find out which as rapidly as possible."

CHAPTER FORTY-SIX

Twenty minutes later Parker Abbas entered the war room and conferred quietly with David Zahavy. David considered the information and stood up. He motioned to Sarah and Laura. The four of them walked out into the living room/general assembly area to talk quietly so as to not disturb the others.

David tipped his head to Parker "Our friend here has obtained information concerning the informant Michael. It's not good. He is at least a double agent and most likely a direct Satanist spy who voluntarily agreed to work with the Mossad primarily to gain insight into any operations that would endanger his group. So, we can't use him to help us but we can definitely use him for our purposes."

Sarah nodded her head, "He can be used to give the Satanists dis-information which will misdirect their planning away from our raid." She looked at Parker. "How much Intel do we have about his place and security, overt and covert?"

Parker handed her the files. But, he cautioned them that Michael was a very intelligent and street smart counter agent within the realm of his expertise.

Laura raised an eyebrow. "What exactly do you mean by his "realm of expertise?"

Parker stared at her for a moment and then glanced at David. David nodded his approval. Parker focused on Laura, "Michael is not a trained spy. He is an in-place informant whose capabilities primarily center on his relationships and his ability to extract information. As such he is not violent, but he is crafty. He doesn't originate actions, he only reports on Intel that he picks up. His "realm of expertise" doesn't qualify him for anything else, such as wet work or active tailing a source, or anything like that. He is shrewd enough that he can easily spot a tail or a covert watching operation. He can't do anything about it other than act innocent. He can, and does, report to us and to the Satanists about these types of things."

Laura nodded her head, "So he's a minimal asset for us but a major asset for the enemy if he can deduce what is going on beyond his part in an operation, right?"

Parker grinned, "Right, he's useful, but potentially dangerous as a source."

Sarah shrugged, "Okay, we'll consider him a part of the problem and not a part of the solution in this case."

Jack stepped out of the war room. "Come on back in guys, you'll be interested in Charlie's demonic research."

Charlie was virtually attending their meeting from his office at the ComSec area and was represented as a hologram above the work consoles.

Charlie grinned at the newcomers. "Hi guys. I have been doing research into our ability to track demonic incursions in our dimension at the target area of the wall and its tunnels and got some surprising results. There is a periodic appearance of several demonic indicators at one specific area of the tunnels. They will show up for a few minutes en masse and then disappear for several hours or even several days at a time."

Jack asked, "How do you know that? How long have you been tracking this area for demons?"

Charlie laughed, "I don't, Crayton does all the heavy lifting in this operation. As soon as you told me where we were concentrating our efforts I ran a program that isolates the area for the last month. Another program I created last year uses satellites to comb the entire Earth for demonic presences and logs them. I just looked at the log for that area and the last thirty days. I'm now coordinating two of the new Landsat 7 Satellites for detailed information on the tunnels in regard to the findings."

Charlie added information on the latest Landsat which was launched in April by NASA Goddard Space Flight Center. "The new Landsat Images are at twice the resolution of previous Landsat photos. The main improvement of the Landsat 7 is the addition of a new instrument, the Enhanced Thematic Mapper Plus (EMT+). It's an eight-band, multispectral scanning radiometer, which images Earth and extends through the visible into the near-infrared."

Charlie showed them a picture of the new satellite. "Since Israel applied for tunnel detection as a Landsat task here in the Mideast, I just piggybacked my requests on theirs and added Crayton's detection routine to spot demonic activities. I've informed the Mossad that there are definite signs of demonic activity in several of the clandestine arms supply tunnels the terrorists are using to infiltrate weapons into the Gaza Strip."

Parker spoke up. "Yes, thanks Charlie. We appreciated the Intel and you don't need to check those tunnels anymore. They no longer exist."

Jack grinned at that thought, "Charlie, can you send the timing and the exact location of the demonic activity in the tunnels under the Western Wall to us?"

"Already there. Catch you later." Charlie's virtual persona disappeared from the hologram area above the work stations.

CHAPTER FORTY-SEVEN

The operation came together quickly and they rehearsed and replayed it twice before David and Sarah were satisfied that it had a reasonable chance of working. David pinpointed the executive suites that Michael maintained for the group on the eighth floor of the hotel. He showed pictures of the grand suite with its marble flooring, large LCD television sets, and large balcony.

Jack thought about the plan and decided to add a backup. "Let's get Debby Hargrove's sniper capabilities as our high guard in a room that overlooks the balcony and our suites. That will give us additional support in the event we become compromised. Get Stan too, as her backup."

Mark nodded, "Good idea. I'll get the room for them and get them set up.

David stood there and explained the Israeli input and assistance. "This terrorist has a six hundred dollars a day luxury suite with a floor space of over 500 square feet overlooking the old city. The hotel security is adequate but will overlook our activities as requested by the Mossad. The local agents will assist us to make sure no one tips the Satanists off and to prevent any response by the local law enforcement personnel if an alarm is sounded. We don't know what type or scale of personal protection either one of these men will have. But, since this is a homosexual tryst which is normally not tolerated by terrorist groups there may be none. Still, we need to be on our toes for unknown body guards."

Everyone grabbed their gear and headed out in two non-descript Crossover/SUVs for the thirty-five-mile trip from Tel Aviv to Jerusalem. In Jerusalem they turned towards Michael's residence in the hotel which overlooked Liberty Bell Park on Jabotinsky St. They prayed before leaving the vehicles and sent Stan and Debbie to enter separately.

Sarah studied the hotel as they arrived. It was a massive, multi-tiered structure on a hillside. She waited until Jack opened her door to exit the SUV. The quick plan they had created called for her to be a wealthy lady with an entourage. Laura and Alexis had helped her dress accordingly. She had admired her reflection in the mirror afterward and decided she definitely looked the part.

Disdaining any interest in the others as they directed the hotel staff as to the luggage, she marched into the hotel with Alexis and Su Li in her wake. David had already acquired the keys to her suite and was holding the door to the elevator open as she reached it. They had, with a little help from the Mossad, reserved the two executive suites next door to Michael's suite on the eighth floor.

After they had settled into their accommodations Sarah shed the grand dame disguise and redressed in an all-black night suit like the others. She looked at Mark and smiled, "Ah, fame is so fleeting." He grinned. He had obviously liked the way she had looked in the finery.

Like all hurried plans, this one was a simple raid with the complication that they could leave no evidence they were there or that Ahmad Zuliman would realize he had provided any information about their plans to people outside of the Satanists.

Charlie and David took the elevator to the basement by circumventing the electronic lock that prevented normal patrons from accessing the lower levels. They quickly found and exposed the power circuits that fed the two suites. Charlie sat back and studied the circuits. "We've got a problem. The hotel did a major upgrade on their electrical systems in December of last year and it doesn't match the schematics we had for the hotel. Now, at this juncture the entire eighth floor is on this one circuit. To isolate the two suites, we'd have to get a maintenance man that knows the electrical layout of the new system in the hotel."

David was disappointed. "We don't have time to do that." He keyed his comm set and described the problem to Jack. He listened for a few minutes and nodded. "Right, be there in a few minutes." He looked at Charlie. "Button it up; we've got to get back."

They were back in the suite in a few minutes.

Mark looked a little grim but purposeful. He called them over to table in the suite. "We've got to knock them out without the cover of darkness. The problem is that there are so many ways to get video, both live and recorded that we could be compromised after we leave."

Charlie shook his head, "Not so. These two men are violating Arab customs and the mores of their culture. They will have shut down any video or recordings before they meet. I can toss their whole apartment in twenty minutes while you're "talking" with them to ensure there aren't any private recordings in operation. Knock them out so we can put on our little play for them."

Mark grinned, "Okay." He turned to David, "Get the boys in here."

Laura asked Mark, "Okay for when we're in there. But, how are we going to get six people and two demons into their suite via a lit balcony? Also, there could be outside watchers that could see us entering in the light. If we knock out the lights on our balcony and theirs it could trigger an alarm and bring questions if not protectors."

Jack nodded, "She's right, we've got to find a way to get in without having the lights out."

Charlie grinned. "You knock them out and I'll get us in the front door. Just have to neutralize the hall cameras and make sure no one is in the hall when we go in."

Jack pointed at Alexis, "Loop the camera in the hall." He told David, "Get ready to gas them." He looked around where are Judah and Aaron?"

A bedroom door opened and a ghastly voice rasped, "Here we are."

The two creatures that sidled and strutted into the main room were really hideous. One looked like a bad dream with eyes that were slanted and red. The mouth was full of sharp teeth and there were warts all over the face and neck. Grossly exaggerated arms and chest loomed over twisted legs that were thickly veined and blackened by growths. The second one was more normal but had no hair and huge ears surrounding three eyes that radiated evil in their shape and intensity. These eyes were violently red and complemented the long tongue that flickered in and out of a lipless mouth. The second creature was hunchbacked and had claws stained with what looked like dried blood.

Jack stared at the creatures and smiled. "Great makeup guys. If I didn't know you were human I'd swear that you were demons."

The same ghastly voice came out of the first creature. "Thanks Jack. Are we ready for our big scene yet? I've got the chemicals that will ensure Ahmad Zuliman will think we're real and later that it was a bad dream."

Jack saw Alexis come back in the suite and nod to him. "We're just waiting for Ahmad to arrive and David and Charlie to put them to sleep."

Jack keyed his combat microphone and talked to Stan who was along as a backup for his wife and her sniper rifle. "Stan, be aware that we are not, repeat, not going to go across the balconies. Complications require an interior entry after a little night-night gas."

Stan replied, "Ten-four, we are . . ." There was a whining and crackling that drowned out the rest of his message.

Jack knew they had gotten the message and didn't want to stay on the air any more than necessary.

His comm link beeped. He heard Su Li speak quietly from the lobby, "Ahmad is getting on the elevator with a bodyguard right now."

Jack told the group and they watched the view of the hall that Alexis had "borrowed" when she fed the loop picture of an empty hall to the camera. Jack nodded to Alex and she switched the camera back to an active view using a small remote. They watched Ahmad exit the elevator and go to the suite next to theirs. He used a key and entered by himself. The bodyguard stood in the hall for a minute and then retreated to the elevator.

Jack told Charlie, "Do it."

Charlie opened the valve on a pressurized container of the knock-out gas that Russian Special Forces pumped into Moscow's Dubrovka Theater to end a hostage crisis years ago.

The FSB-made version of carfentanyl, was an artificial, opium-like substance that is 10,000 times more potent than morphine and usually used to immobilize large animals. It wasn't really a gas at all but an aerosol, tiny particles that float in the air.

He waited for about a minute as he listened to an electronic listening device against the wall. "They're down."

Alexis switched the camera in the hall to the "empty hall" loop. The six people and the two demons followed Charlie to the next suite door where it took him less than ten seconds to open the lock and the door.

Laura grinned inside her gas mask. If anyone came into the hall right, then they would have a hard time deciphering what they were seeing with everyone in gas masks including the two demons.

Everyone slipped into the suite without being seen. Alexis switched the camera back to the normal mode.

CHAPTER FORTY-EIGHT

Once inside Jack and Mark found the two men in the large bedroom. Michael was on the bed and Ahmad was lying on the floor.

David opened the door to the balcony and switched the climate control to flush the aerosol from the room air. Two minutes later he closed the door and reset the air controls. He took off his mask and nodded. The rest of the team quickly put Ahmad onto the bed next to Michael and set the stage by turning on a light bar with red colored light to make the "demons" look even more horrible.

Charlie took the syringes from Aaron and carefully injected both of the men. Michael would sleep through the whole thing. In about four minutes Ahmad would wake up from his dose of the aerosol and the psychedelic drugs would affect his mind, heightening the dream-like surrealistic feeling.

Charlie then turned to checking the bedroom for any secret recording devices he was sure would be here so Michael would have some personal power over Ahmad. It was a standard gambit done by many illicit couples. It took him less than a minute to find it in a book on the book shelf. He used a micro-viewer to find the point just before Ahmad fell and erased everything after that. He put a probe into the recorder and shorted it out. It would seem like a natural fault and who could Michael tell anyway? He finished up and left the room.

David set up his recording devices and slipped out with the others except for Aaron and Judah. They closed the door and waited. A minute later they heard a strangled cry that was answered by that graveyard voice. They waited tensely listening to the two voices as the minutes crawled by. Then, the door opened and Aaron motioned them into the room.

Jack saw that Judah had used a "sleep aid" to send Ahmad back to sleep. He motioned to the group and they quickly cleaned up the scene and gathered at the front door as Alexis switched the camera to the loop. Quickly leaving the suite and returning to their suite they waited as Alexis retrieved the controller from the camera. She came in and smiled.

While Aaron and Judah cleaned up and became normal again, Charlie monitored the room next door. He pulled the listening device off the wall and carefully plugged the tiny hole the aerosol probe had made in the wall. He came into the main room and announced that the two men were awake and apparently acting normally. They apparently dismissed the change in time because of the demon-induced dream.

David asked Aaron, "Did we get what we needed and are you sure he told the truth?"

Aaron nodded, "You can't believe the detail that man had. Nobody can lie convincingly with the concoction we fed Ahmad. He was obviously currying favor with his "demons" by showcasing his volume of knowledge of their plans. He really believes he will be rewarded for destroying thousands of innocent people and destroying thousands of years of history, not to mention acres of Jerusalem. You've got the whole thing recorded and incidentally, we have less than thirty-two hours to stop it. He also believes that there are others of their group who are doing other secret operations to coincide with their explosions."

Jack shook both of their hands, "Good work guys."

Sarah told David, "We need to analyze his comments as soon as possible. Rose was pushing the urgency button pretty hard." She looked at David, "Go to the front desk and pay the full night's bill. Explain that urgent business has suddenly called me out of town."

David grinned and bowed to her. "Yes Ma'am, Immediately, as you wish."

Jack keyed the combat microphone and called Stan. Still no communication. Looking at Mark he said, "You make sure everyone gets out without a problem. Laura and I will get Stan and Debbie. We'll meet you in the parking lot.

The team extracted from the hotel and reached the parking lot. They talked in quiet but confident tones about the raid.

Jack and Laura walked to the next part of the hotel and rode the elevator up to the top floor. They walked quickly to the room the Hargroves were in. Knocking on the door brought no response. Worried now, Jack took out a dagger and sprang the door lock. The room was dark. A coppery odor assailed them and Jack quietly drew his .40 automatic. Gently pushing the door open he reached in and flipped on the lights.

What he saw knocked the wind out of him like nothing had done before. Stan and Debbie were lying together on the floor of the room and from the amount of blood pooling around their heads he knew immediately that they were dead. Jack cried out to Yahshua in his pain and loss as Laura held her hand over her mouth and stared wide-eyed at their friends. She turned to Jack and fell against him in tears. While he hugged Laura to comfort her he realized that he was completely responsible for the death of his two friends. In his remorse he cried out to God and asked why they had to die. He got no explanation but God's peace rolled over him like a wave relieving his stress. He knew that, at that moment. That Stan and Debbie were with Yahshua right then. Jack reached up with his left hand and wiped his eyes. He gently disengaged himself from Laura and checked for the fallen couple's weapons. Whoever had killed them had taken Stan's pistol and Debbie's rifle. He put his arms around Laura again and stood there for several minutes praying with her for them. He noted that they both looked peaceful like they were just sleeping. They didn't look like anything violent had happened to them. Keying his microphone, he called Mark. "Mark, I've got bad news. I'm sorry to be the one that has to tell you this, but somehow, someone got to Stan and Debbie. They are with the Lord now. Get Sarah and casually come up to room 1018. He closed the door and waited while trying to console his wife.

A few minutes later there was a gentle knock and he let the others in. Laura had gotten over the shock and composed herself by then. Sarah and Mark had been, unfortunately, hardened by their military life styles and were more used to having to function even while losing friends. They immediately moved to the bodies and checked them. Mark looked at Jack, "Small caliber round behind the ear, probably a .22 with a silencer. This was done by professional assassins. It doesn't look like there was any battle and I'd guess that they both died before they knew what happened."

Mark looked around the room. "We need to clean up the scene and take them with us for burial. We'll have to make time to mourn for them later." Everyone silently pitched in to help. Mark used the throw rug their friends were laying on to wrap them both up.

Sarah left and came back with a laundry cart. Placing the bodies in the cart they covered it with the sheets from the bed. There was little other sign they had ever been there. The rug had absorbed all the blood.

Sarah and Mark took the cart down the service elevator and Jack and Laura left by the front doors. Laura was clearly on the verge of crying again but her anger held it together until they reached the vans. She turned to Jack with a puzzled look. "Why just them? Why didn't they come after us too?"

Jack shook his head because he didn't have any answers.

Mark and Jack placed Stan and Debbie's bodies in the storage area of the first van while Sarah told the others what happened.

It was a somber group that returned to the undersea base. Parker told them that the Mossad had a coroner on the new base and he could perform the autopsies. They also arranged for their transportation to Tel Aviv. Recently, Stan had become enamored by the Israeli state and had mentioned that to Jack that he and Debbie wanted to be buried in the Jewish city when his time had come. Jack doubted that he had any inkling that it was going to be so soon. The entire team including the SOG prayed for their souls and wished them well. They would be missed.

Afterward, a short service was held by a Jewish Rabbi and everyone said their personal good-byes to Stan and Debbie.

After a brief period to let everyone work out their emotions over the killing of Stan and Debbie, Sarah called for the core team to meet in the war room. They played the recordings twice and came up with a list of facts. Sarah summed them up. "First, they've already got two five megaton dirty bombs in place. Second, they have two more, courtesy of the old KGB through one of the old satellite countries, all single warheads from a MIRV missile bus. They plan to place the second two tomorrow. Then there are the riots they will generate between the Jews and Arabs of Jerusalem to draw a bigger body count. Then they will detonate all four bombs simultaneously via remote control tomorrow at nine p.m., Jerusalem time. Ahmad thought that there are at least seven demons actively guarding the bombs and providing suppression coverage to prevent detection of the radiation. Lastly, we have a list of the people involved."

David, Jack, Mark, Sarah, and Parker Abbas conferred on the best way to defuse the bombs, defeat the demons, eliminate the Satanists, and do it all without public awareness. It was a tall order and would require exquisite timing to cut the head off of the snake just before it struck.

Parker summed up the considerations. "The Crossfire Team will handle the demons and the Satanists. The Mossad will defuse the bombs and dispose of them during the melee of the crowds outside the tunnels. The IDF will control the crowds sufficiently to prevent their getting too violent or interfering with our operations. Does that sum up the responsibilities?"

Everyone agreed and began to work on the details. They needed to wait until the second two bombs were placed before they attacked.

Parker offered an envelope to Jack. Jack opened it and read the contents. He stared at Parker for a few seconds and then handed the letter to David who studied it. Mark watched all this and asked Jack, "What's the offer?"

Jack grinned slightly because he knew Mark was guessing, but it was very accurate guessing. "The Mossad is offering the services of their Metsada department to "handle" the majority of the Satanists. Essentially all those who will not be directly involved in placing and detonating the bombs. That includes Ahmad and Michael."

Sarah studied the men at the table for a few seconds. "Jack, if you accept their offer, they will do the job but you won't be able to confirm the immediate elimination of these people. I believe that God specifically told us to completely eliminate the entire group. Do you feel confident that you will have completed your commitment to God's will in this matter if they do, what they do so well?"

Jack nodded, "There is that. Excuse me for a few minutes' ladies and gentlemen while I see if it is something I can authorize." Jack got up and went into the living room where he could pray without distraction.

Clearing his mind of everything but his love for the creator of the universe Jack praised Yahveh and all the mercy and grace He had seen fit to bestow on Jack himself and his team. Jack knew that God knew what he was going to ask before he asked it. But, he also knew that the Father desired His children to ask Him for permission. The Bible stated that *"you have not, because you ask not."* Jack asked, in earnest prayer, "Father, will I fulfill your command to eliminate all of the Satanists by allowing the Metsada to assist us in this effort?

Jack then waited for a leading. He sensed a presence and he opened his eyes to see the angel Caleb standing before him. "Hi Caleb. Do you bear an answer to my prayer?"

Caleb nodded, "God is pleased that you asked in humbleness and obedience rather than trusting in your personal judgment. He actually arranged it so that the Kidon assassins would aid you in this matter. I was sent to assure you that God will ensure the total annihilation of the Satanists and you can be at peace concerning their contribution to this matter." Caleb had a small smile on his face. "I am proud to know you Jack, and I, along with others, will be near as you strive to do the Lord's will." Caleb vanished suddenly and the room seemed poorer at the loss.

Jack walked back in and gave the letter to Parker. "My answer is yes, and may God protect them as they do His will."

Parker sighed and nodded. "Very, very good, that will go a long way to establish our relationship with your team. But, I will be going with you this time. I need to be a part of the action with the team. Is there any problem with that?"

Jack smiled, "No problem, we'll be glad to have an extra gun and a local viewpoint too."

Parker beamed with pleasure that he would be in on the actual attack. He thought that he would now see for himself if the demons the team was lauded for fighting were real or just a good marketing tactic to get funding and assignments. He had 100 Shekels riding on the non-existence of such creatures because, "come on, he hadn't seen one and there seemed to be no definitive proof that they were real".

CHAPTER FORTY-NINE

The team waited in two vehicles as close as they could get with official sanction near the wall for the Mossad to evacuate the tunnels and the area around the entrance to them. Sitting in one of the SUVs Jack's cell phone rang. He answered it to hear Carol's voice. "Jack! There is a major new timeline concerning the attack on the Western Wall. The devil is up to his usual tricks. He hasn't asked for permission and the timeline didn't show up until he started to make the move it represents. It looks like he is starting to "flood" demons into the tunnel area to prevent any interference with the bombing. There is still no indication that the enemy knows about our involvement."

Jack laughed softly, making the others in the car wonder what could bring humor to him at this time. "Job security, that's all."

Breaking the connection with Carol, Jack silenced his cell phone so it would not give him away at an inopportune time and keyed the combat microphone. "All units, be aware that the enemy is staffing up significantly. Crossfire Team, go to plan B as we attack. Parker, your troops will probably have to handle the human targets in the tunnels as we may be busy."

The signal from the Mossad arrived and Parker responded, "Right Jack, I'll have them ramp it up. We've got a green light, let's move."

The doors on the SUVs opened and the troops moved swiftly across the area in front of the wall. They tried to not draw attention from the people praying at the wall as they reached the tunnel entrance between the men's room entrance and the bank of pay phones. The combat com-link alerted everyone to an incoming large mass of Muslims moving toward the Jews and Christians near the wall.

Laura shook her head. "That's the start of the riot the Satanists are using to bring larger numbers of people here to maximize their death toll."

As they entered the tunnel system the cool night was replaced by the dryness of the tunnels. Mark commented, "Not if we have anything to say about it."

The team was joined by a large number of IDF forces, many of which were probably Mossad agents. Jack keyed his comm system microphone and said, "Move out, Plan B, take out the demons and protect the Israeli troops that will eliminate the human enemy and defuse the bombs."

The troops split up into two groups and each one headed for the indicated new tunnels where the bombs were apparently located. As they neared the tunnels it didn't take the enemy long to detect them and to attack.

Demons literally flooded out of the two tunnel entrances and were met with a high volume of rifle fire. This took out a number of the demons that had entered our dimension illegally but thirty kept coming.

The surviving demons were a variety of gross, ugly, sinister-looking creatures that reeked of evil and other malodorous stinks. Visually they were frightening and aggressive, especially to a person unfamiliar with their sort.

Parker and many of the Israeli commandos had never seen a demon or even thought they could be physically real. Parker stood there blinking with his mouth hanging open. The emanations from the creatures assailed him on many levels and their invulnerability scared him greatly.

The Crossfire team began to pray and seven sets of golden and silver armor appeared. Each team member had a sword of faith in their hands off of which the esteem, or glory, of God flowed in visible waves. The team members surged forward past the Israelis to do battle with Satan's soldiers.

Laura didn't waste time or effort; she immediately went into high speed. She attacked the demons that seemed to be stuck in time and decimated six in very little time. Three other team members emulated her success and the cavern was filled with whirling blades of glory slicing through the demons so quickly there was a huge fog of red and black sickly smoke from the departing demon bodies.

One of the larger demons backhanded David before he could strike and it slammed him backwards to the ground. That proved to be a bad move on that demon's part. Alexis tore into him in a fit of righteous fury and removed his hands, sword, and head in three quick swipes. She stepped back to protect David as he struggled to get up.

David thought to himself, "That's going to leave a bunch of bruises."

Mark and Jack were working as a team and standing back-to-back against eight demons. As the demons pressed their attack Mark said, "Now!" Both men went into high speed and waded into the demons before they could counter the move. Jack ran his sword through one of the demons at the front and took the head off of another one with the return swipe of his blade. Sliding sideward to his left he cut another demon from shoulder, or something that might have been a shoulder, through the trunk of its body and out the other hip-like shapes on the far side of the oddly-shaped creature. The fourth demon when into high speed to counter Jack's advantage but lost it all as his head was cleaved from his body.

Mark simply cut the first two demons in half at the waist and rotated to his left, avoiding Jack's move, and cut the third one's head off. The fourth demon on his side when into high speed and reached out to grab Mark's sword hand at the wrist. The grip the demon had was so strong Mark couldn't pull his arm away so he hit the demon in the face with his armored left hand. Mark was heavily muscled and knew how to put his entire force into his blows, but the demon seemed unfazed by the punch.

Mark was attempting to free his hand when Jack's sword ran the demon through the neck and severed its head off of its body. As it fell to the floor and released Mark's arm, Mark nodded his thanks to his friend.

Su Li used her training to deceive the demons she came up against by stepping back and then attacking as the demon would move forward. She accounted for the last three demons that way.

Suddenly the cavern was empty of demons and the team's armor faded from view. Jack urged the combined Mossad and IDF teams to disarm the bombs.

Obviously leery of running into more demons they still did they job and opened the casings on two of the four bombs. It took them less than a minute to tell Jack.

"There's something very wrong here. These bombs aren't real. They are just dummy casings."

Mark used his combat microphone to call Charlie. "The Mossad says that the four bombs here at the wall are not the real thing. This whole setup is a major misdirection aimed at either us or the Israelis. I'm pretty sure the enemy didn't do this to lure us here since they didn't know about us until just now. Any ideas?"

Charlie was silent for a few seconds while he considered the situation. "Yeah, Mark, the misdirection was most likely aimed at the Mossad or IDF but according to God, the threat at the wall is real. My training and experience tell me that the bombs are really there but are being hidden by the demons. I would guess that the real bombs are nearby because the Intel was true; God says the Satanists have the bombs and they are going to destroy the wall area of Jerusalem. Dig deeper while I see if I can locate them. You have very little time."

Mark told the team and the Mossad/IDF about Charlie's conclusions. He directed the entire effort to search for the weapons by breaking them into teams with one Crossfire team member on each team to handle the demons.

Alexis went with one team deeper into the present cavern while the other teams spread out into the neighboring galleries. She stayed in prayer while they walked quickly through the chamber and was rewarded by the reappearance of her armor near the end of the chamber. The light flowing off of her sword alerted the group.

A large black demon stepped through into our dimension and crushed one of the Israelis with one blow of his sword. Bullets didn't affect him but Alexis' sword did. She parried a massive blow and quickly rotated to her right. Her sword bit into the demon's neck and beheaded it. It dissolved into greasy black smoke as three more demons appeared to challenge her. One of them died immediately as three of the IDF soldiers fired on it.

Showing great courage, several of the Israelis followed Parker in a flanking move around the two demons that were focused on Alexis. One of the demons saw the move and slashed backwards with its sword. The blow hit Parker's left shoulder and knocked him to the ground. If he hadn't been wearing his body armor he would have been killed outright.

Shaking his head to clear the fuzziness caused by the terrific blow, Parker couldn't see anything but cavern wall ahead of them, but that was where the demons had come from. Parker struggled to his feet with his left arm hanging uselessly at his side. He ignored the battle behind him and felt along the wall with his right hand. His hand disappeared through one section and he stepped forward into darkness. He fumbled getting out a light but was able to switch on his Night fighter flashlight. He sensed, more than saw things in the dark. He discerned vague shapes to his right. With his heart in his throat he turned the flashlight toward the shapes. As he turned, the darkness vanished completely as Alexis armor lit up the space as she stepped through the false wall. What she and Parker saw chilled them to the bone.

CHAPTER FIFTY

The four bombs were arranged on separate tables but the inherent violent death they represented was a tangible thing. Alexis keyed her combat microphone and called the rest of the teams. "We've found them at the end of the original tunnel."

The Israelis moved quickly to the bombs and began to disarm them.

With a rush of air and a foul odor more demons started to appear and Alexis confronted three of them to the right side of the tables. Two more appeared on the other side of the bombs and attacked the Israelis who fired on the demons with no effect. The Israeli men and women tried to avoid the attacks and still concentrate on disarming the nuclear weapons while Alexis went into high speed and dispatched the first three.

The other two demons were attempting to drive everyone away from the bomb tables when Su Li and Laura entered the hidden alcove and engaged the demons in battle. One of the demons, smaller but very fast managed to trip Su Li and chopped down at her neck before she could recover.

The black blade ran into a chrome one as Laura parried its blow and deflected the strike into the ground. Alexis' shining blade ran the demon through the chest from the back, quickly ending its career with prejudice.

More of the IDF and Crossfire team charged into the alcove and surrounded the bomb technicians as they frantically worked to defuse the four weapons. Unlike movies and TV, these bombs didn't have a brightly lit countdown timer or even any indicators of their detonation time. Simply a LCD readout that read ARMED in Russian.

As many more demons appeared outside the alcove, Jack, Mark, and David battled them to prevent their interference with the defusing process. As the demons threatened to overwhelm them by sheer numbers in the near darkness of the cavern bullets started to smack into the team's armor.

214

Jack told the Israelis to focus their firepower on the onrushing Satanists.

The battle raged for several minutes while Jack prayed earnestly for heavenly help to defeat the enemy and save the city. Abruptly dozens of angels appeared in the cavern and the alcove and took the battle to both the human and demonic forces alongside the team and the Israelis.

All at once, all the remaining demons disappeared, leaving the Satanists by themselves. The fifteen Satanists didn't even have time to consider surrendering before they died in a hail of bullets and angelic swords.

Jack turned and stepped into the alcove where the bombs were and saw that there were casualties but that the technicians were putting the covers back on the nuclear warheads.

Parker had suffered an attack which left his left arm bleeding and hanging by his side but he had smoking gun in his right hand and a grim smile on his bloody face. "We were able to disarm all four of the warheads and will get them out of here immediately if your team will please stay with us and protect us from any more of those demons." This was an earnest plea from a man who no longer had any doubt as to the reality of spiritual warfare in the world.

Jack assigned Laura, Mark, Alexis, and David to accompany the technicians as their support teams showed up with wheeled carts and covers to remove the warheads from the cavern.

Mark commented to Jack quietly on the side as the transfer from the bomb tables took place. "What bothers me is why the Satanists didn't just detonate one or more of the bombs during the battle."

Jack shook his head, "I don't know the answer to that but I think Yahveh had something to do with it."

As the bombs were being removed Jack knelt down next to Su Li who was sitting on the floor of the alcove. "Are you alright?"

Su Li smiled wanly, "I think so, but I have a large bruise on my left shoulder and an even bigger loss of confidence in my ability to combat demons."

Jack helped her to her feet. "We all have those moments. Just pray and lift it up to the Lord. I know you'll find peace and most likely an extended session with Hugo to restore your confidence."

Su Li laughed. She looked introspective for a moment. "Hey, do we get overtime for the time we spend in training with Hugo? I mean, no time goes by here but we spend days or weeks in heaven training."

Jack could see she was kidding but was encouraged by her attempt at humor. "I'll talk to the boss and see about compensation for you."

Su Li looked at him. "You mean Laura?"

Jack laughed, "No, I mean Yahshua." He led her out of the almost empty alcove and through the cavern to the exit. Walking out into the night he filled his lungs with the fresh air and called the team together.

It was a banged up group with David and Su Li limping or protecting various parts of their bodies as they moved away from the wall. Laura looked around and saw almost no one in the area. "Do you think our battle scared them away?"

Parker walked up to them and answered her. "No, the IDF cleared the area due to the pending riot by mobs of Arabs and Israelis that the Satanists stirred up to cover their actions and increase the body count after the bombs went off."

Mark shook the man's hand. "You showed a lot of bravery in there what with the battle against the demons swirling around you and four nuclear weapons on the verge of exploding in your lap."

Parker smiled wryly. "About that." he said quietly, "Apparently the Satanists weren't all that competent with nuclear weapons. The Russian weapons had three fail-safes that they had to overcome. The Satanists removed two of the fail-safes but didn't know about the third one. That was the one that would have allowed them to detonate the bombs remotely rather than on a timer as they had planned to do. We actually had thirty more minutes when the bombs were defused. Thank God for amateurs...,"

One of the Mossad agents walked up to them and handed Parker two notes. He read the first one and shook his head. He looked at the team members he ruefully smiled. "It seems that Marco Marino has heard about out little battle here and is decrying the needless loss of life of the Satanists. He is demanding an investigation into the slaughter and states that he will bring the culprits to trial." Think he means us?"

Jack nodded, "Remember, we will all be hated for the name of Christ."

Parker thought for a moment, "Yes, well there is that. I rather thought I would skirt that particular problem. But it seems as if I will be included now. Now, the second note is about your fallen comrades. It seems that the Satanists weren't the ones that killed them. Analysis of the untampered videos from the hotel showed two men who went into their room and came back out with a long package, probably Ms. Hargrove's rifle. Both men tried to hide their faces but we were able to identify them. They belong to a Russian Mafia group that was associated with one deceased Sam Sturgis."

Jack shook his head, "Debbie killed him and his people killed her and her husband in reprisal."

Mark's jaw was clenched. "I thought they were done with us after we took care of their demon problem."

Jack looked at his best friend in the world. "I think we may have time to resolve this vendetta thing before we are done on this Earth. My questions are: how did they know she was his executioner, how did they know where they would be, and, how did they kill them without their fighting back."

"We will find out." Mark's tone didn't brook any defiance. "I really loved those two people and they may just be the first our group that the Russian Mafia wants to get rid of. Remember, the Russian Premier wanted to "erase" us after our last vacation on Russian soil."

Jack's frosty look would have given a demon pause. "We need to give them something else to convince them that hunting us down is a bad idea."

217

CHAPTER FIFTY-ONE

After the team was debriefed by the Mossad they returned to their base. It was a time for relaxing and remembering their fallen friends.

Three days later, a patched up Parker Abbas asked the core team for a short meeting. He had his left arm in a sling and a folder with him. He greeted everyone and sat down in the assembly area. He looked at the group which he now held in high regard for their contributions to his country.

"I have been honored to bring you the Mossad and the Israeli government's sincere thanks for your efforts in the Satanists matter. I also bring you news about the killing of the Hargroves. It seems that the powers that be owe your group a debt of gratitude for your continued efforts over the last several years in the defense of our country."

Parker smiled a small smile. "While you were battling demons and Satanists to prevent the bombing of the temple mount my organization had been tasked by the director of the Mossad to "resolve" the matter of the Hargrove's assassins and determine how and why they were taken out and the manner in which they were killed."

He opened the folder. "We were able to find and arrest the two men as they attempted to leave Israel at a border crossing into the Gaza Strip. They are with the Russian Mafia and they are only known by their first names which are Oleg and Mishka. We were able to subdue them although they didn't come quietly. Mishka traded shots with three of the Kidon and died for his efforts. Oleg suffered three broken limbs but he was kept alive long enough to answer some of our questions."

Mark commented, "I hear that questioning by the Mossad can be painful.

Parker sighed, "Sometimes our interrogation techniques are less than healthy for the person being questioned. Oleg was able to tell us that the leadership of their organization directed them to find and eliminate the people that terminated Sam Sturgis while he was under their protection. His death was a black eye for them and revenge is required in these cases."

"It seems that fate played a large part in the death of the Hargroves. Like us at the Mossad, and you with Charlie Wu's computers, the Russians have the capability to tap into the cameras of the world and do facial recognition. Mrs. Hargrove was seen in a Tel Aviv video getting into the same vehicle that you used in your trip to Jerusalem. Bad luck because Oleg and Mishka were in Jerusalem looking for Mrs. Hargrove when their computers spotted the vehicle headed their way on the night of the raid. It was a sad coincidence that Ms. Hargrove used that vehicle again. Oleg and Mishka intercepted your group just as you arrived at the hotel. They concentrated on Ms. Hargrove as their primary assignment."

Parker shook his head. "They ascertained the room the Hargroves were staying at and then used a gas which was surprisingly similar to the one you were using several floors below to knock out your targets. Oleg and Mishka then entered the room and found the unconscious couple. Being assassins they terminated both people and took their weapons as proof of fulfilling their first assignment. The other members of your team were to be next. But, they were warned to leave the country immediately by an unknown contact which we believe is connected to the IDF. The IDF and the Mossad are investigating as we speak. I will return the Hargrove's weapons to you in two days."

He looked up from the folder with a sad look on his face. "You have my deepest condolences for your loss and I hope that this investigation has laid some of your concerns to rest."

Mark looked at Jack. "Thank you, Parker. We very much appreciate your agency's involvement on our behalf and their efficient resolution of the assassins of the Hargroves. One question, can you get us a breakdown of the upper level of the section of the Russian Mafia that dispatched Oleg and his partner to kill our team?"

Parker nodded, "I think you will find all that information in here." He handed the folder with the disk drives in it to Mark as he rose to say goodbye for the moment.

As Parker Abbas walked away from the group he silently figured that there would be true hell to pay in Russia very soon.

The Crossfire Team will return in
"End Times Crossfire".

If this story has awakened you or moved you to seek the love of Christ and His power for your life, whether you've never accepted Jesus as your savior or you've fallen away, repeat the following prayer and begin a most wonderful journey into eternal life with Him today.

Father God in heaven, As You said in Your Holy Word, (Romans 10:9) that if we confess the Lord our God and believe in our hearts that God raised Jesus from the dead, we shall be saved.

(The prayer on the next page is a sample prayer when asking Jesus into your heart as your Savior. You can also pray this in your own words.)

Salvation Prayer

Dear God in heaven, I come to you in the name of Jesus. I confess to You that I am a sinner, and I am sorry for my sins and the life that I have lived; I need your forgiveness. I believe that your only begotten Son Jesus Christ shed His precious blood on the cross at Calvary and died for my sins, and I am now willing to turn from my sin.

Right now I confess Jesus as the Lord of my life and my soul. With all my heart, I truly believe that your Holy Spirit raised Jesus from the dead. Today I accept Jesus Christ as my personal Savior and according to Your Word, right now I am saved.

I thank you Jesus, for your unlimited grace which has saved me from my sins. I thank you Jesus that your grace that never leads to license, but rather it always leads to repentance. Therefore Lord Jesus, transform my life so that I may bring glory and honor to you alone and not to myself.

I Thank you Lord Jesus, for dying for me at Calvary and giving me eternal life.

Amen.

If you just said this prayer and you meant it with all your heart, believe that you are now saved and have been born again.

You may ask, "Now that I am saved, what do I do next?" First of all you need to get into a spirit-filled, bible-based church that teaches the Scriptures, and you need to study God's Word.

Once you have found a church home, you will want to become water-baptized. By accepting Christ you are baptized in the spirit, but it is through water-baptism that you publically announce your obedience to the Lord Jesus. Water baptism is a symbol of your salvation from the dead. You were dead but now you live, for Jesus Christ has redeemed you for a price! The price was His atoning death on the cross. May God Bless You!

Island Crossfire

Books by Stephen L. Thompson

TheCrossfire Series

Colorado Crossfire
International Crossfire
Israeli Crossfire
Believer's Crossfire
Spirit Crossfire
Faith Crossfire
Chinese Crossfire
Texas Crossfire
Dark Crossfire
Island Crossfire
Jagged Crossfire
Violent Crossfire
Russian Crossfire
Nuclear Crossfire
End Times Crossfire
Revelation Crossfire
Gates of Hell Crossfire
Assassin's Crossfire
Albatross Crossfire
Global Crossfire
Far East Crossfire

The SFO Series

Station Force One - Onset